# Deo Vindice

*"The Resurrection"*

Michael A. Jefferson

*To the ancestors*

# Contents

# Acknowledgement

It has been a long journey from the moment I first thought about writing this book until now. It was during a Civil Rights Law seminar in law school that a professor posed the question: If you were president following the American Civil War, what actions would you have taken to ensure the safety of blacks and the respect for the rule of law in the former Confederacy? The question was thought-provoking and my mind went racing. It hasn't stopped until now.

There are so many people I wish to thank for the successful completion of this book. To the members of my circle for their unwavering support, constructive criticism and friendship. These good men are: Gregory "Ace" Brunson, Kermit Carolina, Larry Conaway, Gary Highsmith, Steve Jefferson, and Bob Pellegrino, author of *I see Color*.

To A.J. O'Connell, for her awesome editing skills. To Kristin Horneffer, for assisting me with research. To Sarah Whalen, for her input in the early stages. To Doron Ben Ami, for the spectacular cover design. To Stephen Harrington, for bringing various scenes of the book to life on our website through his remarkable paintings.

To my longtime friend, and owner of WOW Creative Design, Jackie Buster and her incredible team, including Zack Black.

To my brothers who wear the purple and gold – the members of the Omega Psi Phi Fraternity, Inc. – thank you for 31 years of brotherhood. Friendship is essential to the soul.

To my mom, for always believing in me and my dad, who is gone but will always be remembered. To my wife of 27 years, Pamela: thank you for your support. To my two sons, Michael II and Malcolm-Fidel, both gifted writers in their own right.

Finally, to the Creator for helping me see it through.

## — ONE —

# 1964

The shiny black limousine pulled away from the stately mansion in Demopolis, Alabama. Most of the racially-diverse house staff lined the manicured driveway to bid farewell to Tina Richards and her eleven-year-old son Cody. The two were off on a two-week vacation to Beaumont, East Texas, to spend time with her parents and grandmother. But her first stop would be Birmingham to visit her second cousin, Stewart Carson.

"Steve?"

"Yes, Miss Richards?"

"Make a stop at Harry's on the way."

"Sure thing, ma'am."

"Steve?"

"Yes, ma'am?"

"Cut the ma'am crap. You make me sound like an old woman. Do I look like an old woman to you?"

"Absolutely not, ma'am." Tina smiled.

Although thirty-nine, Tina could pass for twenty-nine. A former model, Tina stood five feet eight inches tall and possessed an hourglass figure. She was a strikingly beautiful, dark-skinned woman, who wore a natural hair style. Steve, her driver, was a handsome, white, twenty-three-year-old, who had a crush on her.

"Steve?"

"Yes..." Steve hesitated, careful not to make the same mistake twice. "Yes, Miss Richards," he answered with a smile.

"How did your parents enjoy their visit to our little paradise?

1

"Well, Miss Richards, put it this way. The way my mom describes it, the South is not for them. They consider themselves Northerners — New Jersey folks. But they are impressed with how you Southern folks are taking care of their only son."

Fresh out of college, Steve came south looking for work. He was not unlike most whites his age; work was hard to find in the North. The South's booming economy created vast employment opportunities. Blacks dominated the white collar sector and many of the best-paying blue collar jobs, however, the service industry provided many opportunities. Over the years many young whites like Steve, along with immigrants from Central America and the Caribbean, made their way to the South in search of better wages and an improved way of life.

"So, Steve, tell me — does our little paradise possess too much shade for your parents' taste?" Tina wouldn't let it go.

"Honestly, Miss Richards, probably so. My mom's old school. She grew up in the Southwest — Arizona — and moved east years ago to be with my dad when his job relocated him to New Jersey."

Most Southerners and Northerners considered the southwestern part of the country to be the least progressive, the least diverse and also the poorest. While few blacks lived in the North, many travelled there for business and even to vacation. Hardly any blacks made their homes in the southwestern states of West Texas, New Mexico, Arizona, Utah, and Colorado. For many blacks, these five states could have been in another universe.

"I'm surprised none of your parents' old school ways wore off on you, Steve." Tina spoke in code and Steve got the hint.

"Well, Miss Richards, I want to be a citizen of the world much like yourself."

"You must travel, Steve. Anytime you get the opportunity to travel, do so, dear."

"That's why I came south, Miss Richards, and I don't plan to leave any time soon. I love this place. I love the food, the Southern accent; folks are cool, for the most part. The cities are magnificent. They're safe and clean. There's plenty of work and so many beautiful sites."

"Like my mom?" The voice belonged to Cody, who up to that moment remained rather inconspicuous.

"Excuse me, little man," said Steve, laughing and turning red. He pulled into a small parking lot off the road and adjacent to a brick building with a sign on it which read "Harry's General Store."

"Never mind," interrupted a smiling Tina before Cody could answer. "The usual, Miss Richards?"

"Yes, Steve. Salem — menthol." Tina, while not a regular smoker, would from time to time buy a pack of cigarettes in case she got the urge. Over the last two years the urges came more frequently.

"I'll be right back, Miss Richards."

"Oh, and Steve, bring me something cold to drink. Do you want anything, Cody?" asked Tina.

"I'll take a root beer, please," said Cody.

"Get yourself something as well, Steve. Here you go." Tina handed Steve a ten-dollar bill.

"Cool — I'll be right back folks." Steve exited the car. "Damn." The spring heat rushed his body. "Now this is hard getting used to," he muttered loudly to himself.

"Excuse me Steve?" asked Tina, whose window was slightly rolled down.

"Oh, nothing, Miss Richards — a little warm."

"You'll get used to it, dear." Tina turned her attention to Cody.

"How are you feeling, Pumpkin?" Tina and her son were alone in the limo.

"Stop calling me Pumpkin, Mom — I mean ma'am," Cody started to giggle. Tina smiled and rolled her eyes.

"I've been calling you Pumpkin for as long as I can remember and you'll always be my Pumpkin."

"But Mom — you call me Pumpkin in front of everybody." Tina ran her hands through her son's thick black hair. "I love you, Pumpkin."

"I love you too, Mom, and I think Steve does, too." Cody's face displayed a sly grin.

"Oh, please, child. I am too old for that boy, and besides, that sort of thing doesn't play too well in the South."

"You mean black and white couples, Mom?" Cody asked.

"Yes, Cody. It's not illegal or anything like that, Pumpkin, but there are certain traditions in the South and in our family. It goes back a long time, sweetheart."

"Would you be mad if I married a white girl, Mom?"

"Cody, it's complicated, so just do us all a favor and marry a smart, black girl."

"She has to be pretty like you, Mom."

"Thank you, Pumpkin."

"Did I tell you all my friends at school like you?"

"Yes, you told me Cody, several times. You should tell your classmates to pay more attention to the teacher and less to your mother."

"All set." Steve was sweating when he returned to the car. He opened the driver's door and let the cool air rushing from the vents caress his face. He gently placed the items from the store on the front seat next to him, sat down and let his head fall backwards.

"Maybe you should drink some of your pop before we drive off."

"Good idea, Miss Richards. Here you go, little man." Steve twisted off the bottle cap and handed Cody his root beer soda.

"Thanks, Steve."

"Here you go, Miss Richards." Steve handed Tina her change and cigarettes. "Wow that sounded like a frog," said Steve. Right before they'd driven off, Cody had let out a loud burp.

"Cody, say excuse me," a startled Tina yelled.

"Excuse me, Mom, but I couldn't help it."

Steve laughed.

Ninety minutes after their initial stop the limousine pulled up to a magnificent structure - the "Gold Building," located in downtown Birmingham. A huge purple granite stone emblazoned with the words "CARSON-HAMILTON" encrusted in glittering gold paint greeted visitors to the building. The colored tints on the building's windows gave the structure a beautiful golden appearance. "Should I drive around to the side, Miss Richards?"

"No, Steve, this will be fine."

"She has to make an entrance, Steve," snapped Cody, rolling his eyes.

"I like the walk. It's good for your health," said Tina as she tucked her pack of cigarettes into her purse.

"Give me a sec, Miss Richards." After parking the vehicle, Steve climbed out of the driver's seat. He played his part well. Steve quickly fixed his cap and straightened out the rest of his black, chauffeur attire. He opened the rear door for his passengers. Tina stepped from the vehicle and heads began to turn. Some people even stopped. Steve's hankering green eyes concealed by his dark shades, followed his curvaceous boss until she and Cody vanished into the crowd.

To gain entrance to the building from where Steve parked, the pair had to walk through an open-air plaza filled with pedestrians and elaborately-dressed food carts with decorative tables and brightly-colored umbrellas. It was after 1 p.m. and the place had a festive ambiance — jam-packed with black folks enjoying lunch or returning from lunch.

The Gold Building was fifty-five stories high and served as the work place for some of Alabama's largest companies and organizations, including the powerful Council of State Governments in the South – also referred to as the C.S.G.S.. The building also served as the Birmingham office of Tina's second cousin, the forty-four year-old governor of Alabama, Stewart Carson.

Tina and Cody made their way through the large crowd. One pedestrian whispered, "there's Tina Richards." Many onlookers nodded their heads in her direction, and she smiled and nodded back. One woman came up to her and introduced herself. "Hi, Miss Richards — my name is Mitsy — Mitsy Goines, and I am an admirer of you and your family. I hope and pray you are doing well since your husb...," the woman's voice trailed off as she glanced at Cody who was staring back at her. "Well I'm sure you understand." She nodded convincingly at Tina. Tina politely smiled and nodded her head.

Before moving on, the woman turned again to Cody. "You are such a handsome young man and I love your outfit." Cody wore khaki shorts with a blue and white striped shirt and navy colored sneakers. The woman gently touched Cody's face and said goodbye.

"Thank you," said Cody in a polite, shy voice. Tina waved goodbye to the stranger and entered the building.

"Tina, over here." A familiar voice caught her attention. It was Gladys, a moderately attractive, sharply dressed, middle-aged black woman who served as the governor's chief of staff and confidant.

"Gladys - you didn't have to meet us down here."

"I wanted to, Tina. Hi, Cody"

"Hi, Miss Gladys."

"You get taller every time I see you."

"I wish it were true," Cody put his head down.

"Now don't you worry. Before it's all said and done, you'll be as tall as your fa..ther." Gladys's voice faded. "I'm sorry, Tina," whispered Gladys.

"It's okay, Gladys. He knows you meant nothing by it."

"You think so, Miss Gladys?" Cody's face lit up as he responded to Gladys's initial observation about his height.

"Why, of course I do."

The party of three stepped onto the private elevator. It landed at the top of the building. The three walked down a quiet hallway and entered the governor's outer office. "He'll be right with you. I have some work to finish. I'll see you before you leave."

"Thanks, Gladys."

"Anytime, Tina. By the way, girl...," Gladys leaned closer to Tina "you look stunning. I met someone who might be the right one for you." She smiled and winked at Tina as she left the room.

"Oh cut it out, Gladys; you do?" asked Tina, with a hint of curiosity. Both women laughed.

Tina and Cody made themselves at home in the spacious outer office belonging to the governor. Cody had fallen in love with the place during his first visit seven years ago. It resembled a small museum. The shelves contained scores of books, numerous artifacts and several sporting event trophies from the governor's days as a top collegiate soccer player. Beautiful art decorated the walls. Tina loved the plush setting as well. She felt at home in the presence of her favorite cousin.

"Hey, superstar."

"Uncle Stew." Cody flew into Carson's waiting arms. Although, Cody was Carson's second cousin once removed, he referred to Carson as his uncle.

"I miss you, champ," said Carson.

"I miss you too, Uncle Stew," said Cody.

"I got a surprise for you." He smiled at Cody.

"What is it, Uncle Stew?"

"Give me a sec, Cody, let me check out at this Alabama angel." Carson gave Tina a once over while Cody turned his attention to the governor's impressive library.

"Oh stop it, Stew. Between you and Gladys." Tina was beaming.

"No, I mean it, Cuz, your peach and white outfit is hot. You are a head turner, Cuz."

Tina did a half turn as if she was on a fashion runway and struck a playful pose.

"Did she make an entrance, Cody?" asked Carson.

Cody glanced directly at Carson with raised eyebrows and his head tilted to the left. His facial expression sufficiently answered Carson's question.

"How's Bonnie and the kids, Stew?" asked Tina.

"All is well on the home front this week, Cuz." Carson raised his brow with both hands - palms up and raised his shoulders slightly.

"So you're off to see Uncle Ulysses and Aunt Connie, huh? Well, make sure you give them my warmest regards and, of course, Aunty Ari too. How is she, Tina?"

"Gram is Gram." Tina's voice faded. Tina chose not to go into too much detail about the family matriarch. It was best to tread lightly when talking about her grandmother. "They all miss you, Stew." Tina's spark returned.

"I miss them. I wouldn't be here if it wasn't for the family," said Carson staring at the beautiful portrait of his grandfather David Foginet and his great aunt Araminta Foginet.

The two were twins. His grandfather died in 1956. Aunt Araminta or Aunty Ari, as she was called by most of the family, was eighty-nine years old and still had her faculties, wit, and much internal strength.

The "Twins," as they were called, were the children of Aurelius Foginet (pronounced Foe-jah-nay) and Lisa Stewart - the First Couple of the South. Following the deaths of their famous parents, the Twins used their parents' legacy and sizeable fortune to build the family dynasty: the Carson-Hamilton Empire. The name is derived from Carson's father and Araminta's husband. The governor's mother, Lisa Foginet-Carson, was the daughter of David Foginet. She and Tina's mother, Constance J. Hamilton-Forrester, were first cousins.

"How are we doing in the polls?"

"To tell you the truth I wish we were doing better, Cuz." Carson was attempting to get a place on the 1964 Republican ticket as the vice presidential candidate. The Party wasn't too happy with the current Vice President Paul Kinsey, a white man and a former senator from Pennsylvania. He embarrassed the Party by repeatedly making comments many construed as racist. The Democrats presented a significant challenge, and the Republicans needed the South more than ever. Kinsey's inability to control his bigoted tongue caused serious problems for the Party. Carson's name was on a short list.

If Carson could land on the ticket, he could launch his own bid for the presidency in four years. He would become the first president elected from the South in over 100 years and the first black ever elected to the office. One black, Gramen Edwards, had already served as president of the United States, shortly after the Great War. He ascended to the presidency from the office of the vice president after the untimely death of the sitting president. He served for two years and did a respectable job.

Carson's place on the ticket would be a major coup for the family. Sixteen years ago, Araminta's son and Tina's uncle, Edgar Hamilton, was mentioned as a V.P. candidate, while serving his second term as governor of East Texas, but the Party backed another candidate. The Party's decision infuriated the Twins. It cost the Party the South and ultimately the election. The Twins considered breaking with the Party altogether, but felt the timing wasn't right.

To make up for the slight, Lucy Foginet-Edwards, David's oldest daughter, was given a senior position in the Party, and her first cousin Hamilton was made the national chairman of the Party. He was the second black to serve in that capacity. Hamilton later held other high-profile appointed positions in the government. He finally settled into his present position with his cousin Foginet-Edwards as co-president of the highly influential Carson-Hamilton Trust, but it was Tina who ran the day-to-day operation as the organization's senior vice president. She was considered one of the most powerful individuals in the South.

"Tina, I'm getting hammered on my foreign policy experience."

"Is that what you were working on when we arrived? I heard you on the phone."

"Sort of. This investigative journalist — a woman from Georgia named Teddy Gunn — are you familiar with the name?" He never gave his cousin a chance to respond. "Well, anyway, she got herself jammed up in South Africa. She's over there covering the trial and detention of this fella named Nelson Mandela. He's the leader of the main opposition group the African National Congress," said Carson.

"Stew, I know who Mandela is, and just so you know, the international press is calling the trial 'the Rivonia trial.'[1] The proceedings started last fall."

"Wow, Cuz, I'm impressed, but I shouldn't be, huh? You've always had a serious interest in world affairs. Maybe you can help me with — oh, never mind." Carson immediately dismissed the thought. It wasn't a good idea to put Tina in his private political circle, not now anyway. Tina chose not

---

[1] The Rivonia Trial took place in South Africa between 1963 and 1964. Ten leaders of the African National Congress (ANC), an anti-apartheid group, were charged with 221 acts of sabotage and conspiracy against the South African government. During the trial, ANC leader Nelson Mandela famously stated that "democracy and a free society" is an "ideal for which I am prepared to die" (Supreme Court of South Africa, Pretoria, April 20, 1964). He and others received life sentences in prison as a result. *For further reading, see* The State vs. Nelson Mandela: The Trial that Changed South Africa *by Joel Joffe (Oneworld, 2007).*

to respond. She knew it wasn't a good idea either.

"As I was saying, Cuz, the racist bastards who run the government over there locked her up on a bullshit spying charge," Carson finished his account of Gunn's situation.

"The sister is good - damn good, Stew. She's a graduate of Wheatley. A few years behind me. About a decade ago she exposed the role of the CIA in Iran and Guatemala. She also broke the story on the agency's role in Cuba. Do you remember?" asked Tina, clearly impressed with Gunn's work.

"Yeah, I remember — and now she's on their asses in South Africa," said Carson shaking his head.

"Do you need us to intervene?"

"Not yet, Cuz. I think I got this."

" I might be able to get some mileage out of this if her release is seen as a result of my efforts. Plus, I need her to help me with another problem."

"What's up?" asked Tina.

"The situation in Germany is back in the news."

"The issue about you having a kid out of wedlock," Tina started to whisper in German.

"I caught some of that, Mom." Cody was in earshot of the two adults.

"Sorry, Stew, he's learning the language. What can this journalist do for you over there?"

"Hell, Tina, she can get to the bottom of that bullshit. Sorry, Cody." Carson was now speaking German as well.

"Par for the course, Uncle Stew."

Carson chuckled. "It's essential I do all I can to get Gunn out of jail and back to this country. Once she's free maybe she can help me put an end to this wedlock rumor crap. Thank God Bonnie, doesn't believe this bullshit."

"Well, let me know how I can help," said Tina.

"Will do, Cuz, and thank you." Carson motioned Tina to a corner of the room away from Cody.

"How's he dealing with his dad's death?" Carson continued the dialogue in German.

Tina's late husband, Cody's father, had been a rising political star in the South. At the time of his death, Stanley Richards was poised to take a seat on the powerful executive committee of the C.S.G.S. previously known as the Southern Regional Council or S.R.C.. This was the most powerful governing body in the former Confederacy. Members of the body's executive committee wielded tremendous power over every aspect of political and economic life in the former states of the Confederacy. Founded by Aurelius Foginet, the family had long maintained a powerful presence on the executive committee.

Nearly two years ago, Richard's body was found in a Mississippi hotel room with a bullet wound to the head. The gun had his prints on it, but no one believed it to be a suicide. The cause of death was ruled accidental. In spite of her best efforts, Tina failed to solve the mystery. A year after his death she received a package containing documents pertaining to the C.S.G.S.. A note attached to the documents read "these documents should help you find what you are looking for." After months of pouring over the documents, she still could find nothing.

"He's doing okay, and I want to thank you, Stew." Tina continued the dialogue in German. "You've been wonderful. I don't know how we would have made it this far without you." Tina and Carson were close. After graduating at the top of her class from the world renowned Wheatley University, she decided to study abroad in England. She was twenty-two. Carson was a twenty-seven-year-old junior diplomat working with his father Blaine Carson, who was a high-ranking diplomat assigned to postwar Germany. Tina and the younger Carson became close and spent the summer and holidays together in Germany. He was the first to teach her the basics of the German language.

When the Twins got word of the two cousins spending so much time together Tina was told to come home. Araminta told one family member, "the girl is just like her mother and that boy is just like his daddy." For Aunty Ari the relationship between her granddaughter and her great nephew appeared a bit unnatural. Her twin brother agreed.

"Well, Stew, it's been wonderful. I wish we had more time, but we must be going. Our train leaves in about an hour."

"Heck, Tina, you've only been here for 30 minutes."

"Actually, it's been close to an hour. You were on the phone forever," said Tina smiling.

"Uncle Stew, where's my present?" screamed Cody from Carson's private office.

"Come out here. Remember I told you one day I would tell you about your great-great-grand parents? Well, I can do something better. Your mother tells me you like to read."

"I sure do, Uncle Stew."

"Well, here's something you can read while on vacation." At that moment Carson's hand appeared from behind his back holding a book which appeared to be in mint condition. He gave it to Cody. It's pronounced "dayo-vin-dee-chee," said Carson.

"Dayo-vin-dee-chee," Cody sounded out the words in a whisper. "What does it mean?" asked Cody

"It means Under God, our Vindicator." said Carson.

"What does the phrase mean?" asked Cody, perplexed by his uncle's response.

"Read the book, young man, and we'll talk about it when you return." Carson glanced at Tina, and they both smiled.

"Ah Gladys. Right on time. Their car is waiting," said Carson. Gladys suddenly froze and stared at both Tina and her boss. "My, my, my I can't believe how much the two of you look alike. I'm sure you hear it all the time." Gladys was talking about the striking resemblance between Carson and Tina. Gladys mentioned it before, but probably didn't remember. Both of them smiled. It was an awkward moment and the truth was they've been hearing about their resemblance for as long as they both could remember.

"Take care, Stew, and call me if you need me to do anything for the campaign. Love you, sweetie," said Tina.

"See ya, Uncle Stew, and thanks for the book."

Steve had pulled around to the side of the building. Tina and Cody waved goodbye to Gladys who stood in the side doorway of the building. First Cody, then Tina climbed through the opened door of the limousine held by Steve. "I take it you enjoyed yourself?"

"We had a splendid time, Steve," answered Tina.

"My uncle gave me a book."

"Oh yeah — what's it called?" asked Steve.

"Dayo-vin-dee-chee." Cody tried to pronounce the two words in rapid succession.

"Say again, kid," Steve couldn't quite grasp the title of the book.

"Dayo-vin-dee-chee!" Cody's pronunciation was more deliberate the second time. "It's about my family," said Cody.

"I'm going to start reading it the minute we get on the train, Mom."

"Okay, Pumpkin."

"Mom?" Cody sounded an exasperated tone hearing his mother refer to him by his nickname.

"Excuse me, ma'am — I mean, Miss Richards, but if you don't mind me asking — why not fly to East Texas? I mean, wouldn't it be a lot quicker?" Steve began to put on his seat belt.

"It's my vacation, Steve, and I prefer to take my time. Besides, Cody loves the train."

"It's my favorite way to travel, Steve," said Cody.

"Have you ever taken the H-Line Express, Steve?" asked Tina.

"Can't say I have, Miss Richards. I hear the South has the best transportation system in the country."

"No, Steve. It's the best transportation system in the world."

"I stand corrected, Miss Richards," Steve smiled and bowed his head in a deferential manner.

"Here we are," Steve pulled into the back of the station. "You guys go on and board the train, and I'll get your luggage from the trunk and have it delivered to your car."

"Thanks, Steve. Here you go." Tina gave Steve a twenty dollar tip.

"Why thank you, Miss Richards, but geez you don't..."

"Steve, hush — don't tell your boss what she doesn't have to do,"

"Spend it wisely," said Tina with a wink and a smile.

"Okay, Miss Richards. I'll see you guys in two weeks."

"Bye, Steve." Cody called out as he boarded the train.

"Bye, Cody. Don't give your mom a hard time."

"I won't. I promise." Cody rarely gave his mother any problems. He was considered by most who encountered him to be well-behaved and quite protective of his mom.

"Take care, Steve."

"Bye, Miss Richards."

"Over here, Mom," Cody settled into a large double seat in their private car. After the luggage arrived, Tina went to freshen up. When she returned Cody was staring at the cover of the book, while quietly repeating the title in an attempt to master its correct pronunciation.

"All aboard to Bluff City, East Texas. We'll be making two stops in between: New Orleans and Beaumont. All aboard to Bluff City, East Texas." After several minutes the conductor finally closed the doors and blew the horn. The train slowly began its journey west to East Texas.

Tina appeared relieved. She kicked off her peach-colored pumps, lifted her feet and stretched out her well-formed legs on the seat across from her.

"Good idea mom." Cody said, smiling, while kicking off his sneakers. Tina smiled at her son and slowly drifted off to sleep. The train began to accelerate. Cody took one last glance outside the tinted window, then opened his book and began to read.

# — TWO —

# 1868

**❝**CONVICTED!," one headline screamed. "Down Goes Johnson!," read another. "Wade Takes Oath As 18th President of the United States," said another. For the Radical Republicans[2] in Congress and their supporters, it was a dream come true. One of their own now occupied the highest office in the land. Most observers never thought it would happen. Only a few days before, many in the capital said the Radicals in the United States Senate did not have the votes. There was even talk that big city gamblers from New Orleans had poured bribe money into the process to ensure that President Andrew Johnson kept his job as the nation's Commander in Chief. Even some of the nation's leading newspapers predicted defeat for the Radicals.

The radicals needed 36 votes — a 2/3rd majority. In the end, the vote tally was a stunning 40 votes for removal and 14 against. President An-

---

[2] The Radical Republicans were a faction within the Republican Party that lasted from about 1854 until 1877, the end of Reconstruction. The Radicals fought assiduously against the pro-slavery Democrats, and even against moderate Republicans. For Radicals, abolition of slavery was a priority, and they fought for the rights of freedmen after the war. Radicals also believed that ex-Confederates should have limited political power directly following the Civil War. *Note:* Nowadays, we generally attribute liberal social policies to the Democratic Party, and conservative ones to the Republican Party. However, during the time of the Civil War, it was the richer northeastern states that supported more conservative Republican economic policies (which today's Republican Party also still favor), but due to their lack of dependency on the institution of slavery, both socially and economically, Republicans generally favored more liberal social policies (like the abolition of slavery). *For further reading, see* Statesmanship and Reconstruction: Moderate Versus Radical Republicans on Restoring the Union After the Civil War *by Philip B. Lyons (Lexington Books, 2014).*

15

drew Johnson's[3] presidency ended in disgrace. He was the first president ever to be impeached by the House of Representatives, but it was his trial and conviction in the U.S. Senate that finished him off.

Johnson was primarily charged with violating the Tenure in Office Act[4]. In August of the previous year, while Congress was on its summer recess, Johnson fired Secretary of War Edwin Stanton[5] and replaced him with Union General Ulysses S. Grant[6]. Stanton's department was the primary federal agency responsible for implementing Reconstruction[7] policies in

---

[3]   Andrew Johnson became president in 1865 as a result of Abraham Lincoln's assassination. Johnson often opposed the predominately Republican congress, favoring lenient treatment of ex-Confederates, quick re-admittance of seceded states to the Union, and little to no protection of former slaves. Eventually, on February 24, 1868, Johnson became the first American president to be impeached, but was acquitted in the Senate by one vote. For further reading see High Crimes and Misdemeanors: The Impeachment and Trial of Andrew Johnson *by Gene Smith (Morrow, 1977).*

[4]   The Tenure of Office Act was a federal law that lasted from 1867 to 1887 that limited the president's power to remove executive officeholders without the approval of the Senate. The law was created primarily so President Johnson could not remove Edwin M. Stanton as secretary of war. He eventually did. Thus, when Johnson was impeached, the violation of the Tenure in Office Act was a primary charge. *For further reading, see United States Senate: "Articles of impeachment exhibited by the House of Representatives against Andrew Johnson, President of the United States. March 4, 1868." (Washington, D.C., 1868).*

[5]   Edwin Stanton served as the 27th United States Secretary of War under the Lincoln Administration during most of the Civil War, and until 1868 under President Andrew Johnson during the first years of Reconstruction. Stanton disagreed with Johnson's plan to readmit the seceded states to the Union without guarantees of civil rights for freed slaves. *For further reading, see* Stanton, the Life and Times of Lincoln's Secretary *(Greenwood Press, 1980).*

[6]   To keep Grant under control as a potential political rival, Johnson asked Grant to take Edwin Stanton's place as secretary of war. Eventually Grant returned the office to Stanton, angering Johnson, who then attempted to discredit Grant in the political arena. Grant had been a commanding general who helped lead the Union Army to victory in the Civil War. He eventually became the 18th president of the United States. *For further reading, see* The Man Who Saved the Union: Ulysses Grant in War and Peace *by H. W. Brands (Knopf Doubleday Publishing Group, 2012).*

[7]   The Reconstruction era lasted from the end of the Civil War in 1865 until 1877. During this time, the nation struggled to rebuild the South and transition nearly four million former slaves to a free labor society. Presidents Abraham Lincoln and Andrew Johnson believed the South should be brought back to normal as quickly as possible, while Radical Republicans believed harsh conditions for re-entry should be imposed and the rights of former slaves should first be ensured. Many historians consider Reconstruction a failure because even after the era was over, the South remained largely impoverished and land rights were never successfully negotiated for freedmen. Thus, slavery was replaced with an unjust sharecropping system, and white Democrats re-established a racial dominance system through violence that effectively

the post-Civil War South.

Johnson long believed the Radicals, led by Thaddeus Stevens[8] in the House and Charles Sumner[9] in the Senate, wanted to punish the South and had no interest in helping it recover from the destruction wrought by the war. The Radicals, on the other hand, believed Johnson was too lenient with former Confederate leaders and the South as a whole.

Among other things, the Radicals wanted to ensure the lives, property, and basic rights — including voting rights of blacks living in the South — were respected and protected. They felt Johnson had no interest in such things or their brand of "Reconstruction."

During his tenure in office, Johnson vetoed twenty-two pieces of congressional legislation including the four Reconstruction Acts of 1867-1868.[10] These powerful pieces of legislation divided the former Confederacy[11] into five military districts. Only Johnson's home state of Tennessee, in which he served as military governor, was exempt because it had al-

---

and legally limited the political and social rights of African Americans. *For further reading, see* Reconstruction: America's Unfinished Revolution, 1863 – 1877 *by Eric Foner (Harper Perennial Modern Classics; III edition, 2002).*

[8]    Thaddeus Stevens was a member of the House of Representatives from Pennsylvania and a leader of the Radical Republicans. Stevens, along with other Radicals, argued that the Southern states should be treated as conquered provinces with no constitutional rights. According to Stevens in a Congressional debate over Reconstruction Policy on September 6, 1865 in Lancaster, Pennsylvania, what was necessary in the South was a "radical reorganization in Southern institutions, habits, and manners" and to "revolutionize their principles and feelings." *For further reading, see "Thaddeus Stevens and the Imperfect Republic" by Eric Foner (Pennsylvania History: A Journal of Mid-Atlantic Studies, Vol. 60, No. 2, Thaddeus Stevens and American Democracy, April 1993, pp. 140-152).*

[9]    Charles Sumner was a senator from Massachusetts and, like Stevens, a leader of the Radical Republicans. Sumner fought against what Republicans called "Slave Power," which was the disproportionate political influence that Southern slave owners wielded over the federal government that was used to ensure the survival of slavery. *For more information about Sumner's politics, read the Pulitzer-Prize winning biography,* Charles Sumner and the Coming of the Civil War *by David Donald, Sourcebooks, 2009.*

[10]    The Reconstruction Acts were four bills passed by Congress between March 2, 1867 and March 11, 1868. They established the legal criteria and procedures whose fulfillment was necessary for former Confederate states to be readmitted to the Union.

[11]    Formally the Confederate States of America (CSA), the Confederacy consisted of eleven seceded Southern slave states and lasted from 1861 to 1865. States began to secede from the United States of America following the 1860 election of Abraham Lincoln, who opposed the expansion of slavery. *To explore the implications of the legal issues that resulted from the Civil War, including the lawfulness of succession, executive and legislative powers, and conduct during war,*

ready ratified the 14th Amendment[12] and was readmitted to the Union. The Acts required each state to hold constitutional conventions to ratify new state constitutions, which had to be approved by Congress. The Acts mandated that all men of a certain age had the right to vote and that right could not be interfered with. The Acts also mandated each state of the former Confederacy to ratify the 14th Amendment.

Johnson's vetoes were overridden fifteen times, including his veto of the Reconstruction Acts. Stanton's firing, was for many Radicals, the last straw. When the 40th Congress[13] reconvened in 1868 Johnson was ordered to reinstate Stanton to his old post. Johnson refused, and Grant resigned. The Congress then placed Stanton back in his old position over the objections of Johnson. Then in February 1868, the House moved for Johnson's impeachment. The vote was 126-47.

His trial began in March and lasted three months. Two Radical Republicans[14] served as prosecutors. On May 16, 1868, before a gallery of spectators, the Senate voted first on Article Eleven, the most egregious charge against the president: Johnson's violation of the Tenure of Office Act. The vote was tallied and Johnson's cantankerous presidency came to a sudden end.

So, for the second time in three years, the Constitution and its canons pertaining to succession would determine who resided in the Executive Mansion. Following the assassination of Abraham Lincoln, Johnson, who served as Lincoln's vice president, ascended to the presidency as required by the Constitution. However, there existed no language in the constitu-

---

*see* Justice in Blue and Gray: A Legal History of the Civil War, *by Stephen C. Neff, Harvard University Press, 2010.*

[12] Ratified on July 9, 1868, the 14th Amendment addresses equal rights to United States citizenship and as citizens, equal protection under the laws. The amendment's "Citizenship Clause" was used to overrule the Supreme Court's decision in Dred Scott v. Sandford (1857), which had held that Americans descended from African slaves could not be citizens of the United States. For an educational tool about the Dred Scott Supreme Court case, see Dred Scott v. Sandford: A Brief History with Documents by Paul Finkelman. The book includes excerpts from the Supreme Court's opinion.

[13] The 40th United States Congress met in Washington, D.C. from March 4, 1867 to March 4, 1869, during the third and fourth years of Johnson's presidency. At this time, both the Senate and the House of Representatives held a Republican majority.

[14] Johnson's impeachment committee was made up of Thaddeus Stevens, Benjamin F. Butler, John A. Bingham, John A. Logan, George S. Boutwell, Thomas Williams, and James F. Wilson.

tion that mandated his old job as vice president be filled and there was no language that provided instructions on how it should be filled. So the position of vice president remained vacant.

The Constitution did provide language governing who should succeed the president if in fact the office became vacant and the office of the vice president was vacant. Under such circumstances the office of the presidency was to be filled by the President Pro Tempore[15] of the U.S. Senate, and in1868 that particular position was held by none other than the Radical Republican senator from Ohio: Benjamin Franklin "Bluff" Wade.[16]

---

[15] The president pro tempore, or "president for a time," is the officer of the Senate charged with presiding over Senate sessions in the absence of the vice president. The president pro tempore is third in line of succession to the presidency, after the vice president and the Speaker of the House of Representatives.

[16] Like most other Radical Republicans, Wade was highly critical of Johnson's too-lenient policies. He was a strong supporter of the Freedmen's Bureau, civil rights bills, and the Fourteenth Amendment. At the time of Johnson's impeachment he was president pro tempore. Being that Johnson had no vice president, Wade would have assumed the presidency had Johnson lost his trial in the Senate. *For a classic biography, see* Benjamin Franklin Wade, Radical Republican from Ohio, *Twayne Publishers, 1963.*

# — THREE —

# Acting President Wade

66 Wade! Wade! Wade! Wade! Wade!" The chant from the gallery of spectators went on for what seemed like an hour, but in reality lasted only about five minutes. Lawyers for the defeated Johnson brushed by senators and congressmen and headed to the exit of the Senate chamber. Other legislators rushed to congratulate Wade. History had been made, and Wade stood literally right in the middle of it all.

The crowd surrounded Wade and well-wishers extended their hands to touch the next president. "Well, Bluff, how does it feel to be the acting president of the United States?" asked one senator standing close and using Wade's nickname.

"I'm not sure how I'm supposed to feel. What happens next?" Wade, wearing a thinly-disguised appearance of tranquility, was still taking it all in, and, like many others in attendance, truly had no idea about the ensuing formalities.

"I guess your old friend has yet another task to perform." His colleague said sarcastically, as he turned and motioned his chin upwards in the direction of the gentlemen descending the small stage in the Senate chambers. The senator was referring to Chief Justice Salmon Chase,[17] who had just

---

[17] First serving as senator and then governor of Ohio, Chase became the treasury secretary under President Lincoln and then finally the sixth chief justice in 1864. Chase believed in the abolition of slavery, and therefore was a complete change from his predecessor, Chief Justice Roger B. Taney. One of Chase's first acts as chief justice was to permit John Rock to argue cases before the Supreme Court, making Rock the first African-American attorney to do so. *To get a better idea of Salmon Chase in his role as chief justice from the perspective of his contemporaries,*

21

presided over the trial of President Johnson as mandated by the Constitution. Now Chase, a former senator from Ohio, was faced with the duty of administering the oath of office to his fellow Ohioan, Ben Wade. This had to be the strangest of ironies for the two men.

While both Wade and Chase held strong anti-slavery views (only senators Charles Sumner, Chase, Wade, and John Hale voted against the Fugitive Slave Law of 1850[18]) and each strongly supported women's rights, there was no love lost between the two men. Chase attempted to block Wade's election by the Ohio legislature to the U.S. Senate in 1851. Chase also bested Wade at the 1860 Republican National Convention. The ambitious Chase received forty-nine votes on the first ballot for president while Wade received only three votes. Lincoln subsequently won the nomination over both men.

As the stern faced Chief Justice, wrapped in his black judicial robe, and holding a folder pregnant with historical documents, made his way across the chamber floor, an aide familiar with the relationship between his boss and Wade reminded Chase that it was not his constitutional duty to administer the oath — only a tradition which could easily be disregarded under the circumstances. Chase would not hear of any such talk. At a time when the country needed leadership, this was not the time to allow past and petty differences to interfere with an historic moment.

After restoring order to the Senate chambers, the Chief Justice stood where just an hour before he'd sat in a chair presiding over an historic trial. He now continued to make history. In full view of members of the Senate, members of the House of Representatives, other government officials and ordinary spectators, Benjamin Wade was sworn in as the 18th president of the United States.

---

*see* The Judicial Record of the Late Chief Justice Chase *by John S. Benson, Baker, Voorhis & Co., 1882.*

[18] The Fugitive Slave Law was one part of the Compromise of 1850, the legislation that negotiated American territory between the Free States in the North and the Slave States in the South. The Fugitive Slave Law required that all slaves were, upon capture, to be returned to their masters, even when captured in a northern Free State. Abolitionists referred to it as the "Bloodhound Law" because dogs were often used to hunt down runaway slaves, who could then be exchanged back to their masters for money. *In 1850 in a South Presbyterian church in Brooklyn, Reverend Samuel T. Spear gave a sermon called "The law-abiding conscience, and the higher law conscience: with remarks of the fugitive slave question." In it he talks about how legality does not constitute morality, and uses it as a premise to delicately oppose the Fugitive Slave Law. Reading the sermon will provide an example of the manner in which opposition to such injustices was addressed publicly in the North.*

The news took the nation by storm. Democrats in the North and South were outraged, but there was nothing they could do about their dreadful reversal of fortune. A bona fide Radical Republican now occupied the Executive Mansion. Wade knew the eyes of the nation would be watching his every move. This was also an election year and therefore he had to move with extreme caution so as not to alienate his fellow Republicans. Many Party members believed if Wade became president, he should in fact receive the Party's nomination in 1868. Thus, when the issue of Johnson's impeachment came to light in February of that year, the party agreed to postpone the Republican National Convention scheduled for May 20-21, 1868 to the following month. This, they reasoned, would give the party breathing room to sort out its internal issues and questions, not the least of which was, what to do with Grant?

In the meantime, Wade's most pressing issue was convening his presidential cabinet. He solved this by inviting Johnson's appointees to remain in the cabinet with the exception of Johnson's Secretary of War, John M. Schofield[19]. Stanton regained his old post and duties but Wade had a far more radical plan in store for the incoming Secretary of War — Zachariah Chandler[20] — one he could not reveal unless he was elected to a full four-year term.

On June 14, 1868 the Republican National Convention got underway in Chicago. Grant's supporters came out in full force, but the battle for the presidential nomination, as always, took place behind closed doors, in smoke-filled rooms, and the former Union general was losing.

Grant's difficulty was of his own making. Despite a stellar career as the Union's top ranked general in the second half of the Civil War, he'd made a terrible blunder when he'd served as the Union's military commander

---

[19]  John M. Schofield was a soldier during the Civil War who later served as secretary of war and commanding general of the United States Army. During the Reconstruction era, Schofield was appointed by Johnson to serve as military governor of the First Military District. *For a good book on what day-to-day life in war looked like for an ordinary Civil War solider, see* Hardtack and Coffee: The Unwritten Story of Army Life *by John D. Billings, Bison Books, 1993 (reprint).*

[20]  Chandler was a founder of the Republican Party, an abolitionist, and later, an advocate for the rights of freedmen. He was critical of Lincoln's Reconstruction plan for being too lenient on states which seceded from the Union. He was also active in the campaign to impeach President Johnson. Under President Grant, he served as secretary of the interior. *For a concise look at Zachariah Chandler's understated impact on United States history, see:* Zachariah Chandler: Michigan Patriot: A Brief Look At A Forgotten Hero of America (The Memo Book Series), Volume 1, *by Richard Buchko, CreateSpace Independent Publishing Platform, 2013.*

for much of the area surrounding Kentucky, Mississippi and Tennessee. Grant issued the infamous General Order No. 11[21]. The order sought to disrupt the black market trade in cotton, which Grant believed was heavily influenced by Jews.

General Order No. 11 decreed as follows:

> The Jews, as a class violating every regulation of trade established by the Treasury Department and also department orders, are hereby expelled from the Department [of the Tennessee] within twenty-four hours from the receipt of this order.
>
> Post commanders will see to it that all of this class of people be furnished passes and required to leave, and any one returning after such notification will be arrested and held in confinement until an opportunity occurs of sending them out as prisoners, unless furnished with permit from headquarters.
>
> No passes will be given these people to visit headquarters for the purpose of making personal application of trade permits.

Upon issuing the order, Grant sent a letter to his Assistant Secretary of War at the time, Christopher Walcott, explaining his actions. The letter[22] began:

> Sir,
>
> I have long since believed that in spite of all the vigilance that can be infused into Post Commanders, that the Specie regulations of the Treasury Dept. have been violated, and that mostly by Jews and other unprincipled traders. So well satisfied of this have I been at this that I instructed the Commanding Officer at Columbus [Ken-

---

[21] Issued by Major-General Grant on December 17, 1862 during the Civil War. The order was an attempt to expel all Jews in Grant's military district. The order was an attempt to shut down a Southern black market of cotton, which Grant believed to be run "mostly by Jews and other unprincipled traders" *(see John Simon's The Papers of Ulysses S. Grant, Volume 7: December 9, 1862 – March 31, 1863, SIU, 1979, p. 56).*

[22] See *The Jew in the American World,* by Jacob Radar Marcus

tucky] to refuse all permits to Jews to come south, and frequently have had them expelled from the Dept. [of the Tennessee]. But they come in with their Carpet sacks in spite of all that can be done to prevent it. The Jews seem to be a privileged class that can travel anywhere. They will land at any wood yard or landing on the river and make their way through the country. If not permitted to buy Cotton themselves they will act as agents for someone else who will be at a Military post, with a Treasury permit to receive Cotton and pay for it in Treasury notes which the Jew will buy up at an agreed rate, paying gold.

There is but one way that I know of to reach this case. That is for Government to buy all the Cotton at a fixed rate and send it to Cairo, St Louis, or some other point to be sold. Then all traders, they are a curse to the Army, might be expelled.

This was disastrous for Grant, as one might expect. President Lincoln had the order rescinded within weeks of it being issued, nonetheless many Jews and non-Jews viewed Grant in an unfavorable light. During the convention, Grant attempted to repudiate the order and in doing so, blamed it on a subordinate, however the damage was already done. Wade easily received the nomination and with an appeal for party unity offered Grant the vice-presidency. Grant reluctantly accepted.

With the convention behind them, the Republicans were now ready to take on Horatio Seymour[23] and the Democrats. The 1868 presidential election was the first presidential election to take place after the Civil War. Three former states of the Confederacy, Mississippi, Texas, and Virginia were not yet restored to the Union so their electors could not be counted. In the end, Wade won the election with 214 electoral votes to 80 for Seymour. Wade also took the popular vote by a close margin of 52.7% to 47.3%. Having gained the victory, he and party members sought so badly, Wade wasted little time getting down to business of reforming the South and extending equal rights to all American citizens.

---

[23] Horatio Seymour, a former governor of New York, was the Democratic Party nominee in the presidential election of 1868, which Seymour lost to Republican candidate Ulysses S. Grant.

— FOUR —

# President Wade

Any questions about the intentions of the newly-elected president were put to rest on March 4, 1869. President Wade not only made it a point to invite the foremost African American leader of the day to the inaugural festivities, but he also had Frederick Douglass[24] stand in close proximity to his wife Caroline while he took the oath of office for the second time in less than a year.

Also invited, and quite visible, were the leading abolitionists of the day, William Lloyd Garrison, publisher of *The Liberator* newspaper[25], Wendell Phillips[26], the Grimke sisters Sarah and Angelina[27].

---

[24] After escaping from slavery, Douglass became a leader of the abolitionist movement. Known for his strong oratory skills, Douglass disproved the idea that slaves lacked the intellectual capacity to function as American citizens. Douglass has written several autobiographies; among the most influential is *Narrative of the Life of Frederick Douglass, an American Slave (1845)*.

[25] An abolitionist, suffragist, and journalist, Garrison was one of the founders of the American Anti-Slavery Society. He was the editor of the abolitionist newspaper The Liberator, which he founded with Isaac Knapp in 1831 and published until slavery was abolished by the Constitution. *For a first-hand look at Garrison's ideologies, see his speech, given in 1854, called "No Compromise with the Evil of Slavery." It is publicly available on the Internet.*

[26] Known in the American Anti-Slavery Society as "abolition's Golden Trumpet," Phillips was a skilled orator for the abolitionist movement. Originally a lawyer, he quit practicing law in order to dedicate himself to the movement. *To read more of Phillips' writing, a good book is* The Lesson of the Hour: Wendell Phillips on Abolition and Strategy, *edited by Warren Leming. Published by Charles H Kerr, 2001.*

[27] Angelina Grimke and Sarah Grimke were sisters from South Carolina who were powerful anti-slavery advocates; they became the first women to testify before a state legislature on the

Also in attendance were Lucretia Mott[28], Lydia Maria Child[29], Sojourner Truth[30], Harriet Beecher Stowe, author of *Uncle Tom's Cabin*[31], and the legendary Harriet Tubman[32].

---

question of African American rights. They believed not only that slaves should be freed, but that they should also receive equal rights. The Grimke sisters were among the first abolitionists to also advocate for women's rights and female equality. *See* The Great Silent Army of Abolitionism: Ordinary Women in the Antislavery Movement *by Julie Roy Jeffrey, The University of North Carolina Press, 2000.*

[28] Social reformer Lucretia Mott was elected the first president of the American Equal Rights Association, an organization that advocated for universal suffrage. She was an important broker of the women's suffrage movement as it was wrestling with determining its immediate goal: suffrage for freedmen and all women, or suffrage for freedmen first. *For a good read on the emergence of the women's rights movement within the climate of anti-slavery activism, see* Women's Rights Emerges within the Antislavery Movement 1830-1870: A Brief History with Documents *by Kathryn Kish Sklar, Bedford/St. Martin's, 2000.*

[29] An abolitionist, women's rights activist, Indian rights activist, opponent of American expansionism, novelist, and journalist, Child believed that white women and slaves were similar in that both groups were treated as the property of white men — not individual, autonomous human beings. Child believed that women could achieve more working alongside men rather than in all-female groups, and as such, began campaigning for equal female membership and participation in the American Anti-Slavery Society, provoking a controversy that later split the movement. *For a look at Child's writing, see* Letters from New-York: A Portrait of New York on the Cusp of its Transformation into a Modern City, *University of Georgia Press, 1998.*

[30] An abolitionist and women's rights activist, Truth was born into slavery in 1797 with the name Isabella Baumfree in New York but was able to escape to freedom with her infant daughter in 1826. After going to court to recover her son, in 1828 she became the first black woman to win such a human rights case against a white man. She changed her name to Sojourner Truth in 1843 and crafted what was to become the famous "Ain't I a Woman" speech. In 1864, Truth became employed by the National Freemen's Relief Association in Washington, D.C. where she worked to improve conditions for African Americans. *Read* Sojourner Truth: A Life, A Symbol *by Nell Irvin Painter, W. W. Norton & Company, (Reprint) 1997.*

[31] Stowe was an abolitionist who was best known for authoring the novel *Uncle Tom's Cabin* in 1852, which depicts the gruesome life of slavery and angered Southerners with its honesty. In the years following the Civil War, Stowe campaigned for the expansion of the rights of married women. *Uncle Tom's Cabin* is a most crucial part of United States literature. It depicts slavery's effects on families and helps readers empathize with enslaved characters. Poet Langston Hughes called the book "a moral cry for freedom."

[32] Tubman was an abolitionist, and during the Civil War, a spy for the Union. She used the Underground Railroad, a network of abolitionists, secret routes, and safe houses to make "19 trips" into the south and lead over "300 slaves" to over the course of thirteen missions (figures from PBS "Judgment Day Resource Bank"). After the war, Tubman advocated for women's suffrage. *There are many books written on Harriet Tubman; a highly rated and fairly recent book is* Harriet Tubman: The Road to Freedom *by Catherine Clinton, Back Bay Books, (reprint) 2005.*

Other luminaries such as Susan B. Anthony[33] and Elizabeth Cady Stanton[34] did not receive an invitation due to their opposition to the fourteenth and fifteenth amendments. They argued that women's suffrage was completely ignored by both pieces of legislation.

A surprise guest was Thomas Wentworth Higginson[35], once part of the group known as the Secret Six. This group of wealthy white men helped to finance John Brown's[36] campaign to end slavery, which included his failed raid on Harpers Ferry in Virginia.[37] Unlike the other members of the group, Higginson never fled to Canada or elsewhere. He, in fact, attempted to raise money for Brown's defense. Higginson was never arrested or called to testify. During the Civil War, he led the first federally-authorized regiment of black troops in South Carolina. Wade admired Higginson and was sure to include him in his Reconstruction efforts in a significant way.

Given this inaugural audience, which also included the entire sect of congressional Radical Republicans led by Stevens and Sumner it was clear

---

[33] Anthony was a social reformer who played a major role in the women's suffrage movement. In 1856, she became the New York state agent for the American Anti-Slavery Society. *To read Susan B. Anthony's own writing and speech, read* Failure is Impossible: Susan B. Anthony in Her Own Words *by Lynn Sherr, Time Books, 1996.*

[34] Stanton was a social reformer, abolitionist, and leader of the early women's rights movement. Her Declaration of Sentiments, presented at the Seneca Falls Convention in 1848, is often credited with initiating the first organized women's rights and women's suffrage movements in the United States. *To explore Stanton's own written work, read* The Woman's Bible, *published in 1895 and 1898.*

[35] Higginson was an abolitionist, active in the anti-slavery movement during the 1840s and 1850s. Higginson had been a militant and vocal member of the "Secret Six," a group of John Brown supporters, where he raised money to finance the raid at Harper's Ferry and encouraged John Brown to follow through with the plan. Higginson was also one of the leading male activists of the women's rights movement. *To read Higginson's own words, read* Army Life in a Black Regiment, *originally published in 1869.*

[36] Brown was a white abolitionist, most noted for leading a slave uprising in Harpers Ferry, Virginia. He believed the institution of slavery could only be dismantled through armed insurrection.

[37] In 1859, John Brown, in an attempt to start a liberation movement among slaves, led 21 men in an unsuccessful raid on the federal armory at Harpers Ferry that ended with his capture. His plan had been to seize the weapons and distribute them to slaves throughout the South. Brown was put on trial for treason against the Commonwealth of Virginia, the murder of five men, and inciting a slave insurrection, which resulted in his conviction and a sentence of death by hanging. *For a detailed account of the raid, see* Midnight Rising: John Brown and the Raid that Sparked the Civil War, *by Tony Horwitz, Large Print Press, 2012.*

for all to see the new president was determined to change the course of American history, at least as it concerned the South and the newly-freed slave.

Following the inaugural ceremony, select guests were invited to a reception at the Executive Mansion, which many referred to as the White House. Douglass was one of the first guests to arrive. Many observers who stood outside were shocked to see a Negro enter the president's home as a guest. Douglass savored the moment, deliberately taking his time to exit his carriage. He engaged in a measured walk to the entrance of the Mansion. No effort was made to bar him from the premises.

Walking into the East Room, he made his way over to the first lady. A well-formed and attractive woman, Caroline Rosenkrans Wade[38] looked radiant but a bit tense, Douglass thought.

"You'll get used to it Madam First Lady," said Douglass.

"Excuse me, Mister Douglass," asked the first lady.

"Oh, I was referring to your role as our nation's First Lady," stated Douglass. "I said you'll get used to it."

"You would think I should be used to it by now, Mister Douglass. It's been about a year." The first lady said with a chuckle.

"It takes time, Madam First Lady. Trust me, you're doing fine," replied Douglass.

"I sure hope you're right, Mister Douglass," the first lady said with a sigh. "The task before us is so important for our nation. By the way, Mister Douglass," the first lady continued.

"Call me Fred," stated Douglass.

"If you insist," the first lady said. "You may call me Caroline."

"If you insist," stated Douglass." They both laughed.

"I was about to say, I read the speech you gave to that sewing society in Rochester years ago. It's still one of my favorites."[39]

"Mine too," said Douglass with a smile.

A studious woman, the first lady made it a point to stay up to date on all major matters pertaining to the nation. She was well aware of Douglass and other abolitionist leaders. She was also friends with many in

---

[38] Wife of Benjamin Wade. She was born in Lansingburg, New York, on July 30, 1805. She was married to Benjamin Wade on May 19, 1841. *See The Life of Benjamin F. Wade by Albert G. Riddle.*

[39] On July 5, 1852, Frederick Douglass gave this speech titled "The Meaning of July Fourth for the Negro" in Rochester, New York, at Rochester's Corinthian Hall.

the women's suffrage movement. Her views regarding the latter influenced her husband. She would half-jokingly tell friends she would whisper ideas into her husband's ear while he slept and in the morning, he would wake up with a revelation.

At that moment, the president came up from behind them. "Dear, do you mind if I borrow Mister Douglass for a moment," said Wade.

"I certainly do. We were talking about the monumental task ahead for our nation," stated the first lady.

"Actually, that's what I would like to speak to him about," stated Wade. " There are other guests we must attend to, dear," stated Wade.

"I hope they're as charming as Fred."

"I can't promise you that, my dear." Wade stated with a laugh, glancing at Douglass.

"Until we meet again, Caroline. It was a pleasure," stated Douglass.

"The pleasure was all mine, Mister Douglass," the first lady said.

"Well, Mister Douglass," started Wade, as they climbed the steps leading to the second floor of the Executive Mansion,

"Fred will do fine, Mister President," stated Douglass.

"Excuse me, Mister Douglass?"

"I said you can call me Fred, Mister President."

"Alright Fred, and you can call me Bluff. It's my nickname used by my friends, and I consider you a friend Fred," stated Wade.

"Thank you, Mister President. The feeling is mutual," stated Douglass.

"Right this way," stated Wade as he led Douglass down a long hall and pass a couple of guards and to his office.

The two men entered a well-lit room. Wade began to talk. "You know I didn't care for the last two fellas who lived here. One a pretender, and the other a damn scoundrel," stated Wade. "I see you had your troubles with both of them as well, Fred."

"Well, I considered Johnson useless, Mister President," stated Douglass.

"Bluff, Fred. Please call me Bluff," demanded Wade.

"My apologies Bluff," Douglass nodded once to Wade and continued. "Johnson had no compassion or decency at all. Ignoring those horrible stories told by Negroes who came from the South. Innocent men, women, and children, slaughtered because they wore the indelible mark of the slave. Slaughtered, Bluff, slaughtered like animals by those damn ex-Confederates. The president seemed to ignore the fact that we fought a war to end slavery and the evils produced by such a God awful system."

"Tell me, Fred, why did you support Fremont in the election of '64?"

"Well, Bluff, Lincoln wouldn't go far enough. I got tired of the president and his God-forsaken Ten Percent plan[40], which basically placed the Negro back in the care of our former slave masters," said Douglass. "Later on, it took him forever to get on board with the Thirteenth Amendment[41] and when he finally came around he made it appear it was his damn idea. Bluff, on a smaller note, ole Abe, from what I'm told, amused himself by telling darkie jokes and spending down time at minstrel shows. So I don't regret my actions in not supporting him."

"Fred, I can tell you stories about Lincoln that would shock the hell out of Negroes and whites too. The bastard once said if he could save the Union by not freeing the slaves or save the Union by freeing the slaves he would do so in a heartbeat. Lincoln, I'll tell ya, was one slippery fella," said Wade. "Hell, the man wanted to send all Negroes back to Africa or to some remote island. He said it in my presence. Lincoln, if you ask me, seriously believed in the superiority of the white race," said Wade.

"What about you, Bluff?" The question seemed to catch Wade off-guard. Wade stared briefly at Douglass. "Fred, I don't believe in the equality of men."

"Sir?" Douglass interrupted. Wade now stared straight into Douglass' eyes.

"No, Fred, I believe in the equality of all men and women, too. That's what we are here to build, Fred and now that we are in power, I intend to push our agenda unapologetically. I don't give a God damn about the other side, Fred. I just don't. I believe my presidency has been ordained by the Creator of this here universe, and I intend to make him or her damn

---

[40] The Ten Percent Plan was part of Lincoln's Reconstruction Plan and allowed a Southern state to be readmitted into the Union once 10 percent of its voters swore an oath of allegiance to the Union. The policy was meant to shorten the war by offering a relatively easy route to attaining peace. *For a comprehensive overview on Lincoln's policies, see* Cengage Advantage Books: Making America: A History of the United States *by Berkin, et al., Wadsworth Publishing, Edition 6, 2012, pp. 388.*

[41] The Thirteenth Amendment abolished slavery and involuntary servitude, except as a punishment for a crime. According to Angela Davis, "The 13th Amendment, when it abolished slavery, did so except for convicts. Through the prison system, the vestiges of slavery have persisted." Thus it can be concluded that through the methods of the prison-industrial complex — mandatory minimum sentences, harsh penalties for nonviolent drug offenses that are racially-biased, the continuous construction of for-profit prisons that goes on regardless of crime rates — slavery has not yet been fully abolished. *For further reading, see* Are Prisons Obsolete *by Angela Davis, Seven Stories Press, 2003.*

proud. Now let's get to work."

Wade walked over to his desk. He appeared slightly taller than Douglass first thought. His presence was majestic, and he wore a determined look on his face. "Over here, Fred. Read this while I get this canvas together." Douglass noticed a rather large stack of papers in the president's hand. "Take your time, Fred. This will take a couple of minutes.

"Sure, Bluff," Douglass said as he began to read.

He could see the president unfurling a large white canvas with what appeared to be a drawing on one side. Douglass kept reading the document handed to him by Wade. He soon became startled by its contents.

"Yes, sir, Fred. We are about to make history. Are you ready?" Douglass, still captivated by the document, barely heard the president.

"Did you hear me, Fred?"

"Yes, sir. I mean, Mister, I mean, Bluff. This is unbelievable. Can you do this?" asked Douglass.

"Fred — did you forget so soon? I'm the God damn President of the United States. Now come on over here. I want to show you this chart."

Douglass made his way to the table. The image became clearer and clearer. At the top of the canvas, in bold letters, it read "Fifth Reconstruction Act." Douglass studied the drawing for a few minutes.

"Well, what do you think?" asked Wade.

"Is this what I think it is, Mister President? Can you sell it to the Congress, Bluff?" asked Douglass.

"That's what I was elected to do, Fred," said Wade.

## — FIVE —

# The Fifth Reconstruction Act

**❝**Fred, do you recall the Wade-Davis bill[42] of 1864? Both houses of Congress passed it in July of that year, and that bastard Lincoln had the temerity to pocket veto[43] the bill. I'll tell you, Fred, my dear friend Henry, who co-sponsored the bill with me, had a fit."

"I recall the bill, Bluff," Douglass said.

"Take a peep, Fred. Here's the key to the entire plan for Reconstruction," Wade stated, pointing to the box on the far left of the canvas that read "Military Oversight/Public Safety." "Fred, in order for Reconstruction to work, the Negro's life, property, and rights under the Constitution must be protected. Agree?" Wade asked turning to Douglass.

"Absolutely," said Douglass. "But who do you have in mind for this position, Bluff?"

"I've given the matter a lot of thought, and I think Tom Higginson would be perfect. What do you think Fred? Any thoughts on Tom?" asked

---

[42] Crafted by Radical Republicans Senator Benjamin Wade and Representative Henry Winter Davis, the bill was a proposed plan of Reconstruction of the South. The bill required that more than 50 percent of voters in each of the former Confederate states take the Ironclad Oath, which required them to swear they had never supported either the secession of their state or the Confederacy. The bill passed both houses of Congress but was pocket vetoed by Lincoln and thus never took effect.

[43] A political maneuver that gives the president the power to singularly stop a bill by taking no action. "Veto" is Latin for "I forbid" and gives a governing body, such as the president, the power to singularly stop an official action, such as the passage of a bill. A pocket veto is the exercise of veto power not through official declaration of veto, but rather through complete inaction on the part of a governing body (again, such as the president) when action is required for the proposed action (a bill) to come into effect.

Wade.

"Wow, Bluff, no one can accuse you of being soft on the South." They both laughed.

"It'll give those damn rebels something to think about, Fred."

"Can you get him approved, Mister President?"

"Hell, you just said the magic words Fred — 'Mister President.' I'm the damn President and the buck stops here. Besides, with Stevens in the House and Sumner in the Senate, I don't have a worry in the world about the bill's passage," said Wade. "Now here's the plan," Wade continued.

Over the next thirty minutes, Wade explained the Fifth Reconstruction Act. Tom Higginson would be appointed as major general in charge of all military and police operations in the former Confederacy. Each commander of the five military districts would now answer to him. He would be responsible for establishing a militia in each state and a police force in every county with a population of 25,000 or more citizens. Counties with fewer than 25,000 would consist of deputies who would answer to the Sheriff of the nearest county.

Higginson would be authorized to establish a war college to train senior black officers; an officer candidate school to train junior officers; NCO schools for non-commissioned officers; and a police academy to train local law enforcement officials. There would be at least two military academies in each of the five districts to train new recruits. Currently, there were only 20,000 federal troops in the South. Wade found the number appallingly low and sought to increase the number to over 200,000.

Most significant for Higginson was the power granted to him by the Act to declare a State of Emergency in any one or all five military districts if conditions required. To prevent political manipulation of the Act, the power to rescind the declaration once it was invoked belonged to Higginson alone.

For his part, Higginson could only invoke the declaration for a period of 120 days. Once the emergency order was rescinded, it could only be resurrected by the Secretary of War with the support of the president. However, at any point during the 120-day period, Higginson could request the emergency declaration be extended until the conditions that brought about the emergency had sufficiently passed. Once the order was extended, it could not be rescinded unless he chose to do so or the president and three-fourths of the United States Senate decided the State of Emergency should be terminated.

This was an extraordinary feature of the Act. Even some of the most ardent supporters of the Act viewed this particular feature with some concern. For, if ever invoked, an extended emergency decree would give Higginson or his successor complete dictatorial powers over the states in the former Confederacy. The rationale behind this was to insulate Higginson from any future president or Senate body which proved sympathetic to the ex-Confederates.

Additionally, under the Act there would be seven departments assigned to the reconstruction efforts for the South. Each department would be headed by a commissioner who would answer to the Secretary of War. The Judicial Oversight Department was to ensure fairness for blacks in the court system throughout the South. The Department of Education would work hand in hand with the newly-created Department of Education at the federal level. The Department of Agriculture would teach blacks the latest techniques in farming and food production.

The Department of Revenue Services would help to establish a more efficient way of tax assessment and collection. The Department on Land Reform was an offshoot of the Freedmen's Bureau designed to help facilitate land confiscation from ex-Confederates and land distribution to blacks. The Department of Banking would establish a regional system of banks to assist blacks with financial services. Finally, the powerful Commission on Election and Voter Fraud would work directly with each state's Secretary of State to oversee voter registration, election fraud and voter education. The individual chosen to oversee this department would be entrusted with enormous political power and would be, in effect, the second most powerful man in the South after Higginson.

"Excuse me, Mister President," a voice from behind the door whispered loudly. "Yeah, what the hell is it?" yelled Wade.

"Your guests are waiting," the voice said.

"Well, let them wait," screamed Wade.

"Sir," the voice said, "the first lady is asking for you as well."

"Why didn't you say that in the first place?" Wade's tone softened. "Tell 'em all I'll be right there."

"Will do, Mister President," said the messenger.

"Fred, I gotta go attend to my ceremonial duties but what I need from you is to promote this Act as if your life depended on it. From time to time, I'll ask you to go south as my personal envoy and report back to me directly about the landscape down there. This is one hell of an opportunity we got here, Fred. Are you with me?"

"Say no more, Bluff. I'm at your beck and call."

"That's what I want to hear," said Wade. "Now let's get back to the party, and, Fred,"

"Yes, Bluff."

"The next time you come by to visit please bring along Mrs. Douglass. Caroline and I would love to meet her."

"I'm sure she'll be happy to meet the both of you too, sir."

Douglass followed the president out of his office. He turned back for one last peek at the huge canvas. A big smile came to his face and he shook his head, clasped his hands and looked to the ceiling above. After all his years of struggle, his prayers and the prayers of millions of blacks throughout America were finally answered in the form of President Benjamin Bluff Wade.

# — SIX —

# The Southern Guard

The war left much of the South's infrastructure in total ruin, and without the free labor provided by its former slaves, the task of rebuilding would fall upon the citizens of the former Confederacy. Many returning Confederate soldiers could not believe what had become of their once-beautiful landscape. Even more disturbing to many Southern whites, their former slaves would now have a say in how the South would be governed. This was unbearable for many whites, especially the returning soldiers.

In 1865, six veterans of the Confederate Army decided to form an organization whose principle mission would be to terrorize the black population in and around Pulaski, Tennessee. Their signature trademark was the donning of hoods made of various types of cloth to hide their faces. In the beginning, the organization was a local operation. The membership was made up of disgruntled soldiers and local residents still reeling from the South's devastating defeat and the presence of federal troops occupying their homeland. The presence of blacks going about their daily lives without having to pay the slightest homage to them was too much for many white Southerners to bear.

From the outset, the Ku Klux Klan[44] presented itself as a terrorist outfit.

---

[44] Formally established in 1865 at the end of the Civil War and during Reconstruction, "the Klan" is America's first true terrorist group. It was formed as a social club by a group of Confederate Army veterans in Pulaski, Tennessee, adopting its name from the Greek word "kyklos," meaning "circle," and the English word "clan." They first mobilized as a vigilante group that sought to prevent African Americans from enjoying basic rights, using intimidation tactics like rape, hooded costumes, and gave members puerile titles like "Imperial Wizard," "Grand

Neither the age, gender nor physical condition of their targets made any difference. All that mattered was the color of the individual's skin. KKK members committed unspeakable acts of brutality against black men, women, and children. Pregnant women were butchered and so were small children. Men were lynched and forced to swallow their genitals while crowds of whites cheered. Some blacks were skinned alive. Others were tarred and feathered and set ablaze. No act was too gruesome for their tormentors.

The KKK wiped out entire families. Thousands perished under their brief but brutal reign of terror. Those spared, lived in constant fear of their lives and the lives of their family members, friends and neighbors.

Things got so bad the federal government passed an anti-terrorist bill known as the Enforcement Act of 1870.[45] This act not only protected blacks from the violence of the Klan, it also sought to protect the suffrage rights of blacks. The Enforcement Act did have a powerful impact on curbing Klan violence. However, President Wade strongly believed blacks would be better served if they had the means to protect themselves and safeguard their newly-won rights.

The Fifth Reconstruction Act did just that. General Tom Higginson wasted no time in establishing military training centers in each of the five military districts. Black males fifteen years of age and over received military training and many served in their respective state and local militias. Most whites utterly refused to serve or receive training on an equal status as blacks so decided to forego their opportunity to serve in the militia. This decision on the part of whites would come back to haunt them terribly. Since paramilitary outfits were outlawed, whites who chose not to

---

Titan," and "Exalted Cyclops." The organization sought to overthrow the Republican state governments in the South during the Reconstruction era, especially by violence against African Americans and other civil rights supporters. Later, the group expanded its circle of hatred by becoming severely anti-immigrant (mainly Catholic and Jewish) as well. Throughout its existence, the group has advocated for extremist viewpoints like white supremacy, white nationalism, and xenophobia. *For a holistic view of the KKK that describes the terrorist group throughout the entirety of its most active years, read* Hooded Americanism: The History of the Ku Klux Klan *by David J. Chalmers, Duke University Press Books, Third Edition, 1987.*

[45] Introduced by Republican John Bingham, the act prohibited discrimination in voter registration on the basis of race, color, or previous condition of servitude. The act authorized federal penalties for violating the act and allowed the president to mobilize the army in order to enforce it, if necessary, and use federal marshals to bring charges against offenders for election fraud, bribery, or otherwise preventing citizens from exercising their constitutional right to vote. The full text of the act can be found freely online through various sources.

attend the training centers would have to be fortunate enough to have received training already, or rely on individual training. Most did not see the need for the training and considered it a waste of time.

Many black communities sprang up near the training systems. The lingering fear of the Klan and other white terrorist groups caused many blacks to stay as close to each other as possible. Additionally, many black communities established agreements among their members, which served to protect and advance the agricultural interest and general welfare of their members. Thus, if a male had to leave for military training, other males in the community would volunteer to handle his duties in the field. The agreements would be governed by strict codes of morality to discourage adultery and other violations, which could create discord in a given community. With the exception of a few violations, the system worked extremely well and many black communities prospered.

Individuals received ten weeks of intensive training. Higginson demanded the highest level of training possible. The training program consisted of five two-week sessions. Thousands of black males received this valuable training. Many soldiers in the Union Army stationed in the South considered the training provided by Higginson far superior to any training they received prior to going into battle during the war.

Black males reporting to and from duty filled the roads and railways of the South. White Union officers and non-commissioned officers conducted most of the training. Recruits were given the option to join the Union Army, the field of law enforcement, or the militia reserves.

Those who chose to enter the law enforcement field would receive the necessary training and would later become the constables and police officers in their respective communities. Those who chose to become regular members of the Union Army would sign up for a term of service and be stationed in and around their respective communities but could be sent anywhere based on the needs of the army.

Others chose to remain in the militia reserves. Many of these men enjoyed farming and being with their families and would only be called up in time of need. In most states the latter would receive training at least two weeks out of the year. However, at least three states — Louisiana, Alabama and Arkansas — provided up to six weeks of training per year. This respect for military readiness would later prove to be invaluable.

Some trainees exhibited exceptional military talent and skill. After much deliberation among his staff, Higginson decided to create an elite guard in each of the five military districts. This unit would be a standing army whose primary mission would be to safeguard the capitals and the elected officials in each state in the five military districts. They would number about 5,000 per state. They would remain under federal authority until the military districts were disbanded, and then would become an arm of the state under the authority of the state's governor. They would come to be known as the Southern Guard or "SG." President Wade, upon hearing the idea, could not conceal his gratitude for this arrangement. He immediately sent words of praise to Higginson for his brilliant idea. He also inquired about the training school for officers and NCOs.

Due to the dearth of black Union officers and NCOs, candidates for these schools proved hard to find. Higginson decided to do two things. First, he inquired of all recruits who reported to training about their military background. Those who could show proof of their ranks during the war, maintained those ranks and entered their respective schools. Secondly, he informed trainers to recruit those individuals who displayed leadership abilities during their military training for his officer and NCO schools.

Most of the black officers who served in the Union Army were literate. Most black NCOs were not. In an effort to increase the ranks of black officers, Higginson granted hundreds of blacks selected as officer candidates an opportunity to complete their training if they made a commitment to become literate. Many took him up on his offer, and, with the assistance of dedicated tutors from the North, did in fact become officers after passing a literacy exam given at the end of the year.

Officer and NCO recruits were also given the choice of an assignment. Some chose a career in the Union Army and others chose a career in law enforcement. Most chose to remain in the militia reserves with their rank intact. The SG welcomed those officers and NCOs who displayed exceptional talents.

Since his appointment in the summer of 1869, Higginson had created a militia reserve force consisting of nearly a quarter of a million black males throughout the five military districts. He created a well-trained constabulary force in all but a few counties throughout each military district. He doubled the size of the Union Army in the South, but Higginson's pride and joy was the creation of the elite SG made up of 50,000 crack soldiers — mostly black. They wore dark purple trousers, crisp, white shirts, matching purple blazers with gold colored buttons and dark purple hats. The SG officers had a thick gold stripe running down the sides of their trousers and a gold braided rope adorned their caps. The uniform of the SG enhanced the aura of the organization.

The SG consisted of the best-educated, most talented, best-equipped, and well-trained soldiers in the South. The SG also consisted of men who possessed a certain degree of mental toughness. They took their newfound freedom seriously and would die to defend it. Higginson made it a point to find such men during the recruiting process. Each man singled out as a potential SG recruit had to undergo a rigorous interview hearing. Those considered docile or possessing signs of an obsequious nature did not make the cut.

During a visit to an officer training school in Texas, Higginson took a particular interest in one officer. His training record far exceeded the expectations of his superiors. During the war he held the rank of captain in the Union Army, which by anyone's measurement was quite an accomplishment. Not many blacks achieved that rank and none attained a rank higher than captain.

The man had a quiet way about him. A man of average height, he possessed a well built frame wrapped in dark brown skin. Blessed with a spectacular brilliance, he maintained a steely discipline. His peers relied on him for leadership and he earned the respect of his subordinates. Even white officers and NCOs displayed a remarkable deference toward him, at least in his presence.

His name was Aurelius Foginet, and that name would one day, in the not-too-distant future, send shivers down the spines of ex-Confederates and their sympathizers in the North and South. He would also bring hope and salvation to millions of blacks.

# SEVEN

# Lyle Davenport (Party Boss)

I f Tom Higginson was the most powerful man in the South, Lyle Davenport was a close second. A Southerner by birth, Davenport was sent to live with relatives in Lancaster, Pennsylvania in his early teens. They said he possessed peculiar habits for a young man with such charm and good looks.

His family had strong roots in Pennsylvania's Democratic Party and young Lyle began to frequent many political gatherings where he earned a reputation for being extremely bright and possessing superb organizational skills. He soon began to work on campaigns for some of the major players in Pennsylvania's Democratic circles, including the campaign of future President James Buchanan.[46] Davenport spent much of his time with a small group of adolescent males like himself. They made the most of their free time hanging with the politicians who influenced Pennsylvania's politics. Some of them, including Davenport, procured an older companion, who served as both a benefactor and lover.

As Buchanan's star rose, so did the fortunes of those in his political circle, including young Davenport's. However, in 1857 after Buchanan was elected president, things took a turn for the worse. Buchanan's apparent influence and support of the Supreme Court's decision in the

---

[46] A Democrat, Buchanan served as the 15th President of the United States just before the Civil War, from 1857 to 1861. Buchanan was a "doughface," a Northerner with Southern sympathies, who attempted to maintain peace between the North and the South. These efforts, however, ultimately backfired as neither side felt sufficient support, and Buchanan's presidency ultimately concluded with the secession of Southern states. *For a recent overview of Buchanan's presidency, see* The Worst President: The Story of James Buchanan *by Garry Boulard.*

case involving Dred Scot in 1857[47] was considered blasphemous by many abolitionists, including Davenport's companion, a leading abolitionist in Pennsylvania.

In writing for the Court's 7-2 majority, Chief Justice Roger Brooke Taney[48] took the position the authors of the constitution believed blacks were "beings of an inferior order, and altogether unfit to associate with the white race, either in social or political relations, and so far inferior that they had no rights which the white man was bound to respect."[49] Buchanan had hoped this would solve the question of slavery in the United States. He was wrong.

For many abolitionists, Buchanan had gone too far. Davenport did not consider himself an abiding abolitionist, but he had a complete loathing for the institution of slavery. Upon learning about Buchanan's successful

---

[47]   Dred Scott was an enslaved African American man who unsuccessfully sued for the freedom of himself, his wife, and their two daughters in the *Dred Scott v. Sandford* case of 1857, popularly known as the "Dred Scott Decision." Scott claimed that his family should be granted their freedom because they had lived in Illinois and the Wisconsin Territory for four years previously, where slavery was illegal. The Supreme Court decided 7-2 against Scott, finding that persons of African descent could not be, nor were ever intended to be, citizens under the U.S. Constitution, and thus Scott was without legal standing to file suit in court. It is considered by many legal scholars to be the worst decision rendered by the U.S. Supreme Court in its history. *For more information on the Dred Scott Decision and at how the United States Constitution has been used to legalize racial hatred, see* Slavery, Law, and Politics: The Dred Scott Case in Historical Perspective *by Don E. Fehrenbacher, Oxford University Press, 1981.*

[48]   The fifth Chief Justice of the Supreme Court, delivered the majority opinion in *Dred Scott v. Sandford* in 1857. The framers of the Constitution, Taney famously wrote, believed that African Americans "had no rights which the white man was bound to respect; and that the Negro might justly and lawfully be reduced to slavery for his benefit. He was bought and sold and treated as an ordinary article of merchandise and traffic, whenever profit could be made by it." In 1820, Taney's court had declared the Missouri Compromise unconstitutional, thus permitting slavery in all of the country's territories. *Quote is taken from the text of the Dred Scott Decision.*

[49]   *"In the opinion of the Court the legislation and histories of the times, and the language used in the Declaration of Independence, show that neither the class of persons who had been imported as slaves nor their descendants, whether they had become free or not, were then acknowledged as a part of the people nor intended to be included in the general words used in that memorable instrument. They had for more than a century before been regarded as beings of an inferior order and altogether unfit to associate with the white race, either in social or political relations; and so far inferior that they had no rights which the white man was bound to respect; and that the Negro might justly and lawfully be reduced to slavery for his benefit. He was bought and sold and treated as an ordinary article of merchandise and traffic whenever a profit could be made by it. This opinion was at that time fixed and universal in the civilized portion of the white race."*

attempt to influence Associate Justice Robert Cooper Grier, a Northerner and fellow Pennsylvanian, to support the majority on the Court so the decision would not appear to be based on sectional politics, Davenport's political faith was shaken. He decided to give electoral politics a rest and devote his energies to the abolitionist cause.

By the time Wade was sworn in as president following Johnson's impeachment some eleven years later, Davenport had gained a reputation as a master organizer and staunch supporter of the Radical Republicans. When the time came to appoint someone to lead the party's political efforts in the former Confederacy, Wade turned to Lyle Davenport.

Davenport's triumphant return to his southern homeland was for him a gift from the Creator. He understood the reason for his exile. His involuntary departure from the place he called home was supported and applauded by many who shunned his lifestyle. The tables were now turned, and he held the power. He would now decide who would be run out of town — unless the Secretary of War or the president had anything to say about it.

As the head of the powerful Commission on Election and Voter Fraud, he had the awesome task to protect the suffrage rights of blacks. It would also be his task to ensure the newly freed slave received the political education needed to make informed decisions.

Prior to getting started, he made it a point to meet with General Higginson and his staff. Davenport was accompanied to this important meeting by his brilliant executive assistant Randall McArthur, a black man about five years younger than Davenport, and two other assistants. Davenport and McArthur were also lovers. Higginson was accompanied by his executive secretary, and his newly-promoted colonel and adjunct Aurelius Foginet. Foginet had served briefly as a major but given the dearth of black officers in the Union Army and Foginet's unique talents, not to mention the fact that he outshined all others of equal rank, Higginson wasted no time in making him a full colonel.

The meeting took place in Rabun County, Georgia, the place of Davenport's birth and where he spent much of his youth and adolescence before being sent away. Rabun also had the distinction of being one of only five counties in the state of Georgia which did not secede from the Union.

Davenport had a simple plan. He would establish election and voter fraud commissions in each of the five military districts. Each Secretary of State would serve as de-facto members of his state's respective commission to ensure all elections laws were strictly followed. Each commission would create voter education teams that would fan out across their respective district accompanied by a detachment of the Southern Guard or SG as they were now commonly called. The part of the plan involving the SG required the approval of Higginson.

The teams would hold meetings at churches, schools and, other public settings to educate blacks and whites who chose to participate in the electoral process. Attendees would learn about the duties and terms of each office and how to properly examine the background of a given candidate.

The crown jewel of Davenport's plan was the "Ironclad Oath"[50] prescribed in the Wade-Davis Bill. The Oath was to be administered to all men in the former Confederacy (with the exception of Tennessee) seeking to vote or hold office. Individuals had to swear they never supported the Confederacy in any way, shape, or form. The Oath stated:

> "I, A. B., do solemnly swear (or affirm) that I have never voluntarily borne arms against the United States since I have been a citizen thereof; that I have voluntarily given no aid, countenance, counsel, or encouragement to persons engaged in armed hostility thereto; that I have neither sought nor accepted nor attempted to exercise the functions of any office whatever, under any authority or pretended authority in hostility to the United States; that I have not yielded a voluntary support to any pretended government, authority, power or constitution within the United States, hostile or inimical thereto. And I do further swear (or affirm) that, to the best of my knowledge and ability, I will support and defend the Constitution of the United States, against all enemies, foreign and domestic; that I will bear true faith and allegiance to the same; that I take this obligation freely, without any mental reservation or purpose of evasion, and that I will well and

---

[50] The Ironclad Oath required former Confederate officials and voters, to swear they had never supported the Confederacy. Therefore, by design, the Oath limited the political activity of obvious supporters of the Confederacy like former Confederate soldiers and politicians. Implementation of the Ironclad Oath was supported by Radical Republicans, but rejected by Abraham Lincoln who vetoed it when it was presented in the Wade-Davis Bill of 1864. *For a full text of the Oath, see the* United States Statutes at Large, 37th Congress, 2nd Session. *Commonly referred to simply as the* Statues at Large, *it is the official source for the laws and resolutions passed by Congress.*

faithfully discharge the duties of the office on which I am about to enter, so help me God."

Higginson loved the idea and pledged his full support. The Oath in and of itself would wrest power completely away from ex-Confederate sympathizers. He surmised this was exactly what the president had in mind. With Davenport's plan in full effect, by the time the elections rolled around in 1872 Republicans would virtually control every former Confederate statehouse with the possible exception of Tennessee.

Foginet loved the plan as well but insisted the SG prepare periodic reports of citizen participation in the electoral process. He also wanted reports regarding public safety and voter intimidation. Higginson agreed. Foginet's next request startled both Davenport and Higginson. Foginet requested a non-uniformed officer of the SG serve on each district's election commission in the role of observer. Davenport questioned the need for such a presence.

"It would help with the SG's coordination efforts," replied Foginet. Higginson did not completely understand Foginet's motives, but had come to trust Foginet's insight and supported his rising star's assessment and request.

"Well, what do you think of Davenport?" asked Higginson, turning to Foginet during the ride back to the lodge.

"He's a smart man. Sharp mind - and very organized. I like that especially, sir," said Foginet.

"A little different, huh?" asked Higginson.

"General?" Foginet heard the question but needed more time to think of an honest and appropriate response.

"I guess you don't see that particular lifestyle too often. Do you find his lifestyle problematic, Colonel?" asked Higginson.

"My position on such matters is simple, General. A man — or woman, for that matter, sir, is who he or she is. We cannot and should never sacrifice competence and genius over such trivial matters. That would be imprudent."

"Tell me," Higginson continued, quickly changing the subject, "do you think it's necessary for the SG to be on every election commission, Colonel?"

"No, sir," said Foginet. "I think it's necessary for the SG to be everywhere." Higginson turned and stared briefly at Foginet, who stared straight ahead.

Back home in Rabun, Davenport turned to McArthur. "A rather productive encounter. Wouldn't you say?"

"Are you asking me a question, Lyle?" asked McArthur.

"Well what do you think?" asked Davenport, as he began to remove his clothing.

"I think the General is sincere, but Colonel Foginet is a little intimidating," said McArthur.

"Yeah, and a bit nosey," said Davenport. "Sooner than later his SG will be watching us take a crap. It might be prudent for us to keep a close eye on Colonel Foginet. By the way, did you realize he's the highest ranking Negro soldier in the country?" asked Davenport.

"He's not just any soldier, Lyle," said McArthur. "After General Higginson and General Maguire, he's third in command of the SG and just to be an officer in the SG is quite prestigious," McArthur stated.

"Oh, is it now? I see someone completed his SG homework?" said Davenport, rolling his eyes.

"I think it's prudent to get to know one's allies. Would you not agree?" asked McArthur. Not unlike most blacks who knew of Foginet, McArthur could not help but be impressed by his rising stature.

"I think someone has an eye for the colonel," said Davenport.

"Well, you can't deny his intellect or good looks and strong physique," said McArthur.

"Point well taken, Randall," said Davenport as he rested his chin on the palm of his hand and stared at the corner of the room as if deep in thought. "Now, let's get some sleep. Tomorrow promises to be a big day for both of us." Davenport finally came out of his brief trance.

"I'll be there in a second Lyle. I just want to pen the last few lines of this letter," said McArthur.

"Who are you writing to? If you don't mind me asking, Randall."

"Oh, an old friend of mine. She works for the U.S. Internal Revenue Bureau. She just arrived from Washington. I'm sure you heard the name before. They call her the Wizard," said McArthur.

"Oh, yes. Of course. Some type of math prodigy," said Davenport, feeling relieved. "Well, hurry and finish up. We can both use a good night sleep."

"I'll be right there, Lyle." McArthur put the finishing touches on his letter to Lisa Stewart.

# — EIGHT —

# The Wizard

Shortly after President Wade's inauguration in 1869, a man by the name of Joseph Seligman[51] was offered the post of Secretary of the Treasury but declined for personal reasons. Wade's next choice, Alexander T. Stewart[52], was one of the richest men of his day. Due to a possible conflict of interest with circumstances surrounding his business interest, he was declared ineligible for the appointment. The president then turned to George Sewall Boutwell[53] to serve as the nation's 28th Secretary of the Treasury.

Prior to serving in that post, Boutwell had already served as a State Representative in his home state of Massachusetts; State Banking Commissioner; the 20th Governor of Massachusetts; Secretary of the state's Board of Education; was appointed by President Lincoln as the first Com-

---

[51] A banker and businessman during the Civil War, Seligman was rumored to be responsible for aiding the Union by contributing a large sum of money in bonds.

[52] Stewart was a successful Irish multimillionaire who made his fortune in the dry goods (dried food in the pre-refrigeration era) business. In March 1969, President Ulysses S. Grant offered Stewart the position of secretary of the treasury, but his appointment was not approved by the Senate.

[53] Boutwell, an abolitionist, is primarily known for his leadership in the formation of the Republican Party, particularly the Massachusetts Republican Party in 1855. He was the 21st governor of Massachusetts and later served in the House of Representatives from 1863 to 1869, as secretary of treasury from 1869 to 1873, and then in the Senate from 1873 to 1894. During Reconstruction, Boutwell advocated for African American citizenship and suffrage rights. *To read Boutwell's own account of his years in politics, see* Reminiscences of Sixty Years in Public Affairs, *which was originally published in 1902.*

missioner of the United States Internal Revenue Bureau[54]; and served as a U.S. Congressman from his home state. He would later serve in the U.S. Senate. In the end, Boutwell's abolitionist credentials made him attractive to Wade.

A tireless fighter for the anti-slavery cause, Boutwell would have been Wade's first choice to run the Treasury Department. However, the custom governing appointments to the presidential cabinet at the time dictated two individuals from the same state should not serve in the president's cabinet simultaneously. At the time of Boutwell's appointment Ebenezer Rockwood Hoar[55] also resided in Massachusetts. Hoar did offer to retire, but Wade would hear none of it, and both men did in fact serve in the cabinet.

In his capacity as Secretary of the Treasury it was his job to oversee his old office, the Internal Revenue Bureau. The Commisssioner of Internal Revenue would normally be charge with establishing a tax collection system in the South. Boutwell had other ideas. The fiscal condition of the South following the war made this a tough challenge and Boutwell wanted ed the best minds he could find for this particular mission.

Prior to the war, much of the property was self-assessed by the wealthy landowners. This created fraudulent assessments that provided little revenue. Most of the revenue for states came from the business of buying and selling slaves and the fees associated with this business. With little money, Southern states had a difficult time building and maintaining their infrastructures before the war. Now that the war was over, what little infrastructure that did exist laid in ruin. Prior to the war, Southern states also had little money to build schools, hospitals and other public necessities. After the war, the situation, as one can imagine, was much, much worse.

To handle the task of creating a workable tax collection system, Bout-

---

[54]   The Bureau of Internal Revenue, now known as the Internal Revenue Service (IRS), was established in July 1862, during the Civil War, when President Abraham Lincoln and Congress created the position of commissioner of internal revenue (which exists today as the head of the IRS) and enacted a temporary income tax to cover war expenses.

[55]   Hoar was appointed U.S. Attorney General in 1869 by President Ulysses Grant and served as the first head of the Department of Justice in July, 1870. Hoar was a moderate Republican and opposed federal intervention in protecting African American citizens, believing that Southerners would choose to treat them with respect. Eventually however, Grant could see that Southerners would not willingly comply with new federal law, and came under increased pressure to replace Hoar with someone more radical. In June 1870, without explanation, Grant sent Hoar a letter that requested his resignation from the office of attorney general.

well called on his old friend Arthur Fisk from Massachusetts. Fisk had a solid reputation for matters of banking, tax assessment, and collection, but Boutwell also had a secret weapon. Her name was Lisa Stewart, and she was a young black woman. Years ago she was given a nickname by Boutwell. He called her "The Wizard."

Stewart came to Boutwell's attention when he served as secretary for his state's Board of Education. At the time, the Massachusetts legislature had just voted to integrate its schools, and Stewart was enrolled at the Phillips School, named after the first mayor of Boston, John Phillips. The school was later renamed the Wendell Phillips School[56] after Phillips' son, a renowned abolitionist.

On a visit to the school, Boutwell happened to enter a classroom and observed an instructor engaging a young, beautiful, black girl in college-level mathematics. No other students were present. He inquired as to the situation. The instructor said he was a recent Harvard graduate who had been asked to tutor a child who the headmaster stated was way beyond her peers in the fields of math, science, reading, and writing. The girl, according to the tutor, was by far the most brilliant student he had ever encountered, which included many of his classmates at Harvard. He informed the headmaster that the child should be exploring other avenues for her educational development. The headmaster agreed and told him the girl had already had four previous tutors. Each one left due to the strange pedagogical circumstances they encountered. Boutwell engaged the girl and learned her name was Lisa. She had brown eyes and dark brown skin. She was seven years old.

From that day forth, Stewart's life changed forever. Boutwell later learned Stewart was born shortly before her mother and father escaped from slavery in Maryland and made it safely to Massachusetts. Her father chose to wait until after her birth to escape with his family due to his wife's condition. When his wife regained most her strength, they made their move. Her parents did not want to risk having their child taken from them and sold. Her father was re-enslaved after being captured shortly after the passage of the Fugitive Slave Law in 1850. Stewart and her mother

---

[56] Built in 1834 as school for white children. After Massachusetts required school desegregation in 1855, Phillips became one of the first integrated schools in Boston. In 1863, the Phillips School was renamed the Wendell Phillips School in honor of the abolitionist Wendell Phillips, son of the original namesake, John Phillips. In the 1870s, Elizabeth Smith started teaching at the Phillips School and was thus probably the first African American to teach in an integrated Boston public school.

avoided a similar fate because they were out of town visiting friends when the slavers came. A group of abolitionists cared for them and kept them hidden until the slavers left town. Stewart never saw her father again.

Boutwell moved both mother and child to Groton, Massachusetts, where he and his wife attended to their daily needs. He used his connections to provide Stewart with the best education available at the time. She graduated from high school at eleven, immediately enrolled in college, and subsequently graduated at fifteen with a degree in economics. She was unquestionably the most brilliant child he had ever met.

When Lincoln appointed him to serve as Commissioner of the United States Internal Revenue Bureau, he decided against bringing Stewart with him to Washington due to her young age and concerns regarding her safety. On trips back home he shared with her all there was to know about his position. She also advised him periodically. Needless to say, he heeded her advice. During this time, Stewart interned in a bank in the city of Boston, overseeing complex transactions. Widely respected in her small banking circle, many of the state's top private and public financial experts clamored for an audience with the young prodigy. Boutwell made sure she was paid handsomely for her services. By the time she turned twenty-one, she was rumored to possess a small fortune.

One day she received a letter from Boutwell asking her to come to the nation's capital. She knew it had to be of real importance because she was never asked to come to Washington. Upon her arrival, she was taken straight to the Department of the Treasury for a secret meeting with Boutwell. There she met Fisk, and they were both given their respective assignments. Fisk would serve as the point man for setting up a system of tax assessment and collection but Stewart would handle the day-to-day operations and devise the entire lay-out, reporting only to Fisk or Boutwell. Many in the Massachusetts delegation made it a point to stop by to see her when word got out about her arrival in Washington. Even Senator Charles Sumner paid his respects.

It was May, 1871 when Fisk and Stewart arrived in Pittsboro, North Carolina. The town was chosen as a base of operations because it had been spared the devastation of the war by a simple act of nature. Due to the flooding of the Haw River, Union soldiers could not get to the town.

Fisk and Stewart were met by a large squadron of sharply-dressed SG troops and escorted to a newly-constructed home that would double as their headquarters and living quarters. Stewart loved the spacious accommodations. Fisk, an easy-going man, said, "this will do just fine." Stewart smiled.

Stewart settled in and began to sense something odd, but pleasant about the place since her arrival — the home, the servants, the troops, everything seemed so orderly. She decided to step outside and explore further. She made her way out through the front of the house, and heard what sounded like gunfire coming from the rear. Upon walking around the side of the house, she was met by a small, fair-skinned woman with graying hair, washing linen.

"Good day, Miss Stewart," said the woman.

"Good day...I'm sorry I don't know your name," said Stewart.

"Just call me Nanny or Nan for short," said the woman.

"Excuse me," said Stewart, "but how do you know my name?"

"Oh, we was tol' all 'bout you comin', Miss Stewart," said Nan. "We was tol, a man and a special lady was comin' down ere to pay us folk a visit. We just didn't know it would be you. I means a black gal and a real pretty one. Ebebody is so happy to see you. All the fellas in the SG got their eyes fixed on you."

"Well, thank you, Nan, but what is the SG," asked Stewart as she caressed her short, curly, natural locks.

"Oh the SG is the sudern gard, Miss Stewart. They're ere to protect us. No one messes with dem," said Nan. "They're the ones picked you up from dat train station," Nan continued. "Dey say the SG is ebewhere,."

"Is that right?" quipped Stewart.

"That's right, and dey live in dat building right back dere."

"I think I'll take a walk over there," said Stewart.

"Ok, you safe, round chere, Miss Stewart."

"Nan, please call me Lisa," said Stewart.

"Ok, Miss Lisa, I'll be right chere when you come back. Supper should be ready soon. I hope you is hungry. Even pretty little things gotta eat too," Nan said with a smile.

"I'll be right back, Nan," said Stewart returning a smile and laughter.

Stewart started to make her way over to the large field. A man barked commands at a group of men marching. "Are you lost, ma'am?" a friendly voice asked as he rode up to Stewart on horseback.

"No, sir. Just out for a walk," replied Stewart.

"I'm Sergeant Munroe."

"Hi, I'm Lisa Stewart."

"We know who you are, Miss Stewart; we were not expecting — well, you know."

"A black gal," Stewart finished his thought, playfully using a soft Southern accent.

"Yeah, something like that," said Munroe. "The boys are sho happy to see you," Munroe continued. "Now listen, anything you need, you make sure you ask for me. They gave us strict orders to make sure you are comfortable during your stay, Miss Stewart."

"Well, thank you, Sergeant, uh-"

"That's Sergeant Munroe, ma'am," as he gleefully repeated his name.

"Got it, Sergeant Munroe," Stewart said confidently. "By the way, Sergeant, how many SG are there in these parts?" asked Stewart.

"Well, Miss Stewart, that information is what they call confidential, but I will say this, there are never less than 250 SG soldiers in this area at any given time. The number will probably increase to 1,000 when they make Pittsboro the Capital of the state. Remember the SG is everywhere, Miss Stewart," said Munroe.

"So I've been told," said Stewart.

"'Til we meet again, Miss Stewart," said Munroe, as he began to ride away.

"Excuse me, Sergeant Munroe," said Stewart. Before he could get into his gallop, he swung his horse around.

"Yes, ma'am," he said excitedly.

"Sergeant, is that a shooting range over there?"

"Sho is, ma'am. Would ya like a tour?" Munroe was more than happy to accompany Stewart to the range. He quickly helped her on to the back of his horse. Stewart straddled the horse in her striped teal and yellow skirt. Munroe did a double take.

"What's wrong Sergeant? You never saw a lady ride a horse before," asked Stewart. Stewart knew full well what caught Munroe's attention, but wanted him to explain.

"No, that's not it Miss Stewart," said Munroe carefully. "It just that — well ma'am wouldn't you be more comfortable riding sidesaddle or so, Miss Stewart?" asked Munroe.

"Sergeant, some ladies like myself find this position quite comfortable," said Stewart.

"It's your call, Miss Stewart," Munroe decided not to push back.

"Sergeant?"

"Yes, Miss Stewart."

"How often do you see a man riding sidesaddle?"

"I understand your point. ma'am," said Munroe with a hardy chuckle.

Upon arriving at the range, a few hundred yards from the house where she stayed, a small crowd gathered around the pair.

"This here is Lisa Stewart," said Munroe.

"Glad to have ya, Miss Stewart. We heard all about ya comin," said a young private.

"Right this way, Miss Stewart," said Munroe, clearly making it known to everyone that Stewart was his guest.

"You ever fired a gun, Miss Stewart?" asked Munroe.

"A few times," replied Stewart.

"Want to take a few shots now? I can teach you a few tricks to improve your shot," said Munroe. smiling.

"May I please borrow your weapon, Sergeant?" asked Stewart. Just then a crowd gathered around. Lisa took aim and fired. "A Springfield sixty-one — nice, Sergeant," said Stewart as she loaded the rifle.

"Bulls-eye!" Someone in the crowd screamed. The crowd roared.

"Do it again, Miss Stewart," another onlooker challenged her.

"Does anyone have a Spencer?" The crowd roared its approval. Stewart scanned the crowd, hoping to get an answer.

"Here ya go, ma'am." A young soldier handed Stewart his Spencer rifle.

"Let's see what this can do," Stewart whispered softly to herself but loud enough for those standing next to her to hear.

"Bull-eye!" Stewart took a few more shots to the crowd's delight before heading back to the house.

"You're a natural, Miss Stewart. Damn! Where did you learn to shoot like that, Miss Stewart?" Munroe could not hide his excitement or, better yet, his amazement. "I never saw any woman — and very few men — shoot with such precision, Miss Stewart."

"Let's just say a friend taught me, Sergeant."

"Army fella, ma'am?"

"I'll walk from here, Sergeant." Stewart chose not to respond. She was only a short distance from the house.

"I can take you to the front, ma'am."

"No, this will be fine, Munroe. Thanks for everything."

"Well, I sure enjoyed yo company, Miss Stewart." Munroe helped Stewart off the horse.

"Likewise, Munroe. You take care, and thanks for the lessons," Stewart said teasingly with a smile.

Munroe just smiled and let out a big laugh. "'Til we meet again."

"Goodnight, Sergeant."

Munroe was just one of many soldiers stationed in and around Pittsboro. The SG, while spread out across the state, kept a strong contingent of soldiers in those parts of the state where federal or state business was being conducted. While the police force backed by the local militia seemed to be adequate in most places, the SG would make its presence felt if the need arose. To most black citizens, the SG's presence gave them comfort. For ex-Confederate sympathizers, the SG represented a powerful nuisance.

Over the next few days, Stewart pored over all sorts of documents relating to the demographics, geography, economy, industries, and even prewar history of the state. She would use this formula in every state to develop a practical system of tax assessment. It made Fisk's job incredibly easy.

She made the most out of her accommodations and spent many hours talking with the local residents. Most whites refused to talk with her, but most blacks treated her as royalty. Her beauty invited numerous requests for lunch, dinner, and walks. On a rare occasion she would accept, but for the most part, she chose to remain wedded to her work.

One day, after reviewing some of Stewart's notes, Fisk approached her and inquired as to why she chose to impose such high taxes on individuals with large estates.

"Mister Fisk, the whole idea is to break up these estates and redistribute the land to the newly-freed slaves and poor whites. In the end, this will increase our tax base," she said.

Fisk looked at Stewart with his hand grasping his chin. "Are you telling me the reason for the high tax rate is to force the owner to sell his estate or risk having the property confiscated by the state if he fails to pay the taxes?"

"That's the plan, Mister Fisk," Stewart said.

"I hope I never become your enemy, Miss Stewart," said Fisk.

"I doubt that will ever happen, Mister Fisk," said Stewart. Fisk turned and left the large living room which had become Stewart's main work area.

"Brutal but ingenious," said Fisk as he walked away. "Oh, Miss Stewart, about those other plans — do you think..."

"I'll be meeting with some old friends from Massachusetts next week to discuss our plans for the banks. They're making a special trip and I'll be meeting with your contact from the U.S. Military Telegraph Corps[57] the following week. Everything is set, Mister Fisk — now don't you worry about a thing. We are way ahead of schedule."

In addition to their primary duties, Fisk and Stewart decided to explore the development of a banking system for the states in the former Confederacy, along with an adequate telecommunication system with the help of the U.S. Military Telegraph Corps. Stewart would spend hours of her free time laying the plan out on paper. She worked sixteen-hour days and oftentimes more.

In devising a system for tax collection, Stewart established collection depots throughout major population centers in the former Confederacy and also contracted with local retail establishments in small towns and rural areas to serve as drop-off centers as well. Each depot or retail outlet served as information centers and those working in these centers would be equipped to answer basic questions from residents. Filing deadlines would be strictly enforced and appeals would be handled in a timely fashion. Habitual scofflaws would be prosecuted to the fullest extent of the law and risk losing their property.

By the end of 1871, Stewart, with tremendous support from state and local officials, had painstakingly organized the tax assessment and collection system in North Carolina, South Carolina, Virginia, and most of Georgia. The other states in the former Confederacy were well on their way to being organized, and Stewart's plans for a banking system and telecommunication system moved right along. The timing appeared perfect.

The president's re-election was fast approaching, and the good news kept pouring in. The Klan had been defeated. The Ironclad Oath, once fully implemented, would prevent most Confederate sympathizers from seeking office and those already in office would be removed — by force, if necessary. Thousands more would be prevented from voting. There now existed a reliable and fair system for assessing and collecting taxes, and the former Confederacy was now under the control of an efficient constabulary force, a strong militia and an elite group of crack soldiers who

---

[57] Formed in 1861 following the outbreak of the Civil War, they were responsible for maintaining communications between the federal government in Washington and the commanding officers of the Union Army. *For more information on the U.S. Military Telegraph Corps, see* Lincoln in the Telegraph Office: Recollections of the United States Military Telegraph Corps During the Civil War *by David Homer Bates, University of Nebraska Press, 1995.*

protected state and federal offices and officials. All that remained was to win the election.

Wade kicked off the election year with a dinner at the Executive Mansion. Lisa Stewart was the guest of honor. Douglass and the usual congressional guests were present. Also in attendance was Douglass' wife, General Higginson, Colonel Foginet, Secretary Boutwell, Arthur Fisk, several diplomats, including General Alexander Gorloff, the military attaché to the Russian Ministry. He recently took charge of the Russian Imperial Legation in Washington. During the reception prior to dinner, the president and his guests were treated to an interesting and unusual conversation.

General Gorloff began speaking in his native tongue to a Russian colleague who had accompanied him to the dinner. The conversation piqued the interest of an American officer who stood nearby. The American officer soon interjected and began speaking nearly flawless Russian. The room suddenly fell silent as the startled guests watched and listened to the exchange.

Finally, the president walked over to the American officer. "What seems to be the problem?" asked the president.

"The general hoped there were no ill feelings due to the actions of his predecessor," said the officer. The general's predecessor was Konstantin Katakazi. He had angered many close to the president with his attempts to involve himself in the affairs of state by using underhanded tactics.

"Please assure the general all has been forgiven and I look forward to a harmonious relationship with the Russian government," said the president. The American officer conveyed the message, and the general smiled and immediately offered his hand to the president, who shook it, smiled, and quietly walked away. The general then turned to the American officer and thanked him in Russian.

During dinner, Stewart had the honor of sitting next to the president. Seated next to her was Foginet. "Colonel, when in the hell did you learn to speak Russian?" The president turned in the direction of Stewart and Foginet.

"The world has so much to offer those who travel its many lands and break bread with its many people, Mister President."

"I suppose you're right. How many languages do you speak, Colonel?" asked Wade.

"Several, sir."

"What about you, Miss Stewart? Do you speak another language?"

asked Wade.

"Well, sir, prior to my assignment with the government, I spent a much of my spare time learning the language of Sign," said Stewart.

"Excuse me, Miss Stewart, did you say Sign language?" asked the president.

"Yes, sir, Sign, said Stewart.

"Does anyone in your family have a hearing problem, Miss Stewart?" asked the president.

"No, sir. Not that I'm aware of. I became interested in learning the language after meeting a group of folks from a village called Chilmark in my home state of Massachusetts. It's located on the island of Martha's Vineyard. Many in the group were deaf, and I was amazed by the way they communicated with each other, and I wanted to learn. So I decided to develop my skill and understanding of communication with those who are deaf," said Stewart.

"Fascinating," said Wade. "Can you beat that, Colonel?" he continued.

"No, sir, Mister President. Miss Stewart is a fascinating woman," said Foginet as he stared at Stewart with awe and adoration.

"I'll say," said Wade. "She is indeed."

As the president turned his attention to his other guest, Foginet leaned toward Stewart and whispered, "If it's not asking much, do you think you could teach me to Sign?"

"It takes time, Colonel," said Stewart.

"Well, consider this proposition: if you find the time to teach me to Sign, I'll find the time to teach you Russian, if you don't know it already," said Foginet.

"I don't, Colonel — but I would love to learn," said a smiling Stewart.

"Then we have a deal?" asked Foginet.

"Colonel, just how many students do you currently have?" asked Stewart.

"You'll be the first in a very long time," said Foginet, with a wink and a smile. The two of them looked at each other and chuckled as the president lifted his glass and offered a toast.

"To the Wizard!" shouted Wade.

"To the Wizard," yelled Foginet and the other guests. All Stewart could do was smile, clasp her hands, and politely bow her head in the direction of each guest.

# — NINE —

# Purple Sunrise

After his election in 1868, President Wade ordered General Higginson through Secretary of War Chandler to begin implementing the Ironclad Oath. The Oath was hated by ex-Confederates, who called it the "Damnesty Oath." Wade gave strict orders to Chandler to withhold taking any action against those who initially refused to take the Oath.

"The day will come soon enough," he reasoned.

At the time, Wade did not feel his forces were strong enough in the South to repel the anticipated uprising among ex-Confederates who resisted taking the Oath or who perjured themselves upon taking the Oath. He decided to be patient, and ordered Chandler to inform the head of his political organization in the South, Lyle Davenport, to work with Higginson on establishing a registry of names of those who refused to take the Oath and those who perjured themselves. Davenport, in turn, put McArthur on it. The Oath was enforced on February 12, 1872.

It was 10 o'clock on a cold Monday morning when Unit 2 of the SG began making their rounds. Higginson had been ordered to remove from office every single officeholder who earlier refused to take the Ironclad Oath. Arrest awaited those who lied under oath. Those who resisted the order to leave their respective office faced removal by force. Those elected to national office who either refused to take the Oath or who lied under oath paid a similar price. Their seats in the Congress would be vacated until a special election was held.

Up until this time, the SG, particularly Units 1 and 2, while viewed as a powerful nuisance, were never thought of as ruffians. Unit 1 provided personal protection to any officeholder, other than ex-Confederates, who feared for their safety and requested protection. Unit 2 guarded all federal and state office buildings in the former Confederacy. Most people respected their presence and stayed out of their way. These troops were highly trained and well-equipped. Away from their posts, they were expected to attend school or work on their literacy skills in addition to taking care of their personal obligations. General Higginson encouraged literacy, Colonel Foginet ordered it.

On this particular day, which happened to be Abraham Lincoln's birthday, commanders of the SG were provided a detailed list of those officeholders to be arrested and/or stripped of their power, and removed from their respective office. The lists were prepared meticulously by McArthur, who served as deputy director of the powerful Commission on Election and Voter Fraud (CEVF). With orders and names in hand, Unit 2 of the SG, which was 40,000 troops strong, began fanning out all across the former Confederacy. Most of their targets were taken by surprise and went willingly. Others were removed by force.

In one instance, Jeb Stevens, a former plantation owner, who was recently elected as a Mississippi circuit judge as a Democrat, thought it a good idea to give the SG contingent a piece of his mind when they paid him a visit in the courthouse where he presided.

"You fancy dressed niggas," he began, "ought to realize when court is in session and you need to respect this court and my position as judge. Now go on back to playing soldier or whatever ya'll do and leave this here court room ratt now!," he demanded in a loud authoritative voice, "unless you niggas be looking for some real trouble. Now git," he yelled.

As he concluded, the sergeant in charge of SG contingent, stared at the rotund white man seated behind a desk on a raised platform.

"Are ya hard of hearing boy?" the judge asked. "I said git the hell out of this here court room, and I means now. We are in the middle of some impoant bizness," Stevens continued. The sergeant motioned the squad of seven to rush the bench.

The judge, a man in his late fifties, put up a brief, yet pointless struggle. "Git yo goddamn nigga hands off me cuffee," the judge demanded.

"Ise tired of yo God damn mouth, Judge Stevens. You need to learn this here is a new day for us black folk and you caint talk to us that way any mo," yelled one of the SG, a young muscular black man who got to Stevens first. A loud ferocious smack across Stevens' face followed his words. A vicious punch and another slap followed the first until Stevens' nose and mouth gushed with blood and he fell silent and limp.

Many of the white spectators gasped, most of the blacks cheered as the SG carried Stevens' tamed body out of the courthouse and on to the road. Once there, the soldiers in unison lifted the body of the bloodied judge above their heads and in one motion slammed the heavy mass hard onto the dirt road. The squad of SG stood around Stevens' crumpled body. A member of the squad spoke loud enough for everyone in earshot to hear: "Da'll teach dem how to speak to us for now on."

"Who's next on da list?" asked the young muscular soldier. The sergeant pointed to a large building a hundred yards away. The squad marched confidently up the street to the state office building.

This performance took place all over the former Confederacy. Thousands were arrested and/or forcibly removed from office. Many ex-Confederates did not know what to do. With the militia in each state on full alert as well as local law enforcement, there was nothing anyone could do to stop the actions of the SG. Even in those states like North Carolina and Texas where whites outnumbered blacks, the population remained quiet. For most Southern whites, it was too much of a risk to challenge the SG. All the ex-Confederates and their sympathizers could do for the time being was keep quiet and hope the SG passed them by.

For many blacks living in the former Confederacy, this day was long overdue. The vast majority of blacks had nothing to fear from the SG. Many had relatives in the SG, militia, and local law enforcement. Most blacks saw the removal of Southern whites from seats of power as a good thing and hoped they would never be allowed back. For most, this day would be a day of celebration.

News reached Wade back in Washington D.C. He whispered to his friend Douglass while dining with him and other visitors, "I hope that darkie-joke-telling sonofabitch is twisting in his grave. I had to do the bastard's dirty work but now it's done." Then Wade turned to his other guest and lifted his glass and said in a celebratory tone, "to our sixteenth president — happy birthday Mister Lincoln." He glanced at Douglass and winked his eye. Douglass just smiled and shook his head in quiet approval.

The Redeemers[58] knew it made no sense to challenge the Republican

---

[58] The Redeemers were a faction of the Bourbon Democrats, a conservative arm of the Democratic Party that believed in a particularly liberal form of capitalism. Redeemers pursued a policy of "Redemption," seeking to oust the Radical Republicans from the political arena. As federal troops were gradually withdrawn from polling places, the Redeemers used voter sup-

juggernaut in the South, not now any way. With the events of Purple Sunrise, which is what February 12, 1872 came to be called, Wade had sealed his victory for the 1872 elections. All the Redeemers could do was plan for the aftermath.

---

pression, as well as general intimidation tactics like rape and lynching to gradually recapture back southern governments. In their wake of fraud and violence, many African Americans were driven out of the country with the idea of returning to an African "Mother Land," resulting in a small but substantial flow of emigres to Liberia. The Redeemers, generally led by wealthy landowners and businessmen, dominated Southern politics from the 1870s to 1910. *For a personal look at a "redeemer," see* Wade Hampton: Confederate Warrior to Southern Redeemer by *Rod Andrew, The University of North Carolina Press, (reprint) 2013.*

# — TEN —

# The Redeemers

By August of 1870, all of the states of the former Confederacy were readmitted to the Union in the following order:

Tennessee - July 24, 1866
Arkansas - June 22, 1868
Florida - June 25, 1868
North Carolina - July 4, 1868
South Carolina - July 9, 1868
Louisiana - July 9, 1868
Alabama - July 13, 1868
Virginia - January 26, 1870
Mississippi - February 23, 1870
Texas - March 30, 1870
Georgia - July 15, 1870

Republicans controlled most of the state governments in the South, but blacks were not elected to state and national offices commensurate to their population. Many Democrats, while not in the majority, still held key positions in Southern state governments. On February 12, 1872, only a month before the Redeemers met at the Wormley Hotel, the political landscape in the South changed overnight and forever.

"These niggas are outta control, and it's all because of Benjamin fucking Wade and his nigga-lovin' henchmen Tom Higginson and Lyle Davenport," Henry Thompson began. Thompson, a political ally to former President Johnson, came from Tennessee. Tennessee was not under military rule, thus he and his supporters in the state had more flexibility than the others in the group to operate. "Gentlemen, we got friends in the Union Army. They don't like these niggas struttin' around calling shots either and you can't blame 'em. Hell, who wants to take orders from a nigga?"

"Well, now gentlemen, it ain't gonna do none of us any good just sittin' here fretting about it. We gotta be prepared to do something about it." The voice came from the back of the room. It belonged to S.R. Covington, a former general with the Confederate Army and a scholar.

After the war he began publishing the magazine Home Sweet Home. The magazine became widely popular in the South. It ceased publication after a mysterious fire caused the building that housed the magazine's offices to burn to the ground. It was anyone's guess as to who set the fire, but Covington blamed blacks.

"The niggers did it. They know damn well how I feel about them and their crazy ideas for our beloved homeland," said Covington. After the fire, Covington chose to cease publication of the magazine and returned to teaching in his home state of North Carolina. On this day he held court at the Wormley Hotel[59] with a small but powerful group of the South's leading white citizens, including other former high-ranking Confederate officers and former plantation owners.

The Wormley[60] had just opened in the spring of the previous year. This would be the first of many meetings held by this group who called themselves "The Redeemers" because of their determination to "redeem" their homeland from the Northern Yankees, carpetbaggers[61], and the so-called

---

[59]  Wormley's Hotel was a highly successful five-story hotel, located at 1500 H Street, NW, Washington, D.C. The hotel was a favorite meeting place of politicians. The hotel was the site of the Wormley Agreement, which ultimately helped pave the way to the end of Reconstruction. The hotel, however, was soon demolished and the Union Trust Company was built in its place in 1906.

[60]  A pioneering free-born black entrepreneur, Wormley was owner of Wormley's Hotel. *To read more about Wormley and his unique success, as well as the success that might have been for many more people of color had they not been faced with an oppressive political and societal climate, see* A Free Man of Color and His Hotel: Race, Reconstruction, and the Role of the Federal Government *by Carol Gelderman, Potomac Books, 2012.*

[61]  A term used to describe a Northerner who moved to the South after the Civil War, during the Reconstruction era. Like "scalawag," the term "carpetbagger" was derogatory. It referred to the popular carpetbag luggage that many newcomers carried while traveling. Carpetbaggers were seen as exploitative Northern outsiders taking advantage of the post-war climate by meddling in local politics and buying up plantations at extremely discounted prices.

scalawags[62] in the South. The Redeemers represented the Southern arm of the Democratic Party or Bourbon Democrats[63].

Rufus Hill was a close confidant of John Slidell, a former Confederate diplomat. Slidell was closely associated with the Trent Affair[64]. Hill complained his beloved Cherry Hill plantation in Louisiana was confiscated because he couldn't afford to pay the taxes. "I want that nigga wizard bitch dead — ya hear — dead," he screamed, as he entered the meeting room.

Another well-dressed attendee from Georgia went on about the "evil and foul ways" of Davenport and "his nigga boy-gal," McArthur. "What is this damn country comin' to? All this buggery and unnatural acts taking place right under our damn noses and ain't a God damn soul doing a thing about it."

Another guest, whose appearance suggested he came straight from his duties on the farm, chimed in, "I have a friend — German fella — planter, like myself. He tells me his fine country passed a law last year called sentence 175 — no, no, uh paragraph — that's it — paragraph 175[65] — to punish all the sodomites in their country. From what he tells me they're doing a damn good job of it," he concluded.

---

[62] Scalawag was a derogatory term that referred to Southern whites who supported Union forces during the Civil War, or after the war, supported Northern Reconstruction efforts or the Republican Party. Conservative Southerners considered them to be betraying the South by supporting "Northern" policies like desegregation and civil rights. *To read more about scalawags and how they intersected with black activism, see* Blacks, Carpetbaggers, and Scalawags: The Constitutional Conventions of Radical Reconstruction *by Richard L. Hume and Jerry B. Gough, LSU Press, 2008.*

[63] Active essentially from the 1870s to 1910, the Bourbon Democrats were a conservative sect within the Democratic Party. Bourbon Democrats supported an extremely liberal form of laissez-faire capitalism. They believed in little regulation of business and generally supported the goals of banking and railroads.

[64] The Trent Affair was a diplomatic crisis that took place between the United States and Great Britain. On November 8, 1861, the USS San Jacinto intercepted a British mail ship, The Trent, which had two Confederate envoys on board. They were attempting to travel to Great Britain in order to garner British support for the Confederacy in the Civil War. The British, who had not taken sides in the war, claimed the seizure of a neutral ship by the U.S. Navy was a violation of international law. President Lincoln eventually ordered the envoys be released, averting armed conflict with Britain.

[65] Paragraph 175 was a provision of German Penal Code that outlawed homosexuality between men, and in earlier editions of the law, bestiality, pedophilia, and prostitution. In effect from 1871 to 1994, the law was largely ignored until the Nazis came into power in 1933. In 1871, Paragraph 175 stated: *"An unnatural sex act committed between persons of male sex or by humans with animals is punishable by imprisonment; the loss of civil rights may also be imposed."*

"Gentlemen, gentlemen," shouted another guest, who sported a white suit to match his snow white hair and white walking cane, "All you have to do is stuff some powder in the nigga's ass and I mean stuff it up dere real good and make sure you use a long fuse. Then you put some horse shit in his mouth and tie it shut. After dat, just light the fuse. That'll teach 'em a fine lesson. It'll teach 'em all a fine lesson. We did it all the time back home."

"Why don't ya just dig yourself what we call a nigga hole?" Began a former plantation owner from Mississippi, who wore a long beard, a cheap brown suit and scruffy black shoes. His pistol lay neatly on the table in front of him. "All you do is bind and gag the nigga and bury him in the damn hole right up to his stinking black neck. Then you douse the nigga's head with some molasses, jam or jelly, any sweet-tasting thing will do, spread it on real good and thick then you let the critters have themselves a feast. It might take a few days but they'll chew on the nigga's head 'til he down right dead."

"Well ya'll just save the nigga bitch Stewart for me," interjected Hill. "Ise got real big plans for that smart ass nigga wench — if ya'll gets my meaning," said Hill as he looked down in the direction of his genitals. The other guests roared with laughter. "Had to train a few haughty nigga bitches in my day, by the time I finished, you would've thought I raised those nigga bitches in a house of harlots," said Hill. The crowd cheered him on.

"Let me tell ya'll something about correcting a nigga, specially those prideful niggas..." The man speaking was a former colonel in the Confederate Army. "All it takes is a, long red hot poker. First you get it red hot..."

"That's right, red hot, red hot," screamed one of the guests from the back of the room. "Then you..."

"Okay boys, enough with the chatter." Before the colonel could finish, Covington jumped in. "Gentlemen we got business to handle." Covington was all too familiar with the tone and direction of this conversation. He heard it all before and even had a few stories of his own.

While never openly stated, some in the room suspected Covington of engaging in the same "unnatural acts" many in the room sought to criminalize. Covington had no children and never married. He kept company with his longtime assistant who handled most of his personal affairs. Covington's exploits on the battlefield served to mute any criticism of his masculinity. A capable general he now served as one of the leaders of the

Redeemers.

"The key for us, Gentlemen, is to cut off the three heads of this tyrannical snake. Wade, Higginson and Davenport must go. That is the key. At that point the niggas will be left to themselves." Senator Andrew Garner now had the floor. Thanks to the Ironclad Oath, he was now a former U.S. Senator. Garner's family was one of the richest in the state of Florida before the war.

Angel Wood, the plantation owned by his family, was located in Leon County. It had over 100 slaves, and produced vast amounts of cotton, which made the family wealthy. The county seat in Leon County was Tallahassee, which also served as the state capital. Tallahassee had the distinction of being the only Confederate capital not captured by Union soldiers. "Not a damn Yankee set foot in my town during the war." Garner never grew tired of making this claim. But things were different now — much different, and for all his blustering, Garner knew it.

"The trick," Garner began, "is to get these nigga-lovin' bastards away from the SG. That's key. We can use nigga spies to get that nigga bitch Stewart and that Foginet cuffee." "I want that boy-gal too, that McArthur nigga," Before Garner could finish his point he was interrupted by Thompson.

"Wade and Chandler won't be easy, but leave that to me," continued Garner.

"Leave Higginson to me," said Thompson. "He's stationed in Tennessee, so we don't need to worry about the damn SG down yonder, but ya gotta get Davenport outta Rabun."

"Gentlemen, our friend Mister Thompson is right," Garner started again. "We have to be meticulous in our planning. As much as I hate to admit it, these niggas and their nigga-lovin' friends are a formidable force. This might take a little time, but if we handle our business properly we can lick these sons-of-bitches in due time."

As Garner spoke, the group listened with particular interest. Garner was a respected voice in the old Confederacy and a friend of the late John Milton, the former Governor of Florida, and ardent secessionist. Milton committed suicide as the war came to a close and the South faced certain defeat. During the war, Milton commissioned Garner as a colonel and placed him in charge of furnishing the Confederacy with goods and supplies from his state. The Confederacy was extremely grateful for his administrative skills.

From the details provided, Garner seemed to have covered all his bases. "How can we trust the plan won't be betrayed?" asked one of the guests.

"Now ya'll know what we do to a traitor, don'tcha?" Garner replied with light laughter. "Don'cha?" he asked again. Everyone became quiet. One thing everyone knew, was the price one had to pay for betraying the Confederate cause. "We'll deal with ya like we would if a nigga took favors with one of our white women back on the plantation," he snarled. The room grew eerily silent.

Many of those assembled knew Garner's plan could spell doom for them all. But what could they to do? Wade had completely demolished their power base in the South, and now their former slaves controlled matters with the full support of the president and the U.S. military.

Additionally, many black males and a few females in the former Confederacy were now well-trained soldiers — better trained than both Union and Confederate troops who fought during the war. They were also better equipped. In fact, many would say they were armed to the teeth. If the ex-Confederates didn't do something soon, they would all be forced to move to the North. For many of the men in the room that was unthinkable. The time had come to do or die.

"Any final questions?" asked Garner.

"May I pose a question?" The voice belonged to the youngest participant in the meeting. The young man wore dark trousers and a bright red shirt.

"You're Gabe Owens' kid, aren't you boy?" asked Garner.

"That's right, sir."

"Well, you tell yo daddy I said 'hey' and wish him a speedy recovery," said Garner.     At that moment the young man put his head down and others in the room cleared their throats.

"You probably didn't...." Tears streamed down the young man's red cheeks. "Sir, my daddy died shortly after the niggas removed him from office," said Owens.

"Is that so?" said Garner. "Well, my condolences, son, and don't you worry, now; we'll get things back in order soon enough," Garner said.

"'Bout my question, sir," said the young Owens.

"Ah, yes, son what is yo question?" asked Garner.

"Well, sir, we — and I think I speak for a lot of folks not here, sir," Owens scanned the room for approval.

"Go on, son," said Garner.

"Well, I think we should consider attacking soft targets as well, sir." He continued, "a lot of these places the niggas use to gather are totally unprotected. I think we can send a message to the SG through their loved ones," said Owens.

"Continue," said Garner.

"Well, sir, if we're going to take back our homeland, then maybe we should wage some kind of war right where they live. Let's show the fuckin' SG we're everywhere too, sir."

"Very good, son," said Garner as the other participants nodded their heads in agreement.

"Stick around, son. I'd like to talk to you after this meeting has concluded," said Garner.

"Will do, sir," said Owens.

"By the way, son, what's your name?" asked Garner.

"Daniel," said Owens, "but my friends call me Danny - Danny Boy to be exact, sir."

"Good, very good, Danny Boy," said Garner.

As the meeting concluded and the men began to rise from their chairs, the irony of the meeting place never dawned on any of them. The owner and operator of the Wormley Hotel was a free black man by the name of James Wormley, who had spent time in Europe learning European cuisine. While those assembled were accustomed to black servants, none of them ever openly recognized the fact their accommodations were owned by a man whose race served as the object of their collective contempt.

# — ELEVEN —

# Douglass Returns South

Frederick Douglass arrived in Rabun County, Georgia in May of 1872. Sent by the president as his special envoy, a contingent of the county's leading citizens, including Lyle Davenport, Randall McArthur, and Captain Francis Hope of the SG, met him upon his arrival. Captain Hope was placed in charge of Douglass' security during his stay in the state of Georgia. The Captain brought with him over fifty SG troops and requested an additional 100 militiamen to be on hand for the visit. Hundreds of ordinary citizens, mostly black, greeted Douglass upon his arrival.

Due to logistical concerns, each captain in the SG held sway over their respective jurisdiction. This gave officers of this rank tremendous powers. However, those who held the rank were careful not to abuse their authority. Administrative conflicts between captains were resolved through consensus. Captains who had seniority were also relied upon to settle such disputes.

Douglass was taken aback by the reception. This was his first visit to the Deep South and he didn't expect the conditions to be as such. Dressed in their purple uniforms the SG presented itself as an imposing and impressive force. Douglass had a difficult time distinguishing who the cheers were for, him or the SG. After Purple Sunrise, blacks viewed the SG as their protectors in the former Confederacy. For its part, after Purple Sunrise the confidence of the SG was immeasurable. SG members knew they were loved by blacks, hated by ex-Confederates, and feared and respected by all, and they enjoyed the attention that came with that reputation.

Most Southern whites hated the SG because the SG could check their every move. And while the SG sort every possible opportunity to display just how much they despised their former masters, they demonstrated a great deal of patience and professionalism. Most ex-Confederates had enough sense not to give the SG the opportunity to show who was in charge. Purple Sunrise had resolved that question.

Douglass was taken by coach to the SG compound in Rabun where he joined Lisa Stewart, who arrived from Pittsboro a day earlier. She would accompany Douglass on his visit throughout the South. Douglass had met the Wizard for the first time at the Executive Mansion earlier that year. Her genius and her beauty left a lasting impression. In fact, he had insisted she accompany him on his tour through the South. However, Douglass was well aware of the chemistry brewing between Stewart and Colonel Foginet, to what extent he could not yet figure out. Thus, prudence dictated while in Stewart's company, it would be best to stick to his mission.

During breakfast the following morning Davenport briefed Douglass on the political conditions in the South. Davenport informed him since Purple Sunrise, many towns struggled to fill political offices left vacant by the removal of the "traitors," as he called them. Davenport informed Douglass many of the political seats were now occupied by former slaves elected in special elections held throughout the region. Most of those elected, while not quite literate, managed well in their new post. Some performed exceptionally. Those who struggled too much were removed, and their seats remained vacant. That number was quite insignificant, he informed Douglass.

McArthur told the story of a local black woman, a former slave, who was doing a tremendous job as a judge despite her limitations. A former slave, about forty years old, she was the choice for many in the area where she resided. According to the townsfolk, she had the uncanny ability to settle differences between parties, and to satisfy both sides. Douglass inquired as to how a woman was elected to the position.

"According to the people, she was the best candidate for the job," said McArthur.

"Any protest due to her gender?" asked Douglass.

"Of course Mister Douglass," said McArthur. "But Captain Hope and the SG backed the will of the people, and that was that," McArthur added.

"Mister Douglass, the SG is here for the people and the people are here for us — one can't exist without the other," said Captain Hope, seated at the table. He then lifted his cup of coffee and bowed his head slightly.

"I see," said Douglass.

"Do you?" asked Captain Hope, as he stared warily at Douglass. Hope belonged to the more zealous wing of the SG. A short, burly man, his light brown skin bore the marks of the lash. His rough appearance mirrored his demeanor. Most folks who encountered him stayed out of his way.

Not knowing what to make of Captain Hope's question or his gaze, Douglass decided to fire off another question. "Are women allowed to vote in local elections?"

"Well, Mister Douglass," began Davenport, "there's a lot of experimenting going on here," he continued, with a slight hint of his Southern accent now betraying his roots, "and we figure since the president has made it clear he would one day like to give women the franchise, well,why not start right here in this tiny corner of the South, right next door in Habersham County, Georgia?"

"I see," said Douglass.

"I understand you have similar views, Mister Douglass," said McArthur, "regarding women that is."

"Well," Douglass began, after taking a deep breath. "The president and I agree on many things, including giving women the right to vote."

"Well, now," Davenport chimed in, "I guess you can inform Mister Wade his idea — and yours too, Mister Douglass — has significant support in Georgia, at least the northern part of the state. We'll get the rest of the state and the entire South on board soon enough. Won't we Captain?" asked Davenport.

"That's the plan, sir," said Hope confidently as he stared at Douglass again.

"Where is our first stop on this fine morning?" asked Douglass, sensing the awkwardness of the moment.

"I thought we would start at the Bank of the South," replied Stewart, sensing Douglass' uneasiness with Captain Hope's glare.

"Captain, would you be so kind to prepare the troops?" asked Stewart.

"No problem, Miss Stewart. Ready when you are," said Hope, springing from his chair.

"Is he always so intense?" asked Douglass, turning to Stewart.

"He's one of the nice officers in the SG," Stewart said with a smile. "Don't worry, you'll get used to their presence and ways. The SG is everywhere," said Stewart.

"An' tank da lord fo' dat," replied Dolly – a house servant, standing nearby. She went unnoticed by either Stewart or Douglass.

"You see what I mean, Mister Douglass?" said Stewart.

"Call me Fred," said Douglass.

"Are you starting to get the picture, Fred?" said Stewart.

"I'm starting to," said Douglass with a faint grin and a slight nod. "I'm starting to," he said again in a whisper.

Douglass did not know what to make of the SG just yet. He certainly did not disapprove of them, for their presence was clearly necessary. He just couldn't put his finger on it. One thing he knew for sure, most blacks, including Stewart and not a few white Republicans, admired the SG. Many white Republicans recognized the SG as their protectors as well.

Many supporters of the SG wore some type of purple paraphernalia to demonstrate their loyalty to the SG. Women wore purple ribbons, laces, or scarves. Men wore purple pieces of cloth on their hats, trousers, shirts, or coats. The dress code represented a sign of solidarity, and blacks wore the color purple quite proudly.

# — TWELVE —

# New Beginnings

The Bank of the South was established by law in each state of the former Confederacy with the exception of Tennessee. The idea was the brainchild of Stewart, who, with the support of Fisk and her mentor George Sewall Boutwell, sold the idea to the president. Wade loved it. As it stood, each state would run its own bank free of the big money interest in New York and elsewhere. The bank could be useful to farmers who would be free of predatory lenders.

The bank's deposits were insured by the general fund of its respective state and the taxpayers of that state. Stewart also insisted all state agencies use the bank exclusively for their banking purposes and each town or city with over 25,000 inhabitants do the same. This arrangement would soon prove to be a financial marvel.

Douglass was amazed by the support the bank received from the local citizens. Most blacks appeared to be exceedingly confidant, placing their earnings in the care of the "Wizard's Tomb," as the banks were called. Douglass even opened an account with a generous deposit. The locals cheered him.

Most Southern whites, especially ex-Confederates, chose to keep their money "under the pillow" rather than entrust it with "those ignorant niggas and filthy Jew carpetbaggers from up north," as one white citizen told a local reporter when asked if he would use the bank. He and millions of others like him would soon come to regret their decision.

After leaving Georgia, the next stop for Douglass and Stewart was Tallahassee, Florida. Captain Hope handed over his command to Captain Robert Lacy, one of the few white officers of the SG. Some in the group with Douglass were taken aback when Lacy introduced his wife Anna, a black woman. She accompanied her husband along with hundreds of SG and militia troops to the train depot to meet Douglass. Lacy had grown accustomed to the reaction from most who learned of his relationship with a black woman.

While blacks displayed tolerance for mixed couples, most whites found it despicable. Lacy could not care less. He met Anna in Tallahassee after he joined the SG. They fell in love, and after Florida and the other states of the former Confederacy got rid of the ban on interracial marriage, they took advantage of the new law, one of the first couples in the state to do so. Not many couples followed. Lacy proved to be an exceptional soldier and rose quickly in the SG. The men under his charge respected him because he treated them fairly.

After exchanging pleasantries, Lacy led the group back to the SG compound in Tallahassee. The group enjoyed a quiet dinner and the conversation turned to the new transportation system in the South.

"I must say, Captain, I am impressed with the railway system you guys created here," said Douglass.

"Well, sir, I wish I could take credit for it, but we owe it all to General Higginson. He had the vision to rebuild the railway system throughout the entire region and connect the major cities and towns in the Old Confederacy."

In 1860, about 9,000 miles of tracks existed in the Southern states. By 1870, Higginson nearly tripled that number, using immense pools of labor. His railway construction project drove the economy of the South. The speed of travel also increased exponentially. In 1830, it took two weeks to travel to the border of Louisiana from New York City. By 1870, the same trip took no more than two days.

Higginson even encouraged the states in the five military districts to take ownership in the railway business. Initially all but Texas did. With a combination of public and private financing, the railway system and the South became a booming business.

"It's coming along mighty nicely - ain't it?" asked Lacy. "He put the federal troops to work, and thanks to that young lady sittin' right over there," Lacy motioned with his glass of brandy to Stewart, "there is now a reliable system of tax assessment and collection. No more funny business with the money, if you get my drift, sir," Lacy said to Douglass.

"Yeah, there's a lot of talk about the riffraff going on down here with the railway system and all," said Douglass.

"Well, not anymore, sir. It's under tight control. Good people in charge, too. That's what you need, sir — competent folks. I gotta tell ya, sir — it's made a lot of money for our free men. A lot of men in the militia made a good living helping to put this thing together, sir," Lacy concluded.

"Gentlemen, please excuse us; I want to take Lisa on a tour of the ranch," said Anna.

"By all means, dear," said Lacy, as he and Douglass rose from their chairs.

"I just love that woman," Lacy said, referring to his wife.

"Yes, I can see that," said Douglass. "By the way, how are you received by your troops, Captain?" asked Douglass. "If you don't mind me asking?" Both men took their seats as the women exited the room.

"Oh, not at all," said Lacy. "My troops, think of me like black men should think of all white men — with suspicion, I suppose — but I don't mind. I've grown used to it. Hell, many of these men experienced things that I'll never experience or fully understand, sir. What makes a man want to force another man to do his labor?" Lacy paused and stared upwards as if speaking to himself. Then shook his head. "You have a helluva story yourself, Mister Douglass." Lacy raised his glass to salute Douglass. Douglass nodded his approval. "But you know, sir," Lacy continued, "I just try to be me. I love the SG, and I love my men, and I love our leader," said Lacy.

"Yeah, I hear a lot of good things about the general," Douglass said.

"Uh, excuse me, sir," Lacy interrupted. "I'm speaking about Colonel Foginet. Now don't get me wrong, General Higginson is a fine man who's done some wonderful things for the South, like the railway. But it's Colonel Foginet who makes the SG tick, sir. Make no mistake about it, Mister Douglass. It's Colonel Foginet who defines what we represent. Even the general knows that."

"Where did our lovely ladies go?" asked Lacy without skipping a beat. "Sometimes I get to talking and lose track of time and people," said Lacy.

"It happens to me, too," said Douglass. "Excuse me Captain," said Douglass with a ring of curiosity in his voice. "About Colonel Foginet."

"Why yes, Colonel Foginet," said Lacy, recognizing Douglass' interest in the colonel. "Don't worry, Mister Douglass, you'll meet the colonel soon enough."

"Oh, I already had the honor, but we didn't get to talk much," said

Douglass.

"Well, sir, that's a darn shame," said Lacy. "He sure is fine company. If you get some time with the colonel again, and I suspect you will, ask him about his travels, especially his voyage to Morocco and the Far East. He's like you, Mister Douglass. The man is a real globetrotter," Lacy said with a laugh. "A real globetrotter," he said again, shaking his head.

"Honey, I think Mister Douglass needs his rest. You folks have a long day ahead of you tomorrow," said Anna, appearing with Stewart in the doorway of the dining room.

"And what were you fine ladies talking about?" asked Lacy with a grin.

"Oh, nothing that would interest an officer of the SG or a famous statesman," Stewart replied. Everybody laughed and said goodnight. As Douglass climbed the steps to his room, he couldn't stop thinking about the SG and Colonel Foginet. The man and his admirers piqued his interest.

"I think I underestimated the man," Douglass thought to himself. Little did he know how much he did.

The next day, the group crisscrossed Leon County speaking to its residents as well as individuals who came from nearby counties to get a glimpse of Douglass and Stewart.

"My lord, there are so many telegraph poles in these parts," stated Douglass.

"Don't blame me, sir," said Lacy, jokingly. "We owe it all to the Wizard," turning to Stewart.

"Well, Fred," Stewart started.

"Fred?" Lacy asked curiously, surprised to hear Stewart address Douglass on a first name basis.

"Anyway, Mister Douglass," Stewart placed an emphasis on Douglass' name then smiled at Lacy. "The trick," she continued, "was getting the U.S. Military Telegraph Corps Assistant Superintendents to buy into my plan for stretching communications throughout the former Confederacy. The president was most helpful in helping them see the light, so to speak. I got individual towns to invest in their own telegraph lines and stations. They hired their own operators and charged standard rates. Those towns that opted out were at the mercy of those towns and individuals that saw the benefit of investing in the future. Ex-Confederates were not allowed to buy in. The president does not trust them nor do I," said Stewart. "By the time it was all said and done, we laid three times more mileage in wire than the railroad laid in track," she boasted uncharacteristically. "We expanded the wire for the same reason the general laid so much track," said Stewart.

"And why so Miss Stewart?" asked Douglass, now very interested.

"For military reasons," said Stewart. "Mister Douglass, the general laid the track as a means to transport his military wherever it was needed in the former Confederacy. He just doesn't trust the ex-Confederates. That's the premise I used for laying the communication wire. By the way, both served to expand the economy down here. Let's face it, Fred, a lot of towns and quite a few individuals, including many of our folks, made a nice living off these efforts," Stewart concluded.

"So this happened all over the South?" asked Douglass.

"No, sir, just in the military districts," said Stewart. "The transportation and communication systems are the best in the country," said Stewart. For the first time Douglass heard Stewart talk at length about her work. She wasn't boasting — just laying down the facts, and no one could argue with her. The expanded railway and communication lines improved the states of the former Confederacy dramatically.

"Is that why they call you the Wizard?" asked Douglass.

"That's just one of the reasons, Fred," she said with a smile.

# THIRTEEN

# Alabama - An Armed Camp

66Alabama, here we come," said Lacy as the train on the new railway
system called the "Higginson Line" pulled into Montgomery station.
"Look, folks, I would love to join you, but my business is in Tallahassee.
It was a pleasure Mister Douglass, Miss Stewart. My journey ends here,"
said Lacy, as he helped his wife then Stewart off the train and onto the
platform. "Major Embry will be taking over my command from here," he
yelled as the noise of the crowd became louder with each passing second.

"There's the Wizard," a voice cried out.

"There's Mister Douglass," another voice said.

"Wow! It seems like the whole town is here to greet you good folks,"
said Lacy as Major Embry approached.

"Good morning, folks. My name is Major Jasper Embry. I'll be your
guide from here." The major, a tall, handsome, black man with a commanding presence was clearly a professional soldier.

The major shook hands with Stewart first and Douglass second. He
then walked over to Lacy who saluted him. Lacy made a hand gesture in
Anna's direction. Anna, who accompanied her husband on the trip, and
the major, met during a previous engagement. Each exchanged pleasantries. Then the major motioned to Lacy to walk with him. When they were
a few feet away from the others he whispered to Lacy. Both men glanced
in the direction of Stewart and Douglass. Lacy nodded his head and saluted Embry once more before rejoining his wife.

The major walked up to Stewart and Douglass, "right this way, folks.
There's a coach waiting for you." Neither Stewart nor Douglass could believe their eyes. It was like a sea of purple all around the station. The crowd

was enormous. SG troops lined the entire platform. The crowds stayed behind them. Many waved purple cloths while cheering for Stewart and Douglass. The SG was out in full force, the largest contingent yet to greet Douglass. Many men in the crowd went wild for Stewart, some screaming, "Marry me Miss Wizard." She smiled and waved.

"Hell, this is an armed camp," said Douglass, turning to Stewart.

"You're not kidding, Fred," said Stewart, as she boarded the coach. "My lord, what is going on in Alabama?" Stewart whispered loud enough for Douglass to hear. Douglass boarded the coach and stared at the crowd. The scene was impressive and somewhat intimidating.

When they arrived at the state capitol, most of the state's leading politicians, black and white, waited in the street to greet them. In the center stood the popular governor, Bruce Bainbridge.

"Welcome to Alabama, Mister Douglass and Miss Stewart," said Bainbridge. The governor, dressed in his finest business attire, began introducing both guests to select individuals in the crowd. While there were several white politicians on hand to greet the two esteemed guests, the crowd of onlookers waving the purple cloths was overwhelmingly black, not unlike at the train station.

The narrow steps leading up to the Capitol were lined with SG troops, and the entire area was surrounded by more SG troops. The show of force could not be overstated. As Bainbridge led his guests up the steps, he was followed by Major Embry and other government officials, all eager to meet the famous pair.

"Mister Douglass, what is your impression of the fine state of Alabama?" a reporter asked when the pair reached the entrance of the building.

"Well, son, give me a day or two, and I'll let you know." The crowd around Douglass, including Bainbridge, laughed heartily.

"Miss Stewart, how about you?" another reporter asked. Stewart was not accustomed to speaking with the press, but accommodated the reporter anyhow.

"Well, I like what I see thus far. I tell you one thing, I love the color purple," she replied to thunderous laughter. Her response even brought a smile to Embry's stern face.

"Governor, Governor, do you wish to say anything to our readers about the visit from such esteemed guests?" asked another reporter.

"Well, I think our state is lucky to receive a visit from the president's special envoy and even luckier to receive a visit from one of the smartest and if I might add — prettiest women in the country — Lisa Stewart. We have a lot to talk about so if you guys will excuse us." Bainbridge hurried into the capitol building and made his way towards the twin cantilevered spiral staircase.

Stewart couldn't help but marvel at the design of the twin staircases. "What a work of genius," she exclaimed. "What architectural beauty. Who..."

"His name is Horace King[66], Miss Stewart," said Major Embry, anticipating her question.

"A former slave, Miss Stewart," said Bainbridge who continued the biography. "His work as bridge builder was so respected throughout this state and nearby the legislature passed a special law around 1847 which exempted him from having to leave the state within one year of being granted his freedom. He helped design this building, and he did a substantial amount of work on it."

"Is it true Mister King plans to run for office next term?" asked Senator Langston, one of the few white senators in the legislature.

"Not sure, Senator but time will tell," said Bainbridge.

"I hear he's mighty popular, mighty popular. Some say almost as popular as you, Governor," said Langston.

"Hey, now you just hold on one minute, Spence," said Bainbridge. The crowd around them laughed loudly.

Constructed in 1851, the Alabama state capitol sat atop Goat Hill. The building served as the capital of the Confederacy from February 4, 1861 until May 29, 1861. Jefferson Davis[67] held his inauguration as the president of the Confederacy on the steps in 1861. Both the Provisional and Permanent Constitutions of the Confederacy were drafted in the same building that now served as the office of the first black Governor of the state. Little did anyone know at the time Alabama would never again elect a white person to serve as Governor.

After a small reception, Bainbridge took his two guests, along with Ma-

---

[66] King was a respected architect, engineer, and bridge builder who worked in the Deep South. In 1846, he purchased his freedom from slavery using some of his earnings as an architect. *To find more about Horace King, read* Bridging Deep South Rivers: Life and Legend of Horace King *by John S. Lupold and Thomas L. French, Jr., University of Georgia Press, 2004.*

[67] President of the Confederate States of America, Davis was chosen because of his strong political and military background. *To read Jefferson Davis firsthand, see* The Rise and Fall of the Confederate Government: Volume 1, *published originally in 1881.*

jor Embry, into his private office. He asked Senator Langston to join him in about an hour. Bainbridge, a brown-skinned, stocky man of average height, was born into slavery in 1832 in Lowndes County. He'd managed to purchase his freedom through his work as a master tailor. By law, he had to give part of his income to his owner, but he earned enough to purchase his freedom and that of his wife and child. During the war, he joined Union forces in Northern Alabama and served as a scout for the Union Army. After the war, he settled in Montgomery and became involved in politics. Elected to the House of Representatives in 1868, after Purple Sunrise, he won a special election and became governor.

Purple Sunrise turned the political tide for blacks throughout the former Confederacy. In every state of the former Confederacy with the exception of Tennessee, Purple Sunrise created a huge vacuum in the political arena, and blacks took full advantage of the opportunity.

During the special elections, blacks and their fellow white Republicans won nearly every seat in the Alabama state legislature. The Democrats' power base following Purple Sunrise was completely swept away. The Republican Party in the South, dominated by blacks and their white allies, controlled every single branch of government in each state of the former Confederacy and most local governments as well. This newfound power was reinforced by the ominous presence of the SG.

It didn't take long for Bainbridge and his fellow Republicans to implement real change for black life in Alabama. While significant strides were made prior to Purple Sunrise, the Republicans, with strict orders from Washington, proceeded with absolute caution prior to that event as not to misstep and create political trouble for the president. Thus, prior to Purple Sunrise, ex-Confederates still held some sway on legislative matters. While they were unable to push their white supremacist agenda, they were able to manipulate the rules governing the House and Senate in their respective state legislatures to block progressive legislation. Their obstructionist antics ended on February 12, 1872. Thousands of blacks came to power in the former Confederacy, and they would make good use of it for years to come.

Governor Bainbridge began by telling the small group gathered in his office that his sources informed him the ex-Confederates planned on staging a major military operation, but because he didn't possess any real proof of the plan it was imprudent for him to enact any legislation that would frustrate their plans. He told the group, with the help of Major Embry, he had established a quasi-intelligence operation but the effort failed to produce the intelligence his government needed.

"I think the colonel needs to be made aware of the danger," said Bainbridge.

"Governor you said yourself, you lack the proof," said Douglass. "Maybe it's just a bunch of angry talk from these disgruntled folks who you kicked out of office," Douglass said with a bit of sarcasm that didn't go over Bainbridge's head.

"Fred," started Bainbridge, not waiting for Douglass to give him permission to use his name in the familiar, "this isn't some kind of fuckin' joke, excuse me, Miss Stewart," Bainbridge directed his anger at Douglass.

"By all means continue, Governor," said Stewart.

"We did what we had to do. I don't trust these redneck crackers, never have and never will. Hell, they went to war to keep us in chains. Let me tell you if I had it my way I would remove every damn one of em' from the state of Alabama including their damn wives and children. And don't be fooled by some of these white snake oil salesmen who call themselves Republicans. Some of 'em just pretend to be our friends. Hell, if it wasn't for the SG some of them would be at our throats, too. Did you know some of these white Republicans owned slaves too, Fred? A relative of one of 'em owned me. Damn crackers — they're nothing but beasts in human form. How in the hell do you do the things they've done to other human beings and call yourself human, Fred? They're God damn monsters, and we all know it," said Bainbridge, now standing and pacing the room.

"Mister Douglass, Miss Stewart," began Embry. "I have kept my men on full alert since that day."

"He means Purple Sunrise — and a damn good day it was," said Bainbridge.

"Thank you, Governor, for the clarification," said Embry, turning to Bainbridge.

"No thank you, Major," said Bainbridge.

"We're all anxious, and my troops feel as I do and as the governor does — these white folks are up to no good. Even some of these white Republicans. Our intelligence is decent but a bit jumbled. It has to be coordinated. Once we get reliable information — well, at that point, we can take the necessary course of action," stated Embry.

"What action would that be?" asked Douglass in a cynical tone, as if he didn't know the answer.

"No offence, Fred," Bainbridge started, "but I think you've been away from these here parts too long. These crackers down here — and I suspect a lot of them up where you're at too — will never see us as their equals. Never. The only thing this Southern cracker understands is that thing dangling from the major's hip," Bainbridge kept talking while pointing to the pistol holstered on Embry.

"Don't get me wrong, Fred. I don't despise these bastards because they're white. I despise them because they despise us. They truly believe we belong to them, Fred, to do with us as they please. They're sick, Fred. I'm tellin' you, we are dealing with a diseased mind. These crackers are sick. It's just not normal to treat people the way they've treated us and this race issue is gonna be solved one way or the other. And I for one, Fred, if you don't mind me calling you Fred," Bainbridge didn't wait for an answer, "want us to be on the winning side.

"Let me say one last thing, Mister Douglass, if we don't do what needs to be done, these crackers are gonna regain control of the South, and you best believe they won't hesitate to disenfranchise the Negro — that's what this whole thing is about Fred. To be honest with you, I'm thinking of proposing a change to this here state constitution to give women the right to vote in local and state elections, and just to make sure these ex-Confederates don't use their women as proxies, I'll make their women take the damn oath. How 'bout that? I despise those white bitches, too. They're the first teachers for these sick bastards." Bainbridge's voice became even louder and angrier.

"Governor, your idea of giving women the right to vote is a noble one, and I support it and I'm sure the president would endorse the idea but, I must say, I'm somewhat concerned with this armed presence in your state — no offence, Major,"

"None taken, Mister Douglass," replied Embry.

"Are you suggesting we lay down our arms, Fred?" asked Bainbridge.

"No, Governor, I'm not, but is it necessary to project an image the state of Alabama is in a perpetual state of war?" said Douglass.

"We are!" exclaimed both Bainbridge and Embry in unison.

"Governor, black citizens are now armed. We should turn our attention to improving the conditions for our people. And, let me say, I'm pleased with the progress being made, but your actions can quite frankly be deemed provocative," said Douglass.

"Gentlemen — gentlemen please," Stewart interrupted to calm the rising tensions in the room. "I too have concerns about these former Confederates and some of our Negro folk to be truthful." Everyone paused and looked at Stewart. Her reputation preceded her. She commanded the attention of everyone in earshot when she spoke. "I will personally share your concerns with the colonel. In the meantime, I advise you to get more reliable sources within the ranks of the former Confederates. If they're up to something, only a small handful will know about the plan early on. You must infiltrate the leadership," she suggested.

"How do you propose we do that?" asked Embry.

"The old-fashioned way Major," countered Stewart. "You pay 'em."

"I can't thank you enough, Miss Stewart," said Bainbridge.

"You are quite welcome, Governor. By the way," Stewart stared directly into Bainbridge's eyes, before finishing her thought.

"Yes, Miss Stewart," asked Bainbridge.

"Don't trust anyone," said Stewart.

"I understand completely," said Bainbridge. Just then there was a knock at the door.

"Yes, what is it Trudy?" asked Bainbridge, sounding annoyed as his secretary entered the room.

"It's Senator Langston to see you, sir."

"Tell 'em I'll be with him in just a moment," said Bainbridge.

— FOURTEEN —

# A Matter of Life and Death

After two long days in Alabama, the pair headed to Jackson, Mississippi. The trip was a straight run and a quiet one. Douglass felt betrayed by Stewart during the conversation with Bainbridge, but Stewart knew Bainbridge was right. Bainbridge and Major Embry were in fact paranoid as Douglass thought, but for Stewart that was a good thing. She considered their suspicions to be a healthy paranoia. She also knew if the ex-Confederates regained control of the former Confederacy, black women and their children would catch hell. For Stewart, the present crisis created a life-and-death struggle. And while she held Douglass in high esteem, she frowned upon his moderate ways.

A staunch radical, Stewart could also be flexible. She recognized a place existed in the struggle for moderates, but not in Alabama or anywhere else in the former Confederacy. The former slave owners viewed blacks as their property, to do with as they pleased. To them, killing a black man did not equate to murder. Raping a black woman did not constitute a sexual assault crime. Cheating a black person in the ordinary course of doing business did not amount to fraud. For many whites in the South and North, for that matter, black people belonged to an inferior order on the human evolutionary scale and in the words of Roger Brooke Taney, "...had no rights which white men were bound to respect." While many turned out to see the two honored guests upon their arrival in Jackson, the atmosphere in Mississippi seemed quite different. The SG, while strong in numbers, displayed less intensity. Douglass and Stewart were met by the white Republican Governor Henry Lee Wilcox. He was elected in a special election after Purple Sunrise to prevent any further division in the

Republican Party. The Party became splintered due to infighting by members loyal to former governor and ex-Confederate, James Lusk Alcorn, and former general and military Governor Adelbert Ames.

Many blacks preferred Ames, but they knew it would not be in their best interest to push for a showdown. At the time, nearly 830,000 citizens lived in Mississippi, and blacks represented more than half of the population. Many blacks saw their opportunity in the near future, and they were right. Wilcox would be the last white person to serve as governor of the state of Mississippi.

Blacks in Mississippi viewed education as their pathway to collective advancement as a people. In fact, one of the first colleges for blacks, Alcorn University[68], named after the governor at the time, was founded in 1871. The site of the college used to be occupied by Oakland College, a college for whites, which ceased to operate prior to the start of the Civil War. After the war, the land was sold to the State of Mississippi. Additional land was sold around the college and part of the proceeds went to Alcorn University. Thus, Alcorn University became a land grant college. A sitting U.S. Senator at the time for the State of Mississippi, Hiram R. Revels[69] resigned his seat and became the school's first president. In three short years there would be over 30 colleges for blacks throughout the former Confederacy. Mississippi Vocational College in Mississippi[70], Augus-

---

[68] Originally Alcorn Agricultural and Mechanical College, and now Alcorn State University, Alcorn is a historically black college in Lorman, Mississippi. It was founded in 1871 during the Reconstruction era in an effort to provide higher education for freedmen. At first, the school was exclusively for black males, but women were admitted in 1895. *For a comprehensive history of formal black education in the south, see* The Education of Blacks in the South, 1860-1935 *by James D. Anderson, The University of North Carolina Press, 1988.*

[69] Revels was a minister in the African Methodist Episcopal Church and Republican politician. Revels was the first African American to serve in the Senate, where he represented Mississippi in 1870 and 1871 before becoming an administrator at Alcorn University.

[70] This institution was founded in 1950 by the Mississippi Legislature, which feared that legal segregation of public education was in danger, and therefore created the school to attract African Americans who would otherwise seek to attend Mississippi's white-only intuitions of higher learning. The college is now known as Mississippi Valley State University. *For a historical and sociological look at how education was crafted to limit black progress during the latter half of the nineteenth century, see* The White Architects of Black Education *by William H. Watkins, Teachers College Press, 2001.*

ta Institute in Georgia[71], Biddle Memorial in North Carolina[72], Powell in Mississippi, Payne Institute in South Carolina[73], Wheatley in Florida and Lincoln Normal School of Marion[74] in Alabama are just a few of the schools which one day would become world-renowned institutions of higher learning.

Thanks to the tax system put in place by Stewart, Mississippi, like all the other states in the former Confederacy, now had adequate revenue to spend on public projects like education. Mississippi put aside thousands of dollars in tax revenues to recruit teachers from the North. Many educated blacks and whites flocked to Mississippi for the opportunity. These teachers were well paid and because of the sheer number of volunteers, teacher-student ratios in the lower grades in Mississippi rivaled most schools in the North.

The legislature also desegregated the public schools in the state. This act infuriated most whites, but not much could be done about it. Some in the legislature attempted to appease whites by separating the schools based on gender but most whites frowned upon the idea of integrated schools.

---

[71] The school known today as Morehouse College was founded in 1867 in Atlanta, Georgia, by William Jefferson White, a Baptist minister, along with Rev. Richard C. Coulter, a former slave, and Rev. Edmund Turney of the National Theological Institute. Founded for the purpose of educating black men, the school remains today an all-male black college. *To learn more about Morehouse, see* History of Morehouse College *by Benjamin Griffith Brawley, Cosimo Classics, 2009*

[72] The Biddle Memorial Institute was founded on April 7, 1867, following a first contribution of $1,400 by Mary D. Biddle. Two ministers, Rev. W. L. Miller and Rev. S.C. Alexander held a meeting in the Charlotte Presbyterian Church in North Carolina expressing a need for higher education in the particular area in the South. In 1876 the school became Biddle University, and in 1919, it became the first black college in the South to offer professional courses in education. The school today is known as Johnson C. Smith University.

[73] When the Civil War ended, many African Americans in the South left the churches they had attended with their white owners and established new churches. The African Methodist Episcopal (AME) denomination grew out of this movement. The AME wanted to train people for leadership within the church, and as a result, institutions of education such as the Payne Institute were founded. The Payne Institute was founded in South Carolina in honor of Bishop Daniel Alexander Payne, an advocate of education for former slaves. As the institution grew and moved to the state capital in 1880, it was renamed Allen University.

[74] The Lincoln Normal School was one of the first educational institutions for African Americans. It is rumored that the school's origins lay in the efforts of a former Union soldier who would teach local black children as he lay recovering from his wounds after the end of the Civil War. Regardless, the school stayed open for more than 100 years and was the foundation of Alabama State University.

Most kept their children home, working on the land. Some white children received adequate home schooling or, if their families could afford it, were sent to private schools. In the end, most white children in the state went without a formal education. Many members of the SG also attended school in the evening. Mississippi could easily boast of having the most educated SG troops in the former Confederacy. Mississippi became the first state in the former Confederacy to open a war college for officers. Many SG troops took advantage of this opportunity.

At a visit to the Higginson War College, located on the outskirts of Jackson, and named in honor of the founder of the SG, Stewart and Douglass met with a group of SG officers who had just arrived at the school a little over a month before. When the well-dressed, bespectacled black civilian instructor of the class informed the students Douglass and Stewart had come to the school to discuss "education" in the state of Mississippi, every officer in the room simultaneously pulled a pistol from his holster and laid it on his respective desk. Douglass was stunned.

Stewart had seen the reaction before, but was nonetheless still impressed.

"It's part of the training, sir," said the instructor to Douglass.

"Why?" asked a perplexed Douglass.

"We teach every officer that education-," began the instructor. The officers immediately rose from their seats.

"-is a matter of life and death, sir," barked the officers in unison before the instructor finished his sentence. The officers remained standing until they told to take their seats, and put away their weapons. The instructor smiled, satisfied his point was made.

"Is this type of training happening everywhere?" asked Douglass, turning to the instructor as they stood outside the building.

"Well, we're the first war college, but SG troops are being educated all over the South. It's been that way for quite some time. Colonel Foginet is quite serious about education. He calls education 'our ticket to the future,'" said the instructor.

"I believe that as well. You see, Mister Douglass, when a people have been denied a basic human right such as education for hundreds of years and they get a taste of it, I guess one develops an insatiable appetite for learning. And it must be made clear: if you attempt to deny it at that point, then from the perspective of the new learner and his teacher, I might add, you're inviting your own death. That's the message we must convey," concluded the instructor.

"Well, thank you for the tour, Mister — I'm sorry," said Douglass, not knowing the instructor's name.

"Oh, it's Caraway. Leroy Caraway," said the instructor.

"Thank you, Mister Caraway," said Douglass.

"It's a pleasure to finally meet you as well, Miss Stewart. We hear so much about you in these parts. We can't thank you enough for all you've done for the Reconstruction effort. It truly has made a difference," said Caraway.

"Likewise, and keep up the excellent work you're doing, Mister Caraway," said Stewart.

"Will do, Miss Stewart," said Caraway.

Soon war colleges opened in every state in the former Confederacy with the exception of Virginia. Mississippi also made it a point to send hundreds of its most gifted students, male and female, abroad to Europe, Asia, and South America to learn new skills as engineers, farmers, doctors, architects, financiers, industrialists and a host of other trades and professions. Some of these students would start families and make their homes in countries throughout Europe. Most would bring the knowledge and skills they acquired back home to the South. Mississippi became a model for other states to follow.

Both Stewart and Douglass were impressed by Mississippi's success in the field of education. If any two individuals could appreciate education, the two of them could. Both were born into slavery. Douglass taught himself to read and write and now stood as America's foremost black leader and a special envoy for the president of the United States. The other, a child prodigy who, as a young adult, used her talents to single-handedly revolutionize the tax, banking, and communication systems in the former states of the Confederacy, was now arguably the most celebrated woman of her day.

## — FIFTEEN —

# Ben Forrester

"Wake up, sweetie. Time to go."

"What's going on, Mom?" Cody attempted to gather himself. His short afro appeared a bit unbalanced. "Where's my book?"

"Right here, dear," Tina picked up Cody's book, which had fallen to the floor.

"Thanks, Mom. I must've dozed off."

"Yes you did, Pumpkin, and the next thing you were snoring." Tina smiled and tapped Cody on the nose.

"Was I loud, Mom?" Cody's facial expression betrayed his embarrassment.

"No, sweetie. Besides it's only you and I in here."

"Mom, are we in Beaumont already?" Cody was perplexed. He had taken the train from Birmingham to Beaumont before and the ride seemed much longer.

"No, Pumpkin, we're in New Orleans."

"Why are we getting off?" Cody began to take note of his surroundings.

"We're going to visit Uncle Ben," said Tina.

"I thought..." Cody was confused. He took a deep breath.

"I'll explain on the way to his house." Prior to waking him, she had instructed a porter to remove her bags from the train in New Orleans.

When the train finally stopped, Tina and Cody stepped off and onto a long platform. "Need any help, ma'am?" The baggage handler's Northern accent reminded her of Steve. Tina directed him and his co-worker to take her bags to a cab stand.

"Mom, you changed your clothes." Tina had in fact changed her attire.

She'd slipped out of her peach and cream suit and into a light green skirt with a matching summer sweater.

"Mom, you missed a button." Cody stared angrily at the white baggage handler, whom he noticed eyeing his mother slightly-exposed cleavage.

"Oh, thank you, dear." Tina adjusted her sweater without ever noticing the young man's wandering eyes.

"Right this way, ma'am. I'll flag a cab for you," said the young man.

"Mom, we're not getting picked up," asked Cody walking a little faster now, while casting a wary glance at the baggage handler, whose young face bore a slight smirk.

"No, Pumpkin, I thought since it's so late we could catch a cab. Uncle Ben's house isn't too far from here."

"Wow, Mom, check out at this place." The small group was now in a huge atrium. Cody had last visited New Orleans several years ago. Unable at the time to appreciate the grandeur of the city and its attractions, he was now in awe of its train station. Cody's eyes scanned the huge facility.

The New Orleans Passenger Terminal was less than a decade old. Considered ultra-modern, it was designed by a black father and son architectural team. Upon completion it was considered the finest in the country and one of the finest in the world. Not only did it serve as a hub for the H-Line trains, but it also served as a hub for the world's oldest streetcar system and the city's bus service. The terminal housed some of the city's finest restaurants as well. Painted on one of the terminal walls was a huge mural depicting the events of February 12, 1872. The huge heading at the top of the picture read "Purple Sunrise."

"Mom?" Cody glanced at the wall. "The book — that's one of the chapters in the book."

"Yes it is, Pumpkin. And over there." Tina pointed at another mural. It was the portrait of a tall figure with a light brown complexion dressed in the uniform of an army general. Cody ran over to the mural. The heading read, "General Andre Soule."

"Who's that, Mom?"

"Read the book, Pumpkin."

Cody immediately opened his book and glanced up and down at the chapter headings. "I'm almost at that part, Mom. Was he a member of the family?"

"No, dear. He and your great, great-grandfather were close friends. Read the book, Pumpkin."

"Mom?" Cody's eyes grew wide and his jaw dropped low. "Isn't that Grandpa Foginet and Grandma Stewart?" Cody directed his mother's attention to another wall that displayed a huge mural of Aurelius Foginet and Lisa Stewart. The words at the bottom read "First Couple of the South." Cody whispered the words to himself. The baggage handler turned and began to stare in awe at Tina and her son.

"Is everything okay, young man?" Tina caught the baggage handler looking in her direction.

"I'm fine, ma'am," he said nodding his head and flagging a cab. "Right this way ma'am." The baggage handler directed Tina to a waiting cab. "You guys jump right in and make yourself comfortable. I'll load the bags."

"Thank you, young man." Tina gave the baggage handler a generous tip.

"Wow. Thank you ma'am." As Tina settled into the cab, the baggage handler tapped on the window. "Excuse me, ma'am, I'm a recent college graduate and well I majored in history, the History of the Post Civil War South to be exact. I kinda overheard the conversation between you and your son and, well, ma'am, are you related to the First Couple of the South?"

"Yes, they're my great-grandparents," said Tina awkwardly.

"Ma'am, I know it's late and all and I don't mean to be a bother, but would you mind — well, can I have your autograph?"

On occasion, Tina would be asked for an autograph. Rarely did she refuse. "What's your name, young man?"

"Kevin."

"May I borrow your pen, Kevin?"

"Yes, ma'am — right here." The young man hastily lifted a pen from his shirt pocket and tore out a piece of paper from his small notepad. "Here you go, ma'am." Tina took the sheet of paper and quickly signed her name and handed the paper and pen back to the owner.

"Thank you so much Miss..." Kevin had trouble reading the name. Tina had a stylish signature that made her name difficult to read.

"Richards, Kevin. Tina Richards. And Kevin?"

"Yes, ma'am?"

"Cut the ma'am crap." Tina smiled and winked her eye.

"Oh, okay, sorry, Miss Richards," said a red-faced Kevin with a huge grin.

As the cab made its way from the curb, Cody turned and watched as the excited baggage handler shared his good fortune with his co-workers. Cody stared at his mom in awe. Tina leaned her head back and began softly massaging her eyes with her thumb and index finger. Cody took his mother's arm and placed it around his head and nestled as close to her as he could. A light smile graced Tina's face as she pulled her son even closer to her side.

"Where to, Mum?" asked the black middle-aged cab driver with a Caribbean accent. He appeared oblivious to the exchange between Tina and the young baggage handler. Tina gave the driver an address to a house in the city's French Quarter.

"I'll get you dere in no time, Mum," said the driver. "Travelling late, uh?" Tina did not respond to the driver's question. "You see, Mum, this is how me make my money. All those young white kids from up north don't like working late. They rather go out and party, but, me, I work late for people like you — folks who travel late at night."

"That's good," said Tina while enjoying the view of the opulent city from behind the windows of the cab. New Orleans represented the extraordinary wealth of the South. The city had undergone numerous renovations over the years. Starting around the turn of the century, the old Spanish décor in the French Quarter dating back to the 18th century was demolished. The scenery reminded blacks who now ruled the city of the dark days of slavery. New architectural styles were introduced. Eventually skyscrapers came to dominate the landscape. Ritzy hotels and shops dotted the downtown landscape. No slums or ghettoes could be found. All classes of people lived side by side. Jobs were plentiful. Wages far exceeded the norm in other cities across the country. New Orleans was one of the jewels of the black-dominated Old Confederacy, and it showed.

"Do you come here often, Mum?"

"Yes, I do," said Tina.

"You have family here — yes?" asked the driver.

"As a matter of fact, my brother lives here."

"Dis city is a terrific place, Mum."

"Yes, it is. Have you been here long?" asked Tina.

"Bout ten years mum. I needed the work and dis city has plenty of dat." The cab turned on to Chartres Street. "Almost dare, Mum." The cab pulled up to a huge yellow house that sat on a corner lot.

"Honk the horn, please." Tina instructed the driver.

"No problem, Mum." A white man dressed in a black suit opened the door. He motioned to others in the house to go to the cab. Two young white males made their way to the cab and started unpacking the trunk of the car. Tina thanked the driver and rewarded him with a tip. "Wow tanks alot, Mum. Enjoy your stay," yelled the driver as he pulled away.

Tina and Cody made their way to the front door and passed the man in the suit. "Your brother instructed me to tell you he will see you in the morning. Please make yourself at home, Miss Richards. I'll be downstairs. Call me if you need anything."

"Thank you Lewis. I'll call you if I need you." Lewis served as Ben Forrester's butler. Ben had a house staff of four to seven individuals, depending on the occasion.

"Pumpkin, you can sleep in the room next to mine."

"Okay, Mom. I remember this room," said Cody. "Mom, I'm gonna read a little more before I go to sleep."

"How about a bath first, Cody?

"C'mon Mom?" Tina gave Lewis a look that suggested he should ignore Cody's plea. Lewis immediately instructed a member of the wait staff to prepare Cody's bath.

"Please prepare one for me as well, Lewis," requested Tina.

"Will do, Miss Richards."

The sounds of pots and pans banging in the kitchen awakened Tina and Cody the next morning. The aroma of coffee and fish cooking on the stove made it difficult for the two to remain in bed. The clock read nine o'clock.

"Hey, Sis," Ben embraced Tina as she made her way into the spacious kitchen.

"Hi, Baby Bruh. Appears as if someone has been busy in this place."

"You like it, Sis?"

"I love it, Ben. The cabinets, the floor, the ceiling, my God — the appliances — it's gorgeous."

"A little more work to be done, and I will be finished with this remodeling stuff, Sis."

"Where's my sleepyhead nephew?" Cody walked into the kitchen on cue, rubbing his eyes.

"Hi, Uncle Ben."

"And why are we so tired?" Ben hugged Cody.

"Up late reading." said Cody in a whisper.

"And what is so fascinating about this book, if I might ask?"

"It's the book about our family — *Deo Vindice*.[75]" Cody sprang to life.

"Yes, that is a fascinating book. And how far did you get, Nephew? Wow, Tina our little one has grown so much." Ben didn't wait for an answer. Cody had grown a lot since the last time Ben saw him. "Well, Cody, how far along are you?"

"A few chapters beyond 'Purple Sunrise.' Actually I read that chapter twice, Uncle Ben. I saw a painting of it at the train station. Uncle Ben, why do we call it Heroes' Day and not 'Purple Sunrise'?" Cody was now fully awake.

From 1872 to 1878, February 12 was treated as a day of celebration but had no particular name. Many referred to it as "Purple Sunrise Day." And everyone in the South knew what the day stood for, but there was no official name attached to the historic day. Following the death of Benjamin Wade in 1878, the holiday became officially known as "Heroes' Day" in the South.

In the North, February 12 was celebrated as Lincoln's birthday. Lincoln had no such honor in the South. While the sixteenth president was respected by many black Southerners, his popularity paled in comparison to the eighteenth president, Benjamin Bluff Wade. Wade's birthday, October 27, was widely celebrated in the former Confederacy. It was a special holiday.

"That's a good question, Cody. I believe the official name came about — hmm. Tina, was it 1879 or 1880?"

"I believe 1879, Ben."

"I think you're right, Sis. I guess they wanted to recognize everyone who participated in the great struggle, Cody. We consider all of them heroes!"

"I do too, Uncle Ben." Ben embraced his nephew.

"Now, I want both of you to come sit down over here and enjoy this wonderful Louisiana breakfast. My chef made it especially for you." Ben then ordered his staff to begin serving his guests.

Following breakfast, Tina and Cody returned to their rooms and got dressed for the day.

"I'm in here, Sis." Ben called out to his sister. He heard the clanking of Tina's heels as she made her way across the marble floor in the large atrium.

"Where are you, Ben?" Tina yelled.

---

[75] The motto of the Confederacy was the Latin term "Deo Vindice." When translated it means "Under God, our Vindicator."

"In the study."

"Okay. My God, Ben, you are serious about this remodeling thing. This furniture is beautiful, and the rugs, the shelves..."

"Come sit down, Sis, and tell your baby brother what is troubling you. Ben turned to his butler. "Lewis, I'm not to be disturbed unless it's important. Where's my nephew?"

Lewis put the finishing touches on the room then proceeded to leave. "He's in his room reading, sir. Oh and by the way your neighbor called. She wanted me to let you know that her sister and her niece will be arriving later on today. She was wondering if you could stop by and say hello."

"Thank you Lewis and please make sure my nephew is comfortable."

"Yes, sir," said Lewis.

"Now, Sis, what's on your mind? By the way, that outfit is dazzling."

"Why, thank you, Ben. I've had it for a minute."

"Well, it's the first time I'm seeing it, and you wear it so well. That figure must keep heads turning, Sis."

"Why, thank you, Ben. And I'm sure you do too, Bruh."

"Well I'm not one to complain, Sis." Ben winked at Tina.

Ben Forrester was four years younger than his sister. The two hardly resembled each other. While both were extremely attractive, Ben looked more like his father. He had a light brown complexion. Tina was darker and had a faint hint of her mother's eyes. Ben stood at six foot, two inches with broad shoulders. A former track star, he gave up the sport in college when he became star of the debate team. He attended the world-renowned Powell University in Mississippi.

After graduating from college, he went on to earn a law degree from Powell's law school and later became a certified public accountant. Ben, like his sister, had a brilliant mind. He settled in New Orleans, primarily because the city's cosmopolitan ambiance accommodated his lifestyle. Ben was gay.

For as long as she could remember, Tina served as her brother's protector and confidant. She learned of her brother's sexual orientation during her junior year in college. While home for the holidays, she found Ben sobbing uncontrollably in his bedroom. "What's wrong, Ben?" she'd asked.

"I can't help it, Tina," he cried.

"Help what, Ben? What's wrong? Ben, it's me. What's wrong? Do you want me to call someone?"

"No, Tina. Please don't," cried Ben.

"Well, what's wrong? You can tell me anything, Ben. You know that. Right?" Ben just looked at his sister, then put his head down.

"Tina, you wouldn't understand"

"Understand what? Understand what? Ben, tell me, please," Tina's voice became a whisper.

"I'm attracted to boys, Tina. I like guys, and I can't help it."

Tina was hardly surprised by Ben's revelation. She, as well as others in the family had suspected that Ben was gay for quite some time. What she didn't realize was the pain he'd felt coming to terms with his sexuality.

"Look at me, Ben. Ben — it's me," Tina stared directly at her brother. "So what? That's who you are. Do you understand? That's who you are"

"But what if mom or Dad, Gram... Jesus, Tina, I'm so scared."

"Ben, what makes you so sure they don't know already?"

"What are you talking about, Tina?"

"Ben, all I'm saying is the family is quite tolerant of guys who like guys and girls who like girls. That's just way the family is. You know that."

"But you said they might know about me."

"I said 'what makes you think they don't.' Ben, you know the family knows everything, and if they don't, then it will be our secret until you're ready to tell 'em — okay?"

"Thanks, Tina. You are so wonderful."

"No, I'm not. I just love you, Ben."

"Well, thanks for loving me, Big Sis."

"Don't mention it, Little Bruh. Now, let's go get something to eat."

Ben had a zest for life. His spirit made him well-liked within the family. Both he and Tina were spoiled by their grandmother. Ben was also spoiled by his mother. At thirty-five, Ben served as the president of the Louisiana branch of the Bank of the South which served as the mother branch to all of its subsidiaries in the state of Louisiana. It was second in size only to the East Texas branch. The bank was in effect controlled by C.S.G.S., which was widely influenced by the Carson-Hamilton family.

The Bank of the South was a powerful institution in the southern region of the country. Millions of blacks used the bank exclusively to meet their financial needs. The economy of the former Confederacy was by far one of the richest and most stable economies in the world, largely because its customer base did not allow its money to leave the region. For nearly 100 years the black dollar in the former Confederacy was consistently recycled among the black owned businesses in the region. This made the

Bank of the South one of the largest banks in the world. It even had an investment branch in Ghana and several other African nations, which supported its interest on the African continent.

Several African nations chose to do work with the bank rather than the other international banking institutions due to the bank's willingness to provide loans without imposing harsh terms of repayment. The bank's policy stressed support for democratic governments. It adamantly opposed tyrannical rule.

In one memorable case, the bank made a substantial loan to a developing, democratic African nation. All went well until the democratically-elected government was overthrown by a coup orchestrated by the country's military leaders. The bank immediately introduced austerity measures as a condition of the loan repayment. When the Junta failed to get immediate financial assistance with favorable repayment terms from the other international lending institutions, it was at the bank's mercy.

The actions on the part of the bank led to a financial panic and a popular uprising. The democratically-elected government was restored and the military leaders were arrested and subsequently put to death. It was rumored the death warrant for the Junta leaders was signed in Beaumont.

This action on the part of the bank was a lesson to all clients: the Bank could be your best friend or your worst enemy. The Bank was in the business of helping African nations improve the quality of life for its citizens. Its policies shunned rugged capitalism in favor of mixed economic principles. This made the Bank extremely popular and influential throughout the African continent.

"So, you stopped to see our brother," asked Ben, with a laugh. Ben was referring to Stewart Carson. It was long believed, due to the remarkable resemblance between Carson and Tina, that the two shared the same father.

"Be quiet, Ben. I don't want Cody to hear that."

"He's bound to find out one day," said Ben.

"It's only a rumor, Ben."

"Sure it is, Sis." Ben rolled his eyes. "How is Stewey?" Ben liked Carson, but was somewhat jealous of his relationship with Tina.

"He doesn't like to be called that, and he's doing just fine." Tina snapped.

"Didn't mean to touch a nerve, Sis."

"Ben, forget about that or Stew for a moment. I'm here because I need answers about my husband, and I think you know something or could help point me in the right direction."

"Sis..." Before he could finish, Tina cut him off.

"Ben, you have connects everywhere. That's why Gram depends on you so much. That's why the family depends on you so much. I need your help, Ben."

"Sis?"

"What, Ben?"

"We had this talk a year ago."

"And?

"Sis, let me be straight with you because I love you. The only thing you got out of that twelve-year marriage from hell is that beautiful little boy."

"It wasn't that bad, Ben."

"Tina, the man was never home, not to mention, notoriously unfaithful. He..."

"So was I."

"Yeah, after you woke up and smelled the coffee."

"Two wrongs don't make a right, Ben."

"Tina, the man didn't deserve you, and you're better off without him."

"What about Cody?"

"He is, too."

"Damn, Ben. You actually think my child is better off without his father?"

"I didn't mean it that way, Sis. All I'm saying is Cody could use a better role model. I hear Stew has stepped right in." Ben bit down on his lip.

"You're such a jerk when you want to be, Ben."

"Oh stop it, Tina. I'm just kidding."

"I need your help, Ben."

"Tina, here's all I can say — about four months ago I came into some information about a deal — a deal with this banking cartel."

"Oh no Ben, not them again," Tina put her head back, clenched her jaw and let out a loud grunt, while placing her hands on her head.

"Listen sweetie," said Ben, as he continued. "The deal involved your husband's family. I passed the information on to Gram. She thanked me and told me not to worry about it. Nothing more was said to me about it."

"The cartel? I need to examine those papers again." Tina straightened her posture and began muttering to herself. "Ben, if those greedy bastards..."

"Tina, Gram is already on it. I think she can fill you in on the rest of the story."

"Ben are you hiding something from me?"

"Sis, all I'm going to say is this: allow Gram to provide you with the details surrounding this matter involving your husband and the cartel. If there are any gaps I'll try my best to fill you in. I promise you."

"Why am I always the last to find out?" Tina took a deep breath and exhaled.

"Gram loves you and that little boy of yours, Tina. You know that. She has high hopes for you and Cody. Try and relax. Hey, I got an idea. Why not stay here a couple of days and clear your mind, Sis."

"They're expecting me in Beaumont tomorrow," said Tina.

"Just call ahead and tell them you decided to spend time with your little brother. I'm sure everyone will understand."

Tina paused to give the idea some thought. "Ben, I think I'll do just that. It is my vacation."

"Perfect. We are going to have a blast, Sis, and Cody will just love New Orleans."

## — SIXTEEN —

# Andre Soule

On the eve of the Civil War, slaves represented 50% of the population of Louisiana. The population was approximately 710,000. Louisiana also had one of the largest populations of free blacks, totaling close to 20,000 individuals, many of whom were of mixed blood or biracial. At the time of Stewart's and Douglass' visit, P.B.S. Pinchback,[76] a black man of mixed blood, was acting lieutenant governor of the state, having replaced Oscar Dunn[77], the first elected black lieutenant governor of a U.S. state. Pinchback would later become the first black to serve as governor of a U.S. state when the Louisiana legislature filed impeachment charges against the first Reconstruction governor of Louisiana, Henry Clay Warmoth. Pinchback served for 35 days as governor until the end of Warmoth's term. The charges against Warmoth were eventually dropped.

Given the general make-up of the state's population, the SG was more diverse in Louisiana than any other state in the former Confederacy. In fact, the highest-ranking officer in the SG in the state was Major Andre Soule, a tall, light brown skinned man with freckles and kinky, sandy

---

[76] Born to a white Mississippi planter and a former slave, Pinckney Benton Stewart Pinchback was a Union Army officer and the first African American to become governor of a U.S. state. A Republican, Pinchback served as acting governor of Louisiana from December 9, 1872 to January 13, 1873, 34 days, while Henry Clay Warmoth was being impeached. It was not until 1990 that another African American served as governor of any U.S. state.

[77] In 1868, Dunn served as lieutenant governor of Louisiana, and thus became the first African American to serve as lieutenant governor of a U.S. state. Dunn died in office in 1871 and was replaced by P.B.S. Pinchback. Dunn actively supported universal suffrage as well as land ownership, taxpayer-funded education, and equal protection under the law for all African Americans.

brown hair he wore pulled back and tied in a bush. Soule once told a friend "I hate every drop of white blood" which flows through my veins." Both his maternal and paternal grandfathers were white. During Purple Sunrise, he brutally put down a rebellion by armed whites who resisted the enforcement of the Ironclad Oath.

Louisiana led all the other states in fatalities as a result of Purple Sunrise. The death toll in one incident alone numbered fifty-seven. In total, more than 300 individuals, mostly white, died as a result of Purple Sunrise in the state. Alabama under Major Embry came in a close second with 285 deaths followed by South Carolina under Captain Mansfield Diggs with 103 fatalities. At the end of the day, Soule became the most feared and hated man in Louisiana. He relished his newfound reputation.

Although born free, Soule detested the slave system and those who upheld it. As offspring of mixed parentage, Soule's parents belonged to a class known as "gens de couleur[78]" or free people of color. They'd met as teenagers and with little support from their respective families decided to marry when his mother was eighteen and his father was barely twenty.

Two years after marrying the couple opened a dry goods shop. Over time it became one of the most profitable stores in New Orleans. As a young boy Soule was tutored by his Haitian-born paternal grandmother. She often told him stories about the evils of slavery. As he grew into adolescence he witnessed many of these evils firsthand. His grandmother also taught him to speak French fluently.

A handsome young man, he attracted the attention of females of both races. As a clerk in his parents' store he would often times be called upon to make deliveries to the homes of his customers – many of whom were women. Needless to say he became one of the most popular delivery boys in the area. On several occasions his parents were warned about Soule's supposed interest in the white girls his age. In actuality it was they who had trained their eyes on Soule's tall attractive frame. For his own safety his parents decided to send him overseas to England to further his schooling.

Soule made periodic trips back home from overseas, which he now called his "second" home. A radicalized and worldly Soule came back for good right before the outbreak of the Civil War. In 1862 Soule helped raise a regiment of over 1000 men to fight for the Union cause. His regiment played a prominent role in several battles, including the Siege of

---

[78] See Ira Berlin *Slaves Without Masters: The Free Negro in the Antebellum South*

Port Hudson.[79] After the war Soule tried to revive his family's business, which lay in shambles due to the devastation brought by the war. His efforts were met with mixed results.

In the summer of 1870 after the state of Georgia was readmitted to the Union, General Higginson began his recruitment efforts in Louisiana for his newly-created elite Southern Guard. Soule's leadership skills were immediately recognized. He rose quickly through the ranks. He was one of a few individuals to attain the rank of major in the SG. And he wasted no time letting everyone know who was in charge.

White racial terrorists and their supporters weren't the only ones who became the object of his contempt. Those blacks of mixed blood and blacks in general who denied their blackness, and who sought favor with whites were also held responsible for the perpetuation of "this wicked system," as it was called by Soule.

Soule purged the Louisiana SG of those who harbored this mentality. He called it a "poison that seeps into the minds of men thereby destroying them." Many thought he was one of Foginet's favorites because both men could speak French fluently, but Foginet shared Soule's detestation of self-hatred among blacks. This cemented the bond between the two men. The fact that both men were born in New Orleans, most likely in the same year or just about, may have also played a role in their friendship.

---

[79] See *The Louisiana Native Guards: The Black Military Experience During the Civil War* (Baton Rouge, LA: Louisiana State University Press, 1995).

# — SEVENTEEN —

# Louisiana

Stewart and Douglass left Mississippi with high hopes about the possibilities for blacks in the former Confederacy. In Louisiana, Stewart's scheme for land distribution paid great dividends for black families. Huge parcels of land were divided up and given to former slaves to start anew. The Freedmen's Bureau[80], created by Congress in 1865 to help the newly-freed slaves, was initially charged with the responsibility of land distribution under the Freedmen's Bureau Act of 1866. This bill, vetoed by President Johnson, increased the resentment between the Radical Republicans and President Johnson. When President Wade succeeded Johnson, he strengthened the Bureau.

But it wasn't until Stewart created a system of tax assessment and collection throughout the former Confederacy, that the real work of land distribution began. When General Higginson began reorganizing the military in the South, many black farming communities had to adjust their way of life in order to meet the demands of compulsory service in the state militia. The concept of communal farming grew out of these arrangements

---

[80]   Headed by Union Army General Oliver O. Howard, the Bureau lasted until 1872. It experienced considerable difficulty carrying out its goals as the Bureau encountered resistance from many white Southerners as well as President Johnson, in addition to being chronically understaffed and underfunded throughout its existence. The Bureau was tasked with helping former slaves transition into a "free" society while Southerners enacted Black Codes that restricted movement, labor, and the civil rights of African Americans, creating a state that nearly duplicated the conditions of slavery. *For more information on the Freedmen's Bureau, and particularly how the agency brought more black women into politics, see* Freedwomen and the Freedmen's Bureau: Race, Gender, and Public Policy in the Age of Emancipation *by Mary Farmer-Kaiser, Fordham University Press, 2010.*

and many black communities in time became prosperous because of these innovations. The same concept applied in many black communities that relied on fishing as a means of earning a living.

In New Orleans, Stewart and Douglass visited several hospitals that catered to blacks. While the facilities were adequate, they were far from first-rate. Many of these hospitals, as well as facilities that catered to the mentally ill, were under the direction of the Freedmen's Bureau. Both Stewart and Douglass recognized that in order for blacks to receive adequate health care, the effort to push for such reform would have to come from blacks. Whites, particularly Southern whites, saw blacks as inferior beings and believed their poor health was a result of that fact and nothing more. This attitude about blacks persisted among many whites in the North as well.

The need for black doctors could not be overstated. Not unlike Mississippi, the Louisiana legislature, under the control of Republicans, appropriated funds to send black students to Howard University Medical Center, previously known as Freedmen's Hospital[81], to be trained as doctors. The state planned to open its own training facility in two years. In a few short years, every state in the former Confederacy would have not one, but two, facilities in their respective states for the training and development of black doctors and nurses. The South's healthcare system would one day be the envy of the entire country and rival the best systems throughout the world.

---

[81] Established in 1862, the hospital was originally built to provide medical treatment for African Americas who came to Washington, D.C. during the Civil War, often seeking their freedom. It was the first major hospital to provide medical treatment for former slaves and after the Civil War, six years after its founding, Freedmen's Hospital became the teaching hospital of Howard University Medical School (established in 1868).

# — EIGHTEEN —

# Juneteenth

The Texas State Penitentiary[82] partially opened in the fall of 1849. In 1853, a grant was given to the prison to open a woolen and cotton mill in order to increase revenues for the prison. By the start of the Civil War, prison officials defrayed some of the cost of the prison from the profits made by inmate labor. The profit made by this labor was seen as prisoners paying their debt to society.

All but three Confederate states established a penitentiary in their states prior to the Civil War; North Carolina, South Carolina and Florida did not. For the most part, the penitentiary was used for the most hardened white criminals during the pre-war era in the South. Most of these prisons did not accept black inmates due to the South's ban on race-mixing, and plantation owners created their own system of justice for blacks. Many slave owners paid local jails to provide "correction" for their slaves if the means of doing so on the plantation proved to be ineffective. Few women, black or white, were imprisoned in the pre-Civil War South.[83]

---

[82] The Texas State Penitentiary at Huntsville is the oldest Texas state prison. After the Civil War, Huntsville was the only prison in the former Confederacy and ended up becoming the first racially-integrated public institution within the state of Texas. *For further reading, see* Robert Perkinson's Texas Tough: The Rise of America's Prison Empire, *Metropolitan Books, 2010*

[83] Only in the 1820s did the penitentiary become a means to criminal justice. It was thought that by providing a routinized setting, free of the temptations of society, wrongdoers could rehabilitate. At first, the penitentiary was only popular in the Northern states. For Southerners, serious crime was largely considered to be a Northern problem and not a major concern in the South. Southern crime was often remedied by a system of folk policing where ordinary members of society would ensure justice. Prior to the Civil War, Southern penitentiary systems brought only the most dangerous criminals under state control.

After the arrest of ex-Confederates during Purple Sunrise, General Higginson established a temporary holding facility for these individuals in Walker County, Texas, adjacent to the State Penitentiary at Huntsville. The new convicts came from every state in the former Confederacy.

The new "Sunrise" prisoners, as they were called, pleaded with federal officials not to transfer them so far away from families, but their pleas fell upon deaf ears. The way Higginson saw it, these "traitors and slavers" would at least get a small taste of what it was like to take a man from his family. While the prisoners were adequately cared for, they were not allowed any visitors and their movement inside the facility was strictly limited. The compound was guarded by SG troops stationed in Texas. Those who attempted to escape were placed in the pillory for several hours. The punishment turned out to be very effective in discouraging escape attempts.

Those arrested during Purple Sunrise were subsequently tried by a military tribunal at the facility. Most were found guilty and sentenced to five years. Only a few were acquitted. No other prisoners were held at this facility. Each state was responsible for paying a monthly fee for each inmate from their state. Governor Bainbridge paid six months in advance for each inmate from Alabama and offered Higginson additional money to care for other white inmates from his state. His request was denied. The facility was officially called The Huntsville Detention Camp but soon became known by its critics as Camp Wade.

Shortly after arriving in Huntsville to examine the conditions at Camp Wade, Stewart and Douglass met Captain Hollis Alexander. Alexander was a close confidant of Colonel Foginet and a rising star in the SG. He would accompany Stewart and Douglass on the remainder of their journey to Tennessee. Alexander was the model soldier. He fought for the Union in the Civil War after escaping from slavery in Texas.

On June 18, 1865 he was one of 200 troops who arrived with General Gordon Granger in the coastal city of Galveston, Texas to take control of the state and issue General Order No. 3.[84] This order effectively ended slavery in the state of Texas. While President Lincoln's Emancipation Proclamation, freeing slaves in those states in rebellion with the Union, was issued on September 22, 1862 with an effective date of January 1,

---

[84] Issued on June 19th by Major General Gordon Granger, the order established the Union Army's authority over the people of Texas. The order was issued more than two years after the Emancipation Proclamation; news apparently traveled slowly in Texas.

1863 it had minimal effect in the Confederate states, including Texas, which ignored the order.

On June 19, 1865 General Granger read the order on the balcony of Ashton Villa, one of the first brick structures constructed in Texas. It was a three-story house built in Victorian Italianate style. General Order No. 3 read as followed:

"The people of Texas are informed that, in accordance with a proclamation from the Executive of the United States, all slaves are free. This involves an absolute equality of personal rights and rights of property between former masters and slaves, and the connection heretofore existing between them becomes that between employer and hired labor. The freedmen are advised to remain quietly at their present homes and work for wages. They are informed that they will not be allowed to collect at military posts and that they will not be supported in idleness either there or elsewhere."

On that day Alexander and the former slaves of Galveston rejoiced in the street. Juneteenth[85] celebrations, as they were now called, began the following year in Texas and would be held every year henceforth.

Alexander spent some time in Mexico following the war, but returned to Texas after hearing about the recruitment of black soldiers in the South for militia training. During training his talents were immediately recognized and he became a non-commissioned officer. Under the command of Captain Foginet he was sent to train as an officer and graduated at the top of his class. As Foginet's fortunes grew, so did Alexander's. Foginet appreciated Alexander's thirst for knowledge. He would often find Alexander during off-duty hours, learning to read and practicing his penmanship. Alexander's efforts paid off. He would soon be promoted to the rank of captain.

"Well, Captain what do you make of Texas?" asked Douglass during their inaugural dinner.

"Texas, sir, is my home. That's why the colonel sent me here to watch over these traitors and, of course, you fine people," said Alexander, flashing a grin. A dark-skinned man in his late twenties, Alexander possessed a great deal of charisma and thus had a way with women. His dalliances with white women from time to time angered most whites who knew

---

[85] Combining "June" and "nineteenth," Juneteenth is a popular annual celebration of emancipation from slavery in the United States. The holiday was created after the issuance of General Order No.3.

about them. While the thought of engaging in such affairs just a few short years ago would have caused him to be lynched, there was very little whites could do about it now, and he knew it. Some say he did it to "piss them off."

"Hell," he'd once argued privately to a fellow officer, "these crackers had their way with our women for generations. I betcha it's one of the main reasons they went to war. That's what they meant when they started talking that bullshit about defending their Southern way of life. It was about having their way with black women. Now today some of us might be fuckin' these white gals but at least we're not forcing them against their will. Heck - we're not rapists." Both men nodded their heads in agreement.

"Miss Stewart, it's a pleasure to finally meet you," he paused, admiring the beauty of the woman known as the Wizard. "Oh, and you, too, Mister Douglass," he said apologetically. "Colonel Foginet described you to a tee," he went on, turning back to Stewart.

"Oh, did he?" asked Stewart. "

Well, ma'am. He said you're the finest woman he's ever laid eyes on and the smartest too. That's what he said. You didn't it hear from me, but I think you stole the man's heart." said Alexander.

"Uh, Captain."

"Yes, Mister Douglass," said Alexander.

"I don't think the colonel would be comfortable hearing you say that to Miss Stewart."

"Miss Stewart doesn't mind. I don't think," said Alexander.

Stewart laughed.

"Besides, who's gonna tell?" Alexander asked. "Mister Douglass, I think this here brilliant, beautiful woman is just what the colonel needs. If you don't mind me saying, Miss Stewart."

"No, of course not. Keep right on talking Captain," said Stewart. She turned to look at Douglass with her eyebrows raised, shaking her head slightly and smiling.

Neither Douglass or Alexander knew Foginet and Stewart had maintained communication via secret channels. Both had written several letters to the other since they last saw each other earlier that year at the dinner hosted by the president in honor of Stewart at the Executive Mansion. They would meet again, in a matter of days, in Tennessee, and for both of them that day couldn't come soon enough. Love was in the air.

# NINETEEN

# Ridge Mountain Orphanage

**B**y the time hostilities ended, more than 700,000 people died as a direct result of the war. Nearly 180,000 Negro soldiers fought for the Union Army, and nearly 40,000 of them died during the Civil War, most from infections and disease. The social costs were staggering. The combination of war and emancipation produced thousands of black orphans.

The state of Arkansas established the model for caring for orphans. The Republican-dominated legislature first outlawed segregation in both public and private accommodations, including orphanages. Each county by law had to establish an orphanage in its respective locality. Counties were encouraged to share resources to offset cost. Thus, most counties joined with neighboring counties to create an efficient system that provided services for both children and female adults who had little or no resources to care for themselves. The Freedman's Bureau also assisted mightily in this effort.

Reconstruction efforts in Arkansas was due in large measure to its governor — Jeremiah Chambers — the Radical Republican from Vermont. With the help of the black vote, the immensely popular Chambers would win four terms as the state's governor and would be the last white governor elected in the former Confederate states. The former major in the Union Army modeled his political philosophy after a fellow Vermonter, Thaddeus Stevens.

Upon assuming office in 1869, the 43-year-old Chambers did not waste any time in moving the state out of what he called the "dark ages" and into the "light of civilization." Chambers hated slavery and despised those who sought to uphold it. After Governor Bainbridge, no other governor in the former Confederacy came close to detesting ex-Confederates more than Chambers. The day after Purple Sunrise he not only made February 12th an official state holiday, but he also flew a purple flag from the state capitol building to celebrate the activities of the SG.

Chambers devoted much of the state's resources to assisting blacks in his state. He relied heavily on the SG to keep the peace and even supplied the state militia with resources that made it the best-trained and equipped militia in the entire South, second only to Alabama. The governor took no chances. He feared the SG could be removed by the federal government at a moment's notice since it fell under the federal government's jurisdiction. Thus, by preparing the local and state militias he could rely upon their presence to protect the lives of blacks and some of the gains made in the event such a scenario occurred.

While Chambers was deeply devoted to Wade and the Radical Republicans who controlled the Congress, he knew the political landscape in the former Confederacy could change at any moment, and he insisted on being prepared when and if that fateful day came. The way he saw it, the ex-Confederates would stop at nothing to regain the privilege they once held in the South.

"The smartest thing the president did since taking office was implementing the Ironclad Oath," he once said.

Governor Chambers met with Stewart and Douglass on the grounds of one of the state's newly completed orphanages, a beautiful facility made of brick. "Now, that's what this country should respect and appreciate," said Chambers as he stood pointing to a group of white, black, and Indian children playing together behind the main dormitory.

"How's it coming along?" asked Stewart.

"Well, Miss Stewart, every now and then there is a hiccup or two," said Chambers.

"Excuse me, Governor?" said Stewart.

"How should I put this," said Chambers tugging at his short beard. "I find it difficult at times to change the thinking of the ordinary white citizen toward black people. Many whites can't stand the sight of white children eating, playing, learning or sleeping next to a black child. It's just so foreign to them." Chambers paused. "But you know, Miss Stewart, the bastards are just gonna have to get used to it," said Chambers defiantly. "What do you think about that, Mister Douglass?"

"I agree with you Governor. The bastards are just going to have to get used to it." Everyone burst out laughing.

"Did I miss something?" asked a moderately attractive white woman who seemed to appear out of nowhere.

"Ah, Miss Jamison," said the governor, extending his hand to meet hers as she came rushing to join the crowd. "Folks," the governor began. "This is Miss Elnora Jamison. She is the secret to our success here at Ridge Mountain.".

Shortly after the war, Jamison, like many Northerners, came south to assist in the Reconstruction efforts. A teacher by trade, she now held the title of superintendent of the state's orphanage system. Her office was based at Ridge Mountain.

"There's a lot of work to be done," she began. "And we've heard so much about you, Miss Stewart. They say you can read the thoughts of those in your company. Is this true?" Jamison asked rather perplexingly.

"Not quite. But I do know Mister Douglass is craving a hearty meal," said Stewart as the group laughed aloud in unison.

"Is that true, Mister Douglass?" asked Jamison.

"What can I say? Miss Stewart is a woman of many talents, and yes, she has read my mind rather accurately," said Douglass, laughing with the others.

"Well then, the matter is settled. Is lunch prepared?" asked Chambers.

"The cooks prepared a special meal for our special guests. If you will please follow me," said Jamison, as she led the group to the dining hall.

The group was met at the front entrance by a small troupe of children all dressed in white with purple sashes tied around their waists. They began to sing a song in tribute to their guests. Upon entering the spacious dining room, one could see three dozen wooden tables neatly aligned and each seat filled. Many of the children were giggling and pointing in the direction of their famous guests.

Women dressed in white and black clothing stood adjacent to each table. "They help with supervision. Most came to us destitute. Many of them lost their husbands in the war," explained Jamison.

"How do they get along with each other?" asked Douglass.

"They don't have a choice if they want to stay here," said Jamison. "Every now and then we have to implement correction methods to keep the peace, but things have gotten much better throughout the entire system," Jamison said.

"You see, we completely eliminated the racial caste system here," said

Jamison. "We, like all state and municipal agencies, have adopted the ways and vision of our esteemed governor and president," said Jamison, glancing in the direction of Chambers, who nodded in approval while sipping on his soup. "We feel if we can teach the women — the white woman and their children, to be more precise — then we feel we can change the thinking of future generations," said Jamison.

"What about the men?" asked Stewart.

"That's what the SG and the militia are for," said Chambers.

"Heck," he continued, "we're not nearly out of the woods yet. These damn ex-Confederates are going to fight back. I'll bet they'll strike sometime after the election. The Civil War is not over yet, Mister Douglass. Believe you me. The Southern white man's world has been turned upside down, and they can't abide by the ways of the New South. They believe the Negro belongs in the field working for them — for free. They don't believe in the equality of the races. I even heard one Southern gentleman say Lincoln himself believed in the superiority of the white race. That he did, I told him, but I'm no fan of Lincoln, and that shut him right up," said Chambers.

"Governor, where is the SG, if you don't mind me asking?" asked Douglass.

The governor began laughing. "Don't worry, Mister Douglass, the SG is everywhere in this state. There's a large contingent just a half mile up the road. They send a patrol around every few hours or so. Jamison's fiancé is a lieutenant in the company. They'll be escorting you to the Tennessee border by train tomorrow. As you know, the SG are forbidden by law to step foot in Tennessee. Now, before I forget, make sure you tell the colonel we would love for him to stop by some time. He has a lot of friends in Little Rock. You tell 'em that," Chambers concluded.

"I most certainly will, Governor, and thank you for your wonderful hospitality," said Stewart.

The next morning Douglass arrived early for breakfast in the dining hall. "Will the governor be joining us?" asked Douglass.

"The governor left late last evening under the protection of the SG," said Jamison, who, along with her aides, prepared the hall for the morning meal.

"Why would he leave so late?" asked Douglass.

"It's his way of keeping the enemy off-guard. Besides Little Rock is only a couple of hours away," said Jamison.

"Where's your lovely companion, Mister Douglass?"

"Right here," said Stewart. Jamison quickly turned around.

"Why don't you look sparkling, Miss Stewart," said Jamison. "No wonder why my Jordan told me half the SG wanted this detail."

"Thank you, Miss Jamison," said a smiling Stewart.

At eleven o'clock the front of the orphanage filled with a mix of jubilant children and adults waiting to see Stewart and Douglass off. As they came out of the building a loud cheer went up. A group of girls approached Stewart and presented her with a bouquet of roses. Stewart leaned over and placed a kiss on the cheek of a little black girl.

"Will I be as smart and beautiful as you one day, Miss Wizard?" the little girl asked shyly. Stewart smiled.

"What's your name, Little One?" asked Stewart.

"Jessica, ma'am. But my friends call me Jesse. You can call me Jesse, too, if you want."

"Okay, and you can call me Lisa. But you must promise me you will be good in school, and study hard, and get as much education as you can," said Stewart.

"I promise," said Jesse.

"Me, too," said her friend standing next to her.

"Then both of you will grow up to be smart, beautiful women. Okay?" said Stewart with a smile. Both girls nodded in agreement.

"Okay, now our guest must be going," said Jamison. "We packed you a fine lunch. Be safe and well. And y'all come back and visit us again," said Jamison to Stewart and Douglass as they climbed into their carriage.

"We will," said Stewart.

"And thank you for such wonderful hospitality," said Douglass.Seventy five well-armed SG troops waited to escort the pair to the train that would take them to Hopefield, Arkansas.

"Governor Chambers doesn't want anything to happen to you. Particularly on Arkansas soil," said Lieutenant Jordan Rivers, as he noticed Douglass' reaction to the large entourage of SG troops. As they rode to the station, many of them strained to catch a glimpse of the beautiful Stewart. Stewart smiled and waved. She undoubtedly enjoyed the attention, but not as much as the book she held, *Eugene Onegin,* by Alexander Pushkin.

# — TWENTY —

# Major Whitfield

When their train stopped in Hopefield, Arkansas, the SG troops aboard exited the train and lined the abandoned platform. Douglass and Stewart exited the train and were escorted to the steamboat by a second group of soldiers. The boat would ferry them across the river into Tennessee. While standing on the platform, both Stewart and Douglass sensed an uneasiness about some of the townsfolk who appeared to be milling around the area. Something just didn't feel right. After a brief exchange between the commanders of both groups, the SG commander ordered his troops to abandon the platform. They then took up positions around the area leading to the steamboat. Some even took up positions on the rooftops of nearby buildings. Their presence was imposing, to say the least.

The second group was dressed like Union soldiers except they wore light grey shirts and a purple sash on their waist line and a purple stripe graced the side of their trousers. There was even a small purple band that wrapped around the caps they wore on their heads. They numbered about 40. The commander of the guard was waiting for his guests on the ferry. He wore the rank of major. He looked as if he was a mixture of black and Native American with wavy jet black hair and he appeared to be every bit like the man in charge.

"Good afternoon, folks. I'm Major Whitfield and I'll be your escort while you are in the state of Tennessee. If you'll follow me I'll take you to your seats. The colonel looks forward to seeing the two of you, as does General Higginson. You are now under the protection of the Brigade of the Southern Command but some folks call us the Grey Shirts," he said smiling. "As you know Tennessee is not under federal military control so the SG is prohibited from operating here. Of course it pisses off the colonel and me, too," he whispered. "Hopefully, we'll change that one day. But in the meantime, if either of you need anything, just ask. We are here to accommodate you. Any of you ever been to Tennessee?"

"No, Major, I haven't," said Douglass.

"This will be my first trip to the state," said Stewart.

"I see. Well, we'll do our best to make it a wonderful experience for you both," said Whitfield.

"And what about you, Major?" asked Stewart.

"And please take a seat," said Douglass as the ferry crept away from the dock.

"How long have you lived in Tennessee?" said Stewart finishing her question.

"I was born here, ma'am. My mother was sold to the Chickasaw nation, and my father was a leader on the tribal council. She eventually became his wife, they made a home together, and shortly thereafter I came along."

"So you have the best of both worlds, Major?" Stewart said smiling.

"No one has quite put it like that, Miss Stewart, but I guess you're right," said Whitfield.

When Whitfield was about eight years old, he and his family, along with the people of his tribe, were forced, under the Indian Removal Act of 1830[86], to walk from Memphis, Tennessee to the eastern part of the Oklahoma territory. The journey was known as the "Trail of Tears."[87] His tribe was not the only Native American tribe treated this way. The Seminole, Muscogee Creek Cherokee, and Choctaw tribes all faced a similar predicament.

---

[86]  The Indian Removal Act was passed by Congress in 1830 during Andrew Jackson's presidency. The act gave the president power to "negotiate" the relocation of Indian tribes from the Southern states to federal territory west of the Mississippi River in "exchange" for the complete destruction of their ancestral homelands. *For more information about the removal of Native Americans from their ancestral lands, see the article "No Idle Past: Uses of History in the 1830 Indian Removal Debates" by Jason Meyers, The Historian, Volume 63, Issue 1, 2000, pp. 53-66.*

[87]  The Indian Removal Act forced the dislocation of the Cherokee, Muscogee, Seminole, Chickasaw, and Choctaw nations from their homelands to "Indian Territory" in the west. Native Americans were forced to walk the entire way and the journey became known as the "Trail of Tears" because of the utter devastation wreaked on countless human beings and their cultural heritages. *To read more about the Trail of Tears and the removal of even the Native Americans who had been most willing and successful in adapting to European values, see Trail of Tears: The Rise and Fall of the Cherokee Nation by John Ehle, Anchor Books Doubleday, 1988.*

At one point during the forced march, a young Whitfield became the primary caretaker of a little boy about three years younger than he. The boy's parents, like many others, had died earlier during the march from disease. So the little boy was an orphan. Whitfield made it his duty to watch over the child even though he was but a child himself. During the second week of caring for the boy, they came by a mountain, which was occupied by men who appeared to be wearing uniforms. At first they could hear a lot of jeering, but the haggard group of men, women and children were too hungry to pay much attention to the soldiers. When shots were initially fired, some in the group turned around to ascertain where the shots were being fired from but many, tired, depressed and hungry just kept moving slowly.

Oftentimes during the March, small children on foot lagged far behind the others. Whitfield's parents allowed him to walk with the little boy. They walked a few yards ahead of Whitfield and the little boy. When the second set of shots rang out Whitfield's dad stopped in his tracks and looked around for his son. His mother, sensing the danger, moved quickly back through the crowd, calling out for her son. Just when his father appeared, the little hand Whitfield was holding fell limp. When Whitfield turned around, the little boy was lying face down in the dirt. He had a large gunshot wound to the back of his head. Whitfield's father immediately jumped on top of his son, and his mother fell on top of her husband. The family just laid there until the firing stopped. When they were finally able to get to their feet, they saw at least a dozen members of the tribe lying motionless in the dirt. Half of the victims were small children.

Whitfield refused to leave the lifeless body of his little companion in the desert and so his father carried the small corpse a few miles and buried the small child in a shallow grave. The incident would haunt Whitfield for the remainder of his life.

As a child, Whitfield was raised in the ways of the Chickasaw. His mother spoke English to him at home while away from home he spoke the language of his father. During late adolescence he took a strong interest in tribal affairs but decided to abandon the tribe when the Chickasaw and the four other tribes, collectively referred to as The Five Civilized Tribes[88],

---

[88] The term refers to the five Native American tribes that European settlers generally considered "civilized" as they appeared to adopt some Anglo-American norms (horticulture and Christianity, for example). They include: Cherokee, Chickasaw, Choctaw, Creek, and Seminole.

made a pact in 1861 to fight for the Confederate States during the Civil War. Whitfield chose to fight with the Union. While it was true his tribe and the four other tribes were treated horrifically by the U.S. government and therefore he understood the reasons behind his tribe's decision to fight for the Confederate army, he could not reconcile supporting an entity which viewed both he and his mother and, to a large extent, his father, as less than human and deserving of enslavement.

After the war, he remained with the regular army and rose in the ranks. His background gave him advantages few others possessed. Like Colonel Foginet, it didn't take long for General Higginson to discover Whitfield possessed exceptional talents. When the time came to select who would lead the SG, the two finalists were he and Foginet. Upon being promoted to the rank of colonel, Foginet selected Whitfield as his right hand man and placed him in charge of the prestigious Grey Shirts, who numbered about 250 highly trained combat troops and were responsible for providing security to members of the military high command in the South and all high ranking federal officials who came to Tennessee as well as those state officials who requested security.

Being that the state of Tennessee was not part of any military district, its legislature voted to prohibit any federal para-military unit numbering more than 250 to be stationed in its state. After Purple Sunrise they attempted to modify the law to rid the state of the Grey Shirts but white and black Republicans defeated this attempt on the part of the Democrats. The Democrats, while not in the majority, were still a significant party in Tennessee. This was due in large part to not being subjected to the Iron-clad Oath.

There were less than 65 individuals on the ferry, including the crew. Aside from the Grey Shirts who travelled with the pair, there were at least ten non-uniformed armed military personnel disguised as passengers. Foginet was taking no chances with Douglass — the president's personal envoy and Stewart — the most powerful woman in the South, who just happened to be his love interest.

After a choppy ride across the Mississippi River, the boat landed in Tennessee just outside the City of Memphis. A stagecoach was waiting to take Douglass and Stewart to the train that would take them to Nashville. Both Stewart and Douglass noticed the change in attitude among the white citizens in Memphis. Unlike the white citizens in the other states in the former Confederacy, whites in Tennessee were clearly acting like their usual selves. In the other states of the former Confederacy, whites were a lot more obsequious in their behavior toward black people. This was not the case in Tennessee. They still had a sense of superiority about themselves. They would have to learn humility like the whites in the other states of the former Confederacy.

Nashville was a bustling city of 26,000 people when Stewart and Douglass arrived. It relied heavily on its shipping industry and was a leading port for trade prior to and after the Civil War. It was the first Southern capital to fall into Union hands. This gave the Union a tremendous tactical advantage for the duration of the war.

Stewart and Douglass were met by forty armed Grey Shirts when they stepped off the train. Most passengers and bystanders knew they were important individuals because of the presence of the Grey Shirts, but only a small handful knew who they were. General Higginson made it a point not to announce the visit because of security concerns, but word travelled quickly upon their arrival. Blacks who lived and worked in the vicinity of train station rushed to the scene and tried desperately to get a glimpse of the two celebrities.

## — TWENTY-ONE —

# General Foginet

The headquarters for the Southern Military Command was located on the outskirts of downtown Nashville. Hickory Hill — the estate where the compound now stood — was once owned by a wealthy planter whose fortunes went the way of the war for the South. The mansion itself was beautiful, and the grounds were equally elegant. The large contingent of military personnel coming and going made the place appear busier than it actually was. Much of the work General Higginson was charged with carrying out took place outside of Tennessee.

He left matters pertaining to such work in the capable hands of Lyle Davenport and Randall McArthur, Lisa Stewart, and Colonel Aurelius Foginet. While he entertained important guests and provided updates to his superiors in Washington D.C, namely the President and Secretary of War, he trusted his operatives in the field were doing a fantastic job, and from the looks of things, his analysis proved to be accurate.

When the two guests arrived, they were immediately taken to their respective rooms in the living quarters of the mansion to relax and freshen up after their long trip. Later on in the evening there would be a reception held in their honor. As Stewart unpacked her belongings, she noticed a beautiful bouquet of roses on the table adjacent to the bed. The note placed next to the roses stated "Welcome. Words are inadequate to describe how much I miss you. We will talk soon." A picture of a heart was drawn in place of the writer's signature.

The reception began promptly. The event was the biggest Nashville had seen in a long while. It seemed as if everyone of some importance was in attendance. The two guests were each escorted into the room as their names were called. Each received a tremendous ovation from the enthusiastic crowd. As Stewart approached the dais, she noticed Foginet moving his hands in an awkward motion. Then it struck her he was communicating in Sign language. He told her, "You are a beautiful gift from God." Stewart smiled and approached General Higginson, who extended his hand. Stewart extended hers, and it was met by kiss from Higginson. Many whites in the room were stunned a black woman was treated with such dignity by a white man. Many black guests were taken by surprise as well. But those like Foginet, who knew Higginson, laughed to themselves. He knew Higginson despised the racist culture of the South and used every possible occasion to offend its racist customs.

Higginson sat in the middle of the dining table flanked on the right by Douglass and on the left by Stewart. Foginet sat next to Stewart. Upon being seated, Stewart turned to Foginet, and in perfect Russian said, "Can you please pass the water, Colonel Foginet?" Foginet was stunned, as was the other guest who heard the request spoken in Russian. As he reached for the water she continued in Russian, "be careful, Colonel Foginet, we don't want you to ruin your handsome uniform." They both laughed out loud. The curious observer knew something was brewing between the two of them but at the moment neither seemed to care.

Midway through dinner, Douglass turned to Higginson and whispered something in his ear. The general nodded, stood up and raised his hand, asking the other guests for their undivided attention. He then said he had a special announcement. He asked Colonel Foginet to meet him along with Douglass in front of the dais.

"It is my distinct honor to announce Colonel Foginet has been promoted to the rank of brigadier general in the U.S. Army. I would like Mister Douglass and, if you will, Miss Stewart, to assist in pinning the star which symbolizes the colonel's new rank to his uniform."

This was an unbelievable event. It startled many in the room, even military personnel. Foginet was the first black man ever to be appointed to the rank of general in the history of the nation. That evening, as word spread throughout the city, hundreds of blacks descended upon Hickory Hill to get a glimpse of the new general. General Foginet did not disappoint. With an entourage that included Higginson, Stewart, Douglass, Whitfield, and dozens of Grey Shirts, Foginet walked from the mansion to the gates of the estate where he saluted his supporters. The crowd went wild - "Foginet, Foginet, Foginet." The crowd yelled his name for what seemed like an eternity.

The following evening, Foginet and Stewart met for a private dinner. She presented him with the Nashville Republican Banner, the local paper. The headline screamed "Wade Makes Negro General." Both Stewart and Foginet knew while he deserved his new rank, his promotion also had a lot to do with election year politics. Wade needed the support of black voters in the South, and while there was no question as to his popularity among black voters throughout the nation, he knew Foginet's promotion would seal the deal.

Higginson was also promoted to lieutenant general and General Wright was now brevetted major general. Additionally, Foginet who was the top commander of the SG and Grey Shirts, was now given command of all U.S. Army personnel in the Fifth Military District.

"How have you been, Lisa?" Foginet began.

"It's been exciting but grueling with the travelling and all," said Stewart.

"I love your New England accent," said Foginet.

"I love yours too, General. By the way, what is it?" asked Stewart with a smile.

"Oh, a mixture of my travels to different lands, but mainly Wolof, Arabic and French," said Foginet, smiling. Stewart laughed.

"Well, I see you will be even busier with all of your new responsibilities," said Stewart.

"Not too busy for you, or should I say us, Miss Stewart," Foginet said with a wink.

"It might complicate things," said Stewart.

"What do you mean? I must forego a life with the woman I love?" asked Foginet.

"Please don't play with me, General. My life is full of complications. I don't need any more," said Stewart.

"Lisa, I just don't learn to Sign for anyone." The two of them burst out laughing.

"And I don't learn Russian for just anyone, General," said Stewart.

"In all seriousness, Lisa, I want you for my wife," said Foginet.

"Are you sure that's what you want, Aurelius?"

Foginet smiled having heard Stewart use his first name.

"Yes, I'm sure, Lisa. Will you be my wife?" Stewart took a deep breath.

"Let's talk some more in the morning. There is so much to think about. I'm sorry, General," said Stewart.

"I understand, Lisa," said Foginet.

Stewart excused herself from the table and went to her room. A few hours later Stewart heard a quiet knock at her door. When she opened it, Foginet stood in the doorway. "I just came by to help you make the right decision," said Foginet, smiling. She let him in. He turned and closed the door.

# TWENTY-TWO

# The General and the Wizard

Foginet was joined at breakfast by Higginson, Douglass, Stewart, and Wright.

"I have to prepare a report for the president," Higginson began. "Does anyone feel I should add something of any particular importance?

"Well, sir," started Lisa, "It seems as though there is significant concern regarding the lack of a structured intelligence-gathering apparatus. Governor Bainbridge and Major Embry are just two of the many individuals we've encountered who raised this as a concern. I too believe more can be done in this area," said Stewart.

"What do you think, General Wright?" asked Higginson.

"Well, sir, that might be a bit premature. And the cost is another factor to consider. While I have no doubt such an apparatus can be useful, I'm not too sure the timing is right," said Wright.

"What do you think, Colonel, excuse me, General Foginet?" Higginson asked with a light smile.

"Well, sir, I think it's important that we listen to our folks in the field. They know best, and Bainbridge, while he's a bit high-strung, if you will, I have never known him to be impractical. He's a cautious operator," said Foginet.

"Maybe a bit too cautious," said Douglass. "From what I observed, Alabama is an armed camp. Maybe, just maybe, we should take it easy for a while and focus on improving those systems that have some actual value to our people," argued Douglass.

"All due respect, Mister Douglass, but if we don't improve our intelligence-gathering capabilities, we will not possess much of anything to improve for our people," argued Stewart. "These ex-Confederates are determined to take back the South by hook or crook," she concluded.

"It sounds a bit paranoid to me," said Wright. "Things seem to be under control. The ex-Confederates are disenfranchised and a bunch of them are locked away in Huntsville. Is this necessary?"

"I agree with the General,"

"Which one?" Higginson laughed, as he interrupted Douglass. Wright didn't take kindly to the joke but offered a faint smile.

"I agree with General Wright. I just don't think we should provoke hostilities if we can avoid such things," said Douglass.

"How would they know?" asked Stewart. "The intelligence system I had in mind won't be too easy for anyone to detect," said Stewart.

"How long will it take to construct?" asked Higginson.

"Construction is easy. I already have a design. It's the implementation that will take some time. Maybe six months or so," said Stewart.

"Well everyone, we can talk about it on the ride to South Carolina. The president wants the folks in the South to see his new general. We will all travel east. Then Mister Douglass and I will head north to the nation's capital. The president doesn't think you will be well received in North Carolina and Virginia just yet," said Higginson.

"I agree, General," said Foginet. "When do we leave?"

"In two days. And by the way, General Wright, you'll remain behind and guard the store," said Higginson.

"Will do, sir," said Wright.

"Mister Douglass, do you mind if I have a word with you?" asked Foginet.

"Not at all, General. I'll meet you on the back porch in about fifteen minutes or so," said Douglass.

"Will do," said Foginet.

The train ride east was unremarkable. Higginson and Douglass said their goodbyes to the new couple in Georgia, and Stewart and Foginet made their way to South Carolina. Upon arrival, Stewart and Foginet were greeted by a massive crowd, mostly black but speckled with white faces. The crowd was so enormous that reinforcements from the regular army were called in to assist the SG in crowd control. Stewart and Foginet were held on the train for an additional hour while the crowd was brought under control. When the two finally exited the train, it was pandemonium.

This was their first appearance in public as a couple, and the crowd adored them. They were greeted by a sea of purple flags. At least a dozen purple flags displayed a large gold star in the middle of the cloth to honor the newly-promoted brigadier general.

A chorus of "Foginet! Foginet! Foginet! Foginet!" went on for about ten minutes. Then the crowd started chanting "Stewart! Stewart! Stewart! Stewart!" The two waved and slowly made their way to the stagecoach. They were hustled off to the SG compound, which was located on a beautiful plantation on the outskirts of Columbia.

"You didn't say much at the last meeting back at Hickory Hill," said Stewart.

"No, I didn't, dear," said Foginet. "You see, at this point I don't know who to trust outside of the SG, with the exception of you, of course," he smiled and grabbed Stewart's hand gently. "I want you to do two things for me Lisa," said Foginet. "First, I don't ever want you to abandon the protection of the SG. You must promise me this."

"I understand, Aurelius. But you must promise me the same," she said. He leaned over to kiss her, then quickly remembered they were in the eye of the public.

"I owe you one," said Foginet.

"I'll remind you," said Stewart. "And what's your second request, General?"

"By all means, begin working on the construction of the intelligence apparatus."

"Who do you have concerns about, Aurelius?" asked Stewart.

"It's too early to tell exactly who, but this I do know — those ex-Confederates are up to something, and if we're not careful, those sick bastards will place every last one of us with black skin back in chains," said Foginet.

"What do you plan to do?" asked Stewart.

"I've called a meeting of my top commanders in the SG. I want you at the meeting. I need you at my side," explained Foginet. He continued, "The trick is preventing anything from happening to the president. As long as he's alive, we have a fighting chance. The key for the ex-Confederates is to remove Union troops from the South. That's key for them. They can only do that if they place a sympathizer in the Executive Mansion. Part two is for them to neutralize key personnel, like Higginson and Davenport."

"Yes, Aurelius, and you and I as well," added Stewart.

"Exactly," said Foginet. "So it's imperative that we prepare for the worst-case scenario," said Stewart, looking her fiancé in the eyes.

"I love you, Lisa. You are so brilliant and beautiful," said Foginet.

"I love you more," said Stewart. "Aurelius?"

"Yes, Lisa," said Foginet.

"I hope you don't mind, but I sent a message to Davenport and McArthur when we stopped in Georgia, requesting they come to Columbia to meet with you," said Stewart.

"Is it something pressing I need to attend to?" asked Foginet.

"No, but I think they should be included in whatever plans we make. After all, they run the political machine down here, and they are trustworthy and quite knowledgeable," said Stewart.

"Good point. I'm a little concerned about our white Republican friends in Virginia, North Carolina, and Texas," said Foginet.

"Let's not forget about Georgia," said Stewart.

"You're right, and I won't. Set up the meeting," said Foginet.

"It's already taken care of, my dear," said Stewart with a smile on her face.

Foginet just laughed and shook his head. "I should've known."

# TWENTY-THREE

# Re-Election

66Your impressions, Fred?" asked Wade.

"Excuse me, sir?" asked Douglass.

"Your trip — your impressions. I didn't send you down there for a vacation, Fred. What did you see? What did you learn? What is our support like?" Wade sounded anxious. It was his first meeting with Douglass since he returned from the South. The presidential election was two months away and while Wade was not all that concerned with his chances of winning re-election, he wanted a landslide. He wanted a mandate to rule. He strongly believed the black vote in the South would send a clear message he was on the right side of history, and, more importantly, his policies as they pertained to the freedmen were morally just and in the best interest of the nation. Wade also had additional plans in place for eradicating once and for all the power of the planter class in the South, which he utterly despised.

"Well, Bluff. I gotta tell ya, I was pleasantly surprised. Your master plan is being implemented just as you imagined. I gotta give it to ya, you have a knack for putting the right people in the right place to carry out a specific task," Douglass raised his cup of coffee in a toast to the president.

"Specifics, Fred. God damn it, I need specifics," Wade seemed agitated.

"You want specifics, Mister President, here they are. There are a whole lot of happy black folks down there and a lot of pissed-off white folks. The Southern Guard is everywhere, and they even got some black folks on edge, but they do a damn good job keeping the peace, I must say. There's a paranoid governor in Alabama who sees a conspiracy behind every door. There's a bunch of white Republicans who would easily switch brands if the circumstances were different. They're not trusted by the SG and vice-versa."

"Is that so?" Wade interrupted Douglass. "Go on," said Wade - anxious to hear more.

"The transportation system throughout the region is fantastic as is the educational system they're attempting to build, particularly in Mississippi. Foginet has done a marvelous job insisting members of the SG become literate and well-groomed. He's a much-respected fellow down there. The state banks are doing incredibly well and the people seem to trust that their money is protected. Folks even line up to pay their taxes on time. I was impressed with the orphanage system in Arkansas, and you can't ask for a better communication system. If the South has a weakness, I would say it's the health care system, but I suppose they'll get that together in due time," Douglass paused.

"Do the blacks feel safe? And what about those murdering sons of bitches Klansmen?" asked Wade.

"Bluff, I'm telling you, from what I gather, Higginson has created a 20,000-man militia in every state, and his SG unit under Foginet is top-notch. Put it this way — if they didn't fear the SG before this February past they damn sure fear 'em now," said Douglass.

"Do our folks down there need any more resources? I just don't trust those fuckin' planters, Fred," said Wade.

"Well, they want to set up a better intelligence-gathering system to keep an eye on things," said Douglass.

"Umm," Wade pondered the idea.

"I think Foginet already put Stewart on it," said Douglass.

"Why do you think that is so, Fred?"

"Because, like Governor Bainbridge, they suspect the ex-Confederates have not given up on the possibility of reclaiming the South and putting black folks in chains again," said Douglass.

"And you don't agree with their assessment, Fred?"

"Bluff, the Thirteenth Amendment that guarantees us forced servitude in this country is a thing of the past. Now, I'm not saying there aren't many whites out there who would like to return to those dreadful days, but I'm not so sure if these additional safeguards are necessary now," argued Douglass. "Besides, it makes us appear paranoid."

"Well, Fred, I think that's not such a bad thing. I don't trust those traitorous bastards either," said Wade.

"Tell me, Fred, what do you think about Foginet?"

"Well, sir, I had an excellent meeting with him back in Tennessee. It lasted for about an hour or so. He's a likeable fella. Extremely intelligent. Quite reserved. A good listener. Not much of a talker. It's difficult to tell what's going on in his head."

"Higginson was impressed with him as was I when I met him. They say the man can speak several languages," said Wade.

"He seems to know how to communicate with those who are mute as well. I saw him demonstrating this ability with Stewart," said Douglass.

"Ah Stewart, what a prize, eh Fred? My God, what a mind. You saw him using Sign language, did ya? I bet she learned Russian," said Wade quietly but loud enough for Douglass to hear.

"Actually, sir, I did see her reading a Russian version of a novel by that black Russian fella, the poet Pushkin. Yes, Alexander Pushkin. How did you know she was learning the Russian language, Bluff? If you don't mind me asking," said Douglass.

"Well, to be truthful, Caroline tipped me off after the last time they attended dinner here, when that Russian military officer paid us a visit and he and Foginet communicated in Russian. She told me in the presence of Foginet she knew how to Sign. Well, anyway, Caroline went on and on about how the two of them would make a fine couple. I guess she knew what she was talking about," said Wade, laughing.

"Now about this upcoming election. How does it look for us down there?" asked Wade.

"I want to predict a landslide for you in the South, Bluff," said Douglass.

"Well, what the hell is stopping ya?" asked Wade.

"Not one damn thing, Bluff. I think the South is going to make you proud and give you the mandate to lead our great nation for another four years. At least," said Douglass laughing aloud, "Let's hope so Fred. Let's hope so."

On Tuesday, November 5, 1872, Douglass' prediction was better than expected. The Wade-Grant ticket destroyed the Democratic ticket of Senator James Asheton Bayard of Delaware[89] and Representative William Slo-

---

[89] Bayard was a conservative Democrat who served as senator of Delaware. Bayard believed Southern states should be allowed to secede peacefully and privately hoped Delaware would secede. He opposed abolitionism and believed the Civil War was unnecessary, as Southern states should be allowed independence without opposition.

cum Groesbeck of Ohio.[90] Republicans also held onto control both houses of the Congress. Most significant was the increase in the number of black legislators in both chambers of Congress.

| STATE | TOTAL NUMBER OF HOUSE SEATS | BLACKS ELECTED TO HOUSE | BLACKS ELECTED TO SENATE |
|---|---|---|---|
| Alabama | 8 | 5 | 2 |
| Arkansas | 4 | 1 | 1 |
| Florida | 2 | 1 | 1 |
| Georgia | 9 | 4 | 1 |
| Louisiana | 6 | 6 | 2 |
| Mississippi | 6 | 6 | 2 |
| North Carolina | 8 | 3 | 0 |
| South Carolina | 5 | 5 | 2 |
| Tennessee | 10 | 2 | 0 |
| Texas | 6 | 2 | 0 |
| Virginia | 9 | 3 | 0 |
| Totals | 73 | 38 | 11 |

In the Senate, Alabama, Louisiana, Mississippi, and South Carolina each elected blacks to both Senate seats. All but North Carolina, Tennessee, Texas, and Virginia did not elect a black senator. Arkansas, Florida, and Georgia each elected one black to serve in the U.S. Senate. Thus,

---

[90] A Democrat, Groesbeck served as a member of the Peace Convention of 1861 held in Washington, D.C., which attempted to devise a means to prevent civil war.

there were now thirty-eight black members of the House and eleven black members of the U.S. Senate. Wade could not be happier. Despite not winning Senate seats in North Carolina, Tennessee, Texas and Virginia, blacks still held sway with their white Republican allies to control former Confederate state houses. In fact black governors controlled the executive branch in Alabama, Louisiana, Mississippi, and South Carolina. White Republican governors controlled the other states of the former Confederacy. Additionally, blacks were lieutenant governors in Arkansas and Georgia.

The Presidential Inauguration was held on March 4, 1873. It was a frigid day in the nation's capital and for the third time in five years, the Chief Justice of the U.S. Supreme Court and the president's former political adversary, the Honorable Salmon P. Chase would administer the presidential oath to Benjamin "Bluff" Wade. Standing by Wade's side was his wife Caroline; General Foginet; General Higginson; Lyle Davenport; Randall McArthur and of course the Wizard, Lisa Stewart.

Wade gave much of the credit to this phenomenal victory to these individuals. Lyle Davenport and his assistant Randall McArthur created and brilliantly orchestrated the Republican political machine in the former states of the Confederacy. Stewart's reform efforts in the financial and communication sectors drastically improved the quality of life for millions of citizens across the South. Higginson radically improved railroad transportation throughout the South, but it was his efforts at the behest of the president to arm hundreds of thousands of blacks in the South that won him presidential praise.

Under the leadership of Foginet, the SG became a powerful, well organized, elite group of soldiers which provided much needed protection to black and white voters and officeholders. The Republican candidates' capacity to campaign without fear of being set upon by white hooligans made the entire process democratic and enjoyable. The percentage for black voter turnout was off the charts. In most places, the turnout was well over 90 percent.

Many ex-Confederates saw their future in the South slowly slipping away. Not a few felt if something was to be done it had to be done soon. But those plans would have to wait until the worst of The Panic of 1873 was behind them.

# — TWENTY-FOUR —

# A Red Harvest

The Great Depression of 1873[91], triggered in large measure by the collapse of the Vienna Stock Exchange on May 9, 1873, caused widespread unemployment in the North and West due to the collapse of railroad and building construction projects. American businesses failed by the thousands and corporations lost millions of dollars in profits. But while banks failed in the North, the South was insulated from the economic collapse due to the economic system supported by its state-run banking system.

In fact, while the "panic" was felt in the North and across Europe, the effects were minimal in the South. Many businesses in the South made enormous profits as a result of the economic catastrophe in the North. This was in large measure due to the lending capabilities of the Southern banks. Not a single state-run bank in the South experienced a run on its bank's deposits. By the time the Panic was over, the South was the richest region in the country and one of the richest regions in the world. Many nations sought desperately to create a partnership with this new emerging

---

[91] The "Panic of 1873" was a financial crisis that triggered the first truly global depression, which lasted from 1873 until 1879. It was a consequence of the developed world's industrial, capitalist economy and was brought about largely because of irresponsible speculative spending, mainly in United States railroads. The depression was devastating for Southern blacks as the North became less concerned with civil rights and racism and more concerned with addressing unemployment, labor strikes, falling farm prices, and other economic consequences. *To read more about how the United States political climate and its priorities were affected by the Panic of 1873, see the article "The Politics of Economic Crises: The Panic of 1973, the End of Reconstruction, and the Realignment of American Politics by Nicholas Barreyre,* The Journal of the Gilded Age and Progressive Era, *Volume 10, Issue 4, 2011, pp. 403-423.*

economic power.

While many white Southerners also felt the effect of the Panic due to their unwillingness to support the South's banking system, the mere fact they lived in the South shielded many Southern white families from the hardship experienced by their Northern brethren. Blacks in the South never had it so good. New schools, hospitals, roads, bridges, orphanages, businesses, and public facilities sprung up all over the former Confederacy. Farmers were able to purchase new farm equipment and building material to improve their farms. Europe welcomed black students from the South because it gave their local economies somewhat of a boost and those Europeans who could afford it came to the American South to vacation and enjoy the prosperity of this new and emerging regional power.

As the Northern and Western parts of the nation attempted to deal with the Great Depression, ex-Confederates felt the time had come to make their move. Unlike the Redeemers at the national level, these local groups of ex-Confederates were poorly-organized and easily infiltrated.

Stewart's new system of intelligence gathering, while not fully implemented, was nonetheless beginning to pay off. The system first proved its worth in April of 1873, when a white paramilitary group attempted to start an uprising in Colfax, Louisiana[92]. Thanks to information received days in advance, the area was besieged by black militiamen and federal troops. A company of SG troops was sent in to discourage any further thoughts of rebellion. It worked. The SG surrounded the courthouse and remained on the scene for over a week until the danger passed.

The second incident also occurred in Louisiana, this time in Coushatta[93], the county seat of Red River Parish. In August of 1874, a paramilitary

---

[92]  The Louisiana gubernatorial race of 1872 resulted in a narrow Republican victory and escalated tensions between Democrats and Republicans in the state. The Colfax Massacre resulted, and on Easter Sunday, April 13, 1873, a group of armed white Democrats overpowered Republican freedmen and black state militia members who were defending the Colfax Parish Courthouse. Three white men and an estimated 150 black men died in the conflict. Many of the black men who died were prisoners, not fighters in the conflict, and 48 incidental black men were seized and murdered after the battle. *To read more about the massacre, see* The Colfax Massacre: The Untold Story of Black Power, White Terror and the Death of Reconstruction *by Leeanna Keith, Oxford University Press, 2008.*

[93]  The White League, a paramilitary group composed of white Southern Democrats, formed in Louisiana following the 1872 gubernatorial election, with the goal of eliminating carpetbaggers, and particularly those northern Republicans who became involved in local Southern politics. Around the area of Coushatta, the White League took issue with Marshall Twitchell, a carpetbagger from Vermont turned Louisiana senator. Pretending to be under attack by armed

group of disaffected white Democrats attempted to disrupt the political activities of the Republican Party and Republican officeholders. The plan was to assassinate key Republican officeholders in the Parish. However, when SG troops appeared in public, guarding the designated targets, the plan folded.

For Major Soule, these two incidents served as a precursor of what was to come. Foginet agreed and put all militia and SG on full alert in the South. He also ordered the mass arrest of those suspected of engaging in terrorist activities, but before the order reached the field General Higginson advised him to rescind the order due to political considerations. Foginet was told that, given the upcoming 1874 midterm election, which would be held in three months, a mass arrest may not sit too well with voters and could adversely impact the outcome of the elections. Foginet found this to be totally irrational. The South belonged to Wade and the Republican Party. Black voters would not abandon the Party, nor would they ever question the actions of the SG, who they relied on for their personal protection. He knew something was afoot. But Foginet was a soldier, and when given an order from above, you followed it, with few exceptions.

When he met with his top commanders in the fall of 1872, he ordered each one to compile a list of potential troublemakers, traitors, criminals, and vagrants in their respective states. He also informed the group that the SG must become self-reliant and therefore encouraged each commander to develop an "entrepreneurial spirit" or find someone in his camp who has one and who was capable of spearheading this initiative. He warned all commanders not to go anywhere without the protection of the SG. He ordered each commander to provide a quarter of their active SG troops to serve in the intelligence apparatus being created by Stewart and at least 25 of their most dedicated soldiers to report for special training under Major Whitfield. Finally, he ordered the construction of holding camps in each state, each capable of detaining at least 500 prisoners comfortably.

Foginet had prepared the SG as best he could. If he was wrong, "so what," he reasoned. But if he was right, the ex-Confederates would en-

---

black men, members of the White League rounded up members of Twitchell's family along with three white Republicans, taking them as prisoners. However, while transporting them from Coushatta to Shreveport, the White League decided simply to execute them along with 20 nearby freedmen who happened to witness the murders. Although 25 men were arrested for the massacre, none were brought to trial due to lack of evidence.

counter difficulties in carrying out any subversive military action in the Southern states controlled by the SG. Little did he know, his efforts were being undermined at Hickory Hill.

Colfax and Coushatta were major blunders for the local Redeemers. The actions of the local paramilitary forces forced them to revisit their strategy. They knew they'd lost the element of surprise, but they still had one big advantage — the SG could not operate outside of the former states of the Confederacy. Stewart could not even extend her sophisticated intelligence apparatus beyond the prescribed borders. This would prove disastrous for Wade and the Radical Republicans.

On Monday, October 19, 1874, the Redeemers made their move. As the president was leaving a luncheon in Georgetown held in his honor by the Friends of Liberty, a local group that strongly supported Wade's efforts in the South, three would-be assassins appeared just as he attempted to climb into the presidential stage coach. Unbeknownst to the assassins and the president, three armed blacks — two men and a woman — carrying double-barreled Derringers appeared at the same time one of the assassins began firing in Wade's direction. As the first shot was fired, striking the president in the right shoulder, one of the black men fired at the assassin, hitting him in the eye. He fell to the ground instantly. The black man was fired upon by a second assassin, and he was struck in the forehead. He fell to ground immediately. A second black man fired at the second assassin, and the bullet landed in his chest. The assassin grabbed his blood-soaked shirt and took his last breath. The second black man was hit by a bullet from the third assassin in the neck area and fell over the president. As the third assassin attempted to fire on the president, he was hit in the stomach by a bullet fired by the black woman. Nonetheless, a bullet fired by the the third assassin managed to hit the president in his left leg before he too fell to the ground writhing in pain and slowly dying.

In the end, the president had bullet wounds, one to his right back shoulder area and one to his left thigh. Of the three individuals charged by Foginet to protect the president, two of them lay dead. All three assassins were dead. With the help of bystanders and the surviving black woman, the president was lifted into his coach and taken to a nearby hospital. After seeing the president secured, the woman managed to slip away into the crowd and disappear.

While the president was under attack, General Higginson was returning from an early afternoon meeting with the editor of the *Nashville Banner*.

When his carriage was about two miles from his headquarters, he was set upon by four masked men who surrounded, then fired into the carriage, killing him and his driver. The assassins moved the carriage off the road. Higginson's body was not discovered for another two hours.

Lyle Davenport had received a message his presence was required in North Carolina to resolve a dispute between Republican Party rivals vying for control of the legislature in that state. Knowing how important North Carolina was to solidifying the South, he felt it was important to attend the meeting. He didn't get far. Being in the habit of travelling without the protection of the SG proved fatal. As soon as Davenport crossed the North Carolina state line, his carriage was hijacked by a group of a half-dozen men. By the time they found Davenport's body, it was hacked to pieces.

That same morning, Stewart, who was now stationed in Alabama, had received an urgent message to meet with General Foginet in Tennessee. The message had stated something of grave importance had come up, and he must meet with her face to face to discuss the matter. She found the message strange, and attempted to send a telegram to Tennessee but found the lines to Southern Command were inaccessible. She immediately ordered the SG to bring her to the SG compound. At the compound, word filtered in that the president had been attacked by assassins and was now mortally wounded.

Stewart immediately wrote a letter and gave it to a courier whom she ordered to hand deliver it to General Foginet in Tennessee. Next she instructed Major Embry to bring all high-ranking government officials to the SG compound immediately.

"I would strongly suggest the governor issue a State of Emergency," she told Embry.

"I agree, Miss Stewart," said Embry.

"And, Major —"

"Yes, Miss Stewart," said Embry.

"I advise you to get on the hot wire and inform the entire Southern Command we are under attack." Stewart was not making a request, and Embry knew it.

"Will, do Miss Stewart," said Embry. While the top commanders of the SG were not in the habit of taking orders from anyone outside the chain of command, least of all a woman, Stewart had earned their respect. When she spoke, it was as if the order came from Foginet himself.

As Stewart made preparations in Alabama, the Redeemers' plan was in full effect. In Washington D.C. four black congressman and two black senators were shot in broad daylight. The Redeemers even managed to kill the lieutenant governor of Arkansas, who was visiting the nation's capital. With many of the telegraph lines cut, word of the carnage in D.C. got out slowly. Back in the South, churches and schools were bombed in Virginia, North Carolina, Texas and Georgia. In Mississippi, a group of sixty ex-Confederates attempted to storm City Hall in Jackson. The SG prevailed but lost at least a dozen men.

Right around the time Higginson met his end, Foginet was preparing for a meeting with Major Whitfield. When Foginet walked in his office, one of his lieutenants, a rising star in the Grey Shirts, was lying on the floor foaming at the mouth. An overturned tray of cornbread with molasses topping lay on the floor next to him. At that moment, Foginet's secretary entered the office and screamed at the site of the young officer's lifeless body.

"He said he had an appointment with you, so I let him wait in your office. The kitchen brought over what you requested. I guess he helped himself and," his secretary sensed the full picture. "Oh, my God," she yelled and collapsed to the floor.

Foginet was in fact supposed to meet with the young officer, but had forgotten and never told his secretary. The bread eaten by the officer was intended for him.

"Lock it down," he ordered. By this time, Major Whitfield had arrived.

"What's wrong, General?" he asked.

"There's been an attempt on my life," said Foginet. "Put the Grey Shirts on full alert and lock this damn compound down. No one, and I mean no one, enters or leaves," ordered Foginet, still staring at the young lieutenant lying on the floor.

"Send a squad out to find General Higginson and General Wright immediately," said Foginet. Word still had not reached him about the president, but he suspected something was wrong. "Can we get a communication to Washington?"

"All the lines are cut, sir," a communications officer said.

"Whitfield?"

"Yes, General?"

"Don't let a soul leave that kitchen," said Foginet.

"I got it, sir."

"Sir?" a member of the Grey Shirts approached Foginet. "We sent a squad out looking for General Higginson, but my squad escorted General Wright to the train depot last evening. He's definitely not here in the compound, sir."

"Thank you, Captain. Carry on with your duties. Oh, Captain..." Foginet had come to rely on Captain Blandon. "I'm counting on you," said Foginet.

"I understand General. I know what it means, sir," said Blandon sensing the danger. Minutes later, Foginet went into the briefing room.

"Corporal," Foginet began talking to a young enlisted man.

"Yes, General?"

"I have a special assignment for you. I need you to get a message to Lisa Stewart in Alabama. Do you know who she is?" asked Foginet.

"She's The Wizard, General. Everyone knows that, and she's a damn good-looking lady, sir," said the Corporal, not knowing whether to smile or frown.

Foginet brushed off the compliment regarding Stewart and continued. "Yes, yes, corporal, I guess you know who I'm speaking of, but listen, I'll give you a special pass. If anyone stops you, all you have to do is show them this pass. Do you understand?" asked Foginet.

"Yes, sir," said the Corporal.

Foginet sent three different runners on three different routes to get the communication to Stewart. He knew if she survived the attack, she would have already taken action. His communication reinforced what they had gone over a dozen times. At this point, Lisa Stewart was only one of a small number of individuals he could completely trust. Alone in his office he said a silent prayer asking for guidance, mercy, and strength. He also said a prayer for the South, its people, and for his future wife.

Even with Stewart on his mind, Foginet acted swiftly and decisively. He sent runners north, south, east, and west to get information as to what was going on across the country. He ordered the lines to be repaired and restored immediately. Slowly word came trickling in. The president had been shot multiple times. There was no word if he was dead or alive. Seven black members of Congress were shot dead in broad daylight along with the lieutenant governor of Arkansas. Scores of black men, women, and children were dead due to bombings across the South. Stewart's courier arrived, and Foginet was able to breathe easier.

Foginet quickly sent a message to Fredrick Douglass, who he last heard was in Washington D.C. As the courier left his office, word came in that the body of General Higginson had just been recovered. Foginet was stunned. He dismissed the half-dozen members of his staff from his office. He needed to be alone. He had admired Higginson deeply. He owed his career to the man. For him, Higginson possessed the ideals that all men should aspire to own. He had warned Higginson repeatedly about the danger they were all facing, but Higginson was on the cusp of retirement and did not want "a damn Grey Shirt escort everywhere I go," as he informed Foginet not too long ago. Now he was dead. Shot numerous times in the upper torso while seated in his open air carriage.

Later, the news came Davenport was found butchered in his coach and his driver shot. The Redeemers had decapitated two of the most essential pillars of the administration and had severely injured the most important figure in the entire regime. Clearly, they had won this battle, but the war was far from over.

Having secured the necessary items from both his office and Higginson's office, Foginet made preparations to leave Tennessee with Major Whitfield and a forty-member contingent of the Grey Shirts. He placed Captain Blandon in charge of the remaining Grey Shirts troops and Major Finley in charge of the compound.

In a few hours, he would be in Alabama, but first there were some questions that needed to be asked and answered. "Major Whitfield," Foginet called.

"Yes, General?"

"Accompany me to the kitchen and tell someone to find Sergeant Hatcher from the Telegraph Corps. Tell him he's wanted in the kitchen."

"Will do, General," said Whitfield. Foginet was determined to get to the bottom of the conspiracy, starting with individuals in his own back yard.

The following morning, the papers across the nation blared what news they had of the attempted assassination of the president, the assassination of General Higginson and the assassination of Lyle Davenport. Little was written about the assassination of the seven black members of Congress, including two United States senators and a sitting lieutenant governor — at least not in the major newspapers outside of the South. Many of the black newspapers in the North and South did an exceptional job with its coverage of events — what little they knew — but the major white dailies said little about the assassination of these seven, high-ranking, black, elected officials.

When Foginet arrived at Madison Farms, the SG compound in Alabama later that evening, he spent the first fifteen minutes with Stewart in a private office. He then asked Governor Bainbridge and the entire Alabama congressional delegation to join him in the spacious meeting room. Most of Alabama's delegation heeded Bainbridge's warning and stayed close to home during the summer recess. They returned earlier than expected for the fall elections. Not one was a casualty of what one Delaware newspaper headline almost gleefully called the massacre: "The Red Harvest."

They were joined by Major Embry and two captains from the SG, Lafayette Inge, the senior U.S. senator from the state of Alabama and the junior U.S. senator Morgan Watts. A select few high-ranking officials from the Alabama state legislature were also present. There was not one white face in the room. Bainbridge insisted on it.

When the meeting began, Stewart was asked to provide an assessment of what she knew at the time. She pulled several sheets of paper from a folder she carried and began by telling the group about the casualties in Washington, including the president.

"We know he was shot multiple times. We just don't know his condition yet," she said. "Our sources tell us," she continued, "the vice president was not attacked and an attack on Secretary Chandler was thwarted by a few bystanders," Stewart hesitated, then continued.

"General Higginson was murdered in Tennessee, and Lyle Davenport was murdered in North Carolina," she shook her head slightly and continued, "As for civilian casualties, our sources tell us that over 200 black men, women, and children were killed throughout the former states of the Confederacy, and that number will most likely increase — a lot. The civilian casualties were mostly from explosives, mass shootings, and at least two dozen lynchings. That's all for now," Stewart slowly folded her soft, dark brown hands and rested them on the papers that told the tragic news.

For a moment, there was silence as each participant tried to make sense of the killings. A few of the men openly wept.

"Goddamn Savages," whispered Bainbridge.

Foginet's eyes stared at the ceiling while he used his hand to massage his beard and the bridge of his nose. "What do you think, Senator?" Realizing there were two United States senators in the room and three state senators, Foginet directed his question before anyone could answer. "Senator Inge, please, your thoughts, sir."

Inge was a sixty-seven year old former slave with no formal education, but a self-taught man. He rose quickly through the political ranks in the state of Alabama and was now a U.S. Senator. Prior to running for elected office, he was a respected preacher who folks compared to Solomon of ancient times because of the wisdom he often displayed. He was well respected by everyone in the room. Thus, like Stewart or Foginet, when he spoke, everyone listened.

| State | Total Number of Black Congressmen | Total Number of Black Congressmen Killed | Total Number of Civilians Killed |
|---|---|---|---|
| Alabama | 7 | 0 | 2 |
| Arkansas | 2 | 0 | 8 |
| Florida | 2 | 1 (Sen.) | 22 |
| Georgia | 5 | 1 (Rep.) | 54 |
| Louisiana | 8 | 1 (Sen.) | 16 |
| Mississippi | 8 | 1 (Rep.) | 71 |
| North Carolina | 3 | 1 (Rep.) | 36 |
| South Carolina | 7 | 0 | 43 |
| Tennessee | 2 | 1 (Rep.) | 61 |
| Texas | 2 | 0 | 53 |
| Virginia | 3 | 1 (Rep.) | 41 |
| Totals | 49 | 7 | 407 |

"Well, we got ourselves a major problem folks," he began slowly. "The key to this whole thing is the president. If he's dead or dying, then you must hope Grant didn't make a deal with the devil. If the president lives, then there's still hope to salvage this thing. But what we all must understand," he paused, then repeated himself, "What we must all understand is this — while there are some damn good white folks in this country, like our president, and like the two men who lost their lives yesterday — may God keep them and bless them — there are whole lot more white folks who don't give a damn about us black folks. Many of them hate us for no good reason and most — in the North and South — don't see us and will never see us as their equals."

At this point Bainbridge led a collective nodding of the head by many in the room.

"It is essential," Inge continued, "That, whatever we do, we can never allow this white man, or a black man who thinks like this white man, to ever, and I mean ever, gain political power over us. Now they might not be able to put us back in chains, but I suspect, if left to them, all of us will be relegated to second-class citizenship at the very least. But I trust the General understands this as does Miss Stewart. So I'm going to leave it in the hands of you fine people to make sure this doesn't happen. Now, if you will excuse me, these old bones need some rest."

As Inge starts to rise from his chair, Foginet follows suit. "One last thing," Inge paused then concluded his thoughts.

"I wish everyone a good night, and if you forget anything I said here this evening, don't forget this," Inge was now shaking his index finger. "How we handle this situation will determine the future of black folks in the South in particular and this nation in general for generations to come. Good night, and may God bless each of you."

After Inge made his exit, others offered their thoughts on the events of the past 24 hours. Finally Bainbridge asked, "Well, General, what do you plan to do?"

The room fell silent. You could hear a pin drop.

"Governor," Foginet was now standing. "Right now I plan to get some rest so I can think a bit more clearly about the matters before us. I think it's also prudent we get as much information as we can. In the meantime I've placed the SG on full alert along with all regular army troops and state militia in the Fifth Military District. I've asked the other military governors to do the same. We'll meet again at noon tomorrow, right here, for another briefing. Now, if you folks will excuse me, my bed is calling."

Foginet left the room without giving anyone an inkling of his thoughts. He knew if the president died, the Reconstruction experiment would in all likelihood follow him to the grave. If the president was alive he would need to be moved out of harm's way.

A few minutes after settling in one of the guest rooms of the large mansion on the SG compound, there was a knock on the door. When Foginet answered the knock, standing in the doorway was Stewart.

"What took you so long?" he asked.

"Well, I just don't want to make things so obvious," said Stewart.

"Get over here, young lady," said Foginet smiling, as he took her in his arms, while the door closed behind her.

"You know, General, I'm not getting any younger," said Stewart.

"Lisa, can I just hold you tonight?" asked Foginet.

"Only if you promise to hold me all night long."

Foginet just smiled and and pulled her closer to him.

By the time Foginet awoke the following morning, Stewart was gone. Foginet walked across the room and looked out the window overseeing the huge training field of the compound. He was startled. The compound flooded with SG troops everywhere. Twelve-pound Napoleon cannons as well as twenty-pound Parrot cannons were stationed around the perimeter of the compound. Sharpshooters with Whitworth rifles could also be seen on top of buildings and in trees. Some of the politicians brought their families to the compound out of fear of another attack. Many slept in the available cottages that dotted the compound. Others slept in makeshift tents placed in the strategic areas all over the sprawling compound to accommodate those civilians who sought refuge.

Most of the tents went unused. The black citizens of Alabama took their protection seriously, and the white ex-Confederate terrorists that participated in the killings knew it. They knew while other states in the former Confederacy had their own state militias, Alabama, Arkansas, and Louisiana created well supported and well trained county militias. The low number of civilian deaths during the Red Harvest suggested they'd done something right.

After consuming a light breakfast, Foginet entered the meeting room, which was now transformed into a war room.

"What do you think, General?" asked Stewart. Telegraph lines ran everywhere and the room bustled with SG troops and politicians.

"I had the Telegraph Corps working on this all through the night," said Stewart.

"Wow," said a bewildered Foginet, glancing at Stewart. "Any news from the North?" asked Foginet.

"According to some reports, Fredrick Douglass has issued a statement of condemnation in the capital," said Stewart.

"I've been waiting to hear that since yesterday," said Foginet.

"His statement?" asked Stewart perplexingly.

"No, dear, that he was still alive," said Foginet.

"Well, he's all over the wire," said Stewart.

"Can we contact him?" asked Foginet

"I've been trying all morning," said Stewart.

"Send a message asking if he received my communication," said Foginet.

"When did you contact Douglass?" asked Stewart.

"Right after I sent the three couriers to you," said Foginet. "Come here," whispered Foginet as he gently grabbed Stewart by the arm and walked her over to a corner.

"Lisa, what I'm about to tell you no one else knows," Foginet began. "Remember when I met with Douglass when you came to Hickory Hill?"

"I do," said Stewart with an anxious look on her face.

"Well, I warned him this could happen, and I said I needed to take precautionary measures to safeguard the president's life. Of course, he thought I, like Bainbridge and yourself, was paranoid. But I asked a favor of him. I asked if he ever felt the president life's was in danger to do everything in his power to convince the president to move south until the danger had passed." Foginet now wore a blank veneer on his face.

"And?" asked Stewart.

"Like I said, he thought I was paranoid, but he reluctantly agreed to accommodate my request," said Foginet.

"Aurelius, what did you mean when you said you needed to take precautionary measures to protect the president?" asked Stewart.

"Shhh — not so loud, my dear." He smiled and gently massaged Stewart's cheek.

"Those twenty-five troops each commander had to turn over to Major Whitfield," Foginet looked around the room. "Well, a small number were trained to protect the president and Chandler. Neither the president nor Chandler were informed about the plan because in all likelihood they would have probably said no to the idea," said Foginet.

"That explains it," said Stewart.

"Explains what?" asked Foginet.

"Someone sent a strange message to Major Embry just over an hour ago," said Stewart.

"Do you have it?" asked Foginet.

"I gave it to his secretary," said Stewart. "There he is," said Stewart pointing to a soldier across the room.

"Private," yelled Foginet.

"Yes, General?"

"Please come over here."

As the private made his way across the room Stewart whispered to Foginet, "I'll be right back."

"Where are you..," but Stewart had rushed away. He directed his attention at the private instead. "Private, do you still have the message for Major Embry?"

"Yes, General. I've been unable to give it to him just yet, sir."

"Please give it to me, Private, and I'll make sure Major Embry gets it," said Foginet.

"Okay, sir."

"Oh, Private?"

"Yes, General?"

"Please find Major Whitfield, and tell him his presence is requested immediately."

"Will do, sir," said the private, as he hurried away.

The message was sent from the lone survivor of the three agents sent to protect the president. "Saved a big fish. Couple of hooks in it. One near top and other at bottom. Still breathing. Should make it home. All fishermen drowned, even my friends."

It was a bit choppy and coded but it was clear enough to grasp its meaning. According to the correspondence, the president's attackers were all killed and the president survived the attack with wounds to his upper and lower torso but he should survive. It was signed "W."

When Stewart initially read the message she attempted to decipher the message but so much was going on she thought it best to pass the message on to its intended recipient. Now that she knew Foginet had sent agents to protect the president, she surmised the sender was following protocol. The SG compound in Alabama was the designated headquarters for all agents in the field. Southern Command in Tennessee could not be trusted. Embry and all other SG commanders would have been told to pass on any message signed "W" to Major Whitfield, who served as the point man of the operation.

All Foginet needed was to confirm the accuracy of the message, then determine if Douglass was successful in convincing the president it would be in his interest to leave Washington and come to Alabama under the protection of the Alabama SG. He would get his answer that evening.

## — TWENTY-FIVE —

# Rainy

"Hi. I'm Cody. What's your name?"

"My name is Lorraine but my family and friends call me Rainy."

Rainy was the niece of Ben's neighbor. Ben extended an invitation to Rainy through his neighbor. He thought it would benefit his nephew to have company around his own age while he was in town. Rainy was a year older than Cody. She had just arrived with her parents to spend time with her aunt, her mother's sister. Rainy had dark brown eyes that matched her complexion. She was an attractive, slightly overweight girl who wore bangs in her hair. Her summer outfit consisted of a red and white striped dress with red saddle shoes and white bobby socks.

"How long are you visiting, Rainy?" asked Cody.

"Three weeks, but if momma had it her way she would never leave." Rainy settled into a large brown, soft leather chair adjacent to Cody in Ben's spacious reading room. The tall mahogany book shelves held scores of books. A lavish area rug decorated the polished hardwood floor. A huge picture window provided a breathtaking view of the well-manicured garden and lawn in the backyard.

"What's wrong with where you live now?" asked Cody.

"Nothing, but momma grew up here and my dad is from East Texas. Momma loves Louisiana. She never stops talking about how lucky she was to grow up down here. She goes on and on about life in the South."

"Why did she leave if she loves it so much?" asked Cody.

"I guess it was my daddy's job. He's an engineer you see and he's really smart so his company transferred him to one of their offices in the North — a place called Connecticut. You heard of it?"

"Of course, Rainy. That's the state next to Rhode Island and New York. I learned that in history class last year. That's pretty far from here."

"You sound like momma." Rainy started to giggle.

"Where were you born Rainy?"

"I was born right here in Louisiana. I was born in Baton Rouge — just North of here — we lived there until I was two — then we moved to New Orleans so momma could be closer to her family. At least that's what daddy thinks. We stayed here until I was seven then we moved to Connecticut."

"How come I never met you before?" asked Cody.

"Are you from here?" asked Rainy.

"Nope, I'm from the great state of Alabama."

"What's so 'great' about Alabama?" asked Rainy.

"A lot of things I guess," said Cody. Cody was so accustomed to calling his home state "the great state of Alabama" he never gave it any thought as to why he and others called it 'great'."

"Well that's it," said Rainy.

"What's it?" asked Cody.

"We never met because you live in the great state of Alabama." Rainy spread her arms as she teasingly repeated the phrase used by Cody in describing his home state. In actuality, the state of Alabama was the unofficial capital of the former states of the Confederacy.

It was the headquarters of the C.S.G.S. Many countries, particularly from the Caribbean, Africa and South America maintained consulates in Birmingham or Montgomery. Several major American corporations invested in satellite offices in the state as well. The Alabama branch of the Bank of the South was the third largest in the former Confederacy behind the East Texas and Louisiana branches.

The state's National Guard units were the best-prepared and most efficient in the entire country. Many argued the state's military apparatus easily rivaled the militaries of several foreign countries. Many outside of the South questioned the need for such a show of force. Few Alabamians did.

But the pride and joy of most citizens in the state was the University of North Alabama in Florence. It served as the home of the top collegiate soccer team in the country. A perennial Division I soccer power, the school already had eight national titles. Soccer was the most popular sport in the states of the former Confederacy.

For over eight decades, students from the former states of the Confederacy participated in exchange programs with countries from all over the world. When these students returned home they brought with them the customs and traditions of those countries. Football or soccer as it was called in the United States was a sport played in every corner of the world. It was only a matter of time before it became popular in the former states of the Confederacy.

Stewart Carson was one of North Alabama's most celebrated alumni. During his playing days at the school his team won back-to-back national titles. He was a three-time All American and in his senior year was selected as the top collegiate player in the country. Two years removed from college he suffered a devastating knee injury that ended his professional soccer career.

"Are there many blacks in Connecticut?" asked Cody.

"Not really. But there are a whole lot of whites — too many for momma." said Rainy.

"Do you have any friends in Connecticut?" asked Cody.

"Sure I do," said Rainy.

"Do you have any white friends?" asked Cody

'My best friend is white — her name is Haley. My other friend Jill Burke is white and so is Debbie Wyman. Claudia Davis and Tonya Reid are black and Anna Ortiz is Puerto Rican."

"Puerto Rican?" asked a perplexed Cody.

"Anna's family is from a place called Puerto Rico. Some of them, like Anna, look black and some look like Indians."

"Indians?"Cody interrupted. But Rainy continued.

"I even saw a few who could pass for white. They speak Spanish and English. But the white people in Connecticut don't like when they speak Spanish," said Rainy.

"How come?" asked Cody.

"Maybe because they can't understand the language." Rainy shrugged her shoulders.

"You speak Spanish? asked Cody.

"Anna tried to teach me but it's so much to learn. Anna said I should spend time with her in Puerto Rico then it wouldn't take so long to learn the language. Maybe one day..."

"I speak German," said Cody proudly before Rainy finished.

"German? Why German?" asked Rainy.

"Well - my mom speaks it a lot. She's fluent."

"What's fluent?" asked Rainy

"It means she speaks it well."

"Do you have any white friends Cody?" asked Rainy, switching subjects.

"Can't say that I do. Well, I consider Steve a friend"

"Who's Steve?" asked Rainy.

"He our chauffeur. He's pretty cool. I think he likes my mom."

Alabama had the distinction of having the fewest white American residents among the former states of the Confederacy. Although hate crimes were extremely rare in the region, most whites were less than enthusiastic about visiting the state. Most black Alabamians did little to change their minds.

"Momma says your family is rich. Is that true?"

"Huh?" Cody was taken aback by the question. "I guess so." Cody was feeling a little embarrassed. It was the first time anyone asked him directly about his family's financial status. He didn't know how to respond. Cody began to ponder the question more deeply.

"Momma says I should marry someone who makes more money than daddy. She told me not to tell daddy. It might hurt his feelings." Rainy's words interrupted Cody's thought process.

"Momma says when I grow up I should be a stay-at-home mom with a Ph.D."

"A what?" asked Cody.

"One of those fancy degrees," said Rainy.

"Momma says since she can't have that lifestyle ain't no reason why I can't. But I shouldn't tell daddy because it might hurt his feelings."

"What kind of work does your momma do?" asked Cody

"She's an accountant," said Rainy.

Not unlike many women in the former states of the Confederacy, Rainy's mom had a professional license. Education was widely encouraged among both genders. There were as many women as men in most of the professional fields. Due to the glut that existed in these fields, some individuals began relocating to southern states bordering the states of the former Confederacy. Louisville and Tulsa became prime relocation spots for black professionals from the former states of the Confederacy.

"What about your mom, Cody?"

"My mom is a businesswoman — at least that's how she describes herself."

"What kind of business?" asked Rainy.

"It has something to do with the family. It must be important work because when we're out and about people are always staring at her or stopping her to have a conversation. Some people even want her autograph," said Cody.

"Momma says your mother is quite pretty. Momma says she and your mom have the same body type."

"All of my friends at school think my mom is pretty too," said Cody.

"Momma says your family is famous. Is that true?"

"Well I'm just starting to learn about my family. My uncle gave me a book and..."

"What about your dad?" asked Rainy. Cody was unable to finish his thought before Rainy hit him with another question. The question caught Cody off-guard. He froze for a moment. Few people asked Cody about his father because most already knew.

"My dad died a couple of years ago." Cody recovered and lowered his head slightly.

"How?" Rainy pressed on.

"My mom thinks someone killed him," said Cody.

"Why would someone do such a thing?" asked Rainy. Cody remained silent and stared straight ahead.

"I'm sorry to hear about your dad Cody. You think he's in heaven?" asked Rainy.

"Could be. I try not to think about it much. I just miss him — a whole lot. We used to spend a lot of time together — when he was home. He travelled a lot. He was going to run for governor one day, at least that's what he told me." Cody's upper body fell back in his chair. His head hit the soft leather and he began to reminisce about his dad. Water slowly filled his eyes.

"Do you think your mom will ever get married again?

"I don't know."

Cody shrugged his shoulders and wiped both eyes with his hands. "Can we talk about something else Rainy?" Cody was not in the mood to talk about his father, at least not on this day.

"Sure. Like what?" asked Rainy. She began to sense Cody's uneasiness about the topic regarding his father.

"How about — school?" asked Cody.

"What about it?" asked Rainy.

"Do you like it?" asked Cody.

"Sometimes. I'll be going to the eighth grade next year, then high school. What grade are you in Cody?"

"Grade? What's that?" asked Cody.

"You know — fifth, sixth, seventh grade?"

"We don't have grades down here. Don't you remember, Rainy?" Prior to moving north, Rainy spent nearly five years in the school system of the former Confederacy.

"Yeah, that's right." Rainy whispered to herself. "Well anyway," Rainy's voice returned to normal. "I hope I don't get Mr. Nolan for my home-room teacher this coming school year. Last year he slammed this little, bald head, bucktooth boy right into the lockers and made him cry."

"Why did he do that?"

"Because Darnell was playing around — that's the little boy's name. The other boys were playing too but they were white. They only got yelled at. Darnell got this big lump on his little head. Momma said if that crack-er — that's what she called Mr. Nolan — ever put his hands on me she would whip his white, rusty ass." Rainy covered her mouth quickly with one hand as her eyes scanned the room.

"Momma told the little boy's mother she shouldn't let Mr. Nolan get away with that." Rainy lowered her voice.

"What happened to the teacher?" asked Cody.

"I don't know. Momma and the lady stopped speaking because momma told the lady if she lived in the South they could do something about her son's teeth and it wouldn't cost her a dime. The lady got mad and told momma her son's teeth was none of her business. Momma told the lady she was only trying to help."

Each state in the former Confederacy had a single payer health system. This meant the state was the sole entity that funded the healthcare system in each state. Insurance companies were not allowed to operate in the system. All eligible citizens received free health care, including dental care. Doctors were hired by the state and were paid exceptional wages. In fact, jobs in the medical field offered the best wages in both the professional and technical areas.

Like most state-run entities in the former Confederacy, the health care system was supported by a sizeable tax base and generous contributions provided by the Bank of the South. The region's health care system had no rival in North America and few in the world.

"Do you like the North better than the South Rainy?"

"I don't know Cody. I've been away from here so long it's hard to tell. Mom and dad both want me to attend college in the South. They started saving money already. So I guess I'll be coming back eventually. Momma says when I go to college down here she's moving back with me but I shouldn't tell daddy about her plans just yet."

"Do you ever talk to your dad Rainy?"

"Oh yes. Lots of times. Sometimes we talk in his cave. That's what he calls his private room in the basement. He plays music and reads his books down there. He said he built it so he could enjoy some peace and quiet. I think he built it to get away from momma." Rainy rolled her eyes.

"Okay little ones, time to eat some lunch." It was now noon and the voice came from the kitchen. It was Lewis. Rainy and Cody jumped up from their seats and ran straight to the dining room. "Wash your hands first, children, then help yourself to lunch. The chef prepared a big plate for each of you."

"Can we have seconds?" asked Cody while drying his hands.

"You can eat as much as want," said Lewis. "I hope you're not shy Rainy."

"Oh you don't have to worry about me sir. I'm hardly shy, especially around good food and good company." Rainy looked at Cody and the two of them began to laugh.

# — TWENTY-SIX —

# The Rise of Foginet

"Dear General, I am in receipt of your message and I have been successful in convincing our mutual friend that a vacation is in order. Please make preparations for our friend's arrival. He will be accompanied by his spouse. Other guests, including myself, will arrive later. A separate letter shall follow spelling out more definite times and travel arrangements. Our friend looks forward to your Southern hospitality." The letter was signed "D."

Foginet could not believe his eyes. He wasted no time informing Stewart about the correspondence. It was late, and he expected the second correspondence to arrive the following morning. He called a private meeting with Major Whitfield, Major Embry, Governor Bainbridge, and, of course, Stewart. Everyone was given their respective assignments and no one was to breathe a word of the president's visit.

The follow up letter came as expected the next morning. The compound was in frenzy, but only a handful of individuals knew why. When the train pulled into the Montgomery station, there was not a soul in sight. The SG had closed down the station and created a two-mile perimeter around the area. The Grey Shirts served as escorts. The president was wheeled off the train, and he and the first lady were placed in a coach surrounded by dozens of Grey Shirts. A buzz was soon heard around town the president had just arrived although few people saw him. Some folks dismissed the talk as rumor.

When the coach pulled up to the mansion at Madison Farm, the first lady was in awe. She was overheard saying how beautiful things looked. The president and the first lady were taken to the spacious accommoda-

171

tions of the master bedroom. They would be waited on hand and foot by the servants who ran the house for the duration of their stay.

The next morning, when the president arrived at breakfast, already seated at the table were Foginet, Stewart, Bainbridge, Inge, Embry, and Whitfield.

"My, my, my — you look dazzling, Lisa," said the first lady.

"Thank you, Mrs. Wade. I was about to say the same about you," said Stewart.

"Oh, you're too kind, dear. And please call me Caroline. I'm here for a vacation and these formalities make me feel as if I'm still in Washington." She turned to Foginet, "And how are you, General? You look mighty handsome in that uniform."

"Caroline, must you embarrass the man in front of guests?" interrupted the president. He turned to Foginet, "How are you General?" asked Wade. "I hear you picked up a new language," said the president, smiling and glancing at Stewart with raised eyebrows.

"Now who's embarrassing the general, Bluff?" said the first lady.

"Aw, he knows I'm just messing with him a bit," said Wade. Foginet took the humor in stride. He admired the president and first lady. Foginet considered them both a blessing from above, and keeping them alive was his primary concern for the sake of millions of black people.

"How long has it been, General?" asked Wade.

"Too long, sir, but it's good to see you again. I trust your journey was in keeping with your expectations," said Foginet.

"All this damn secrecy, General. I guess I should get used to it. I also want to thank you for all you've done, General. Fred told me all about it. I want to talk to you later in private," said Wade.

"Sure, sir," said Foginet. "Sir?" Foginet began. "Allow me to introduce some folks here — this is Governor Bainbridge."

"Thank you for your hospitality, Governor. Caroline and I love the place." said Wade.

"It's my pleasure, Mister President. Maybe when you settle in a bit more I'll give you and the first lady a tour of the capital," said Bainbridge.

"I look forward to it, Governor," said Wade.

"This is Major Embry of the Southern Guard," Foginet continued.

"My, my, you fellas have certainly been busy. Keep up the good work, soldier," said Wade.

"Will do, sir," said Embry.

"And this is Major Whitfield of the Southern Command," said Foginet.

"If there is anything I can do for you, Mister President, just ask," said Whitfield.

"Mister President, Major Whitfield will be in charge of your security while you are here. He is directly responsible for training those who came to your aid in Washington," said Foginet.

"Ah, yes, thank you, Major. Well done," said Wade.

"I owe you thanks as well," said the first lady.

"And of course you ...," before Foginet could finish, Wade recognized a familiar face.

"Lafayette!" exclaimed Wade. "My, you are a sight for old eyes. I am terribly sorry about these tragic events, Senator."

"It's not your fault, Mister President. You're a casualty as well," said Inge.

"Let's have lunch and catch up on some Washington gossip," said Wade.

"I look forward to it, Mister President," said Inge. Following the 1872 elections the president came to rely on Inge as one of his chief advisers in the senate, particularly concerning matters in the South. The two men spent hours together in the Executive Mansion discussing politics and exchanging personal stories. There was a mutual respect and admiration. Each considered the other a friend.

"General?"

"Yes, Mister President?"

Wade motioned Foginet closer so he could whisper. "There was this little black woman present on the day I was uh, well you know. Does anyone know what became of her? She truly saved my life, and Caroline and I would love to meet her and thank her."

"No word yet, but Stewart is working on it," said Foginet.

"Then it will surely get done," said Wade with a smile. He knew full well how determinedly Stewart took to any task presented to her. After the introductions and some chit-chat, the group was treated to a delicious Southern breakfast prepared by the one of the best chefs in Alabama.

By the time Sunday rolled around, the news had spread all across the country and throughout much of the world the president was recuperating from his wounds in the state of Alabama under the protection of the SG and the Grey Shirts. He would begin receiving official guests on Monday for matters of great importance only. This was classified as an official vacation, and it could not come at a better time. With most of the members of Congress at home campaigning for office, there wasn't as much work to do in Washington around this time of year. The way the president and the first lady figured, they would remain in Alabama until the beginning of the year.

A week after the attack, news began filtering in about those who were responsible for the attack on the president. All three dead men were identified as Confederate sympathizers from Tennessee. The murderers of Higginson and Davenport were still at large, but good leads came in regarding their identities. At this point the leaders of the conspirators decided to play it safe. They knew it was impossible to kill Wade while he was in Alabama, and the Grey Shirts would now provide protection for any federal elected official from any state in the former Confederacy. After the Red Harvest, their numbers increased tenfold to 2,500. They became a modern version of the Praetorian Guard who provided protection for the Roman emperors.

Due to the sheer number of deaths throughout the former states of the Confederacy directly connected to the Red Harvest, each state stepped up its military presence by strengthening their respective militias. All vowed the next time wouldn't be so easy.

During the second week of the president's stay, he requested a meeting with Foginet. Foginet was informed that Frederick Douglass had decided to come to Madison Farm toward the end of the president's stay and spend the last two weeks of the president's visit with Wade, and accompany him back to Washington. Wade also informed Foginet that he'd decided to promote him to the rank of major-general and the supreme commander of all federal troops in the former states of the Confederacy, the position formerly held by Higginson.

"General, I'm going to take some heat for this, but I don't give a damn. What I do give a damn about is ridding our nation of this rebel scum. I need your assurances you can handle it," said Wade.

"Mister President, may I have a day to consider your offer?" asked Foginet.

"No, you may not, Goddamn it. You're the perfect man for the job," said Wade. "Now, listen, these bastards are not done. They are determined to take back the South and put the blacks under their yoke. You, my friend, are charged with making sure that never happens," said Wade. He continued, "Lafayette — excuse me — Senator Inge and Mister Douglass have a great deal of trust in you and so did General Higginson, God bless 'em. And if those fine gentlemen trust you, as does Caroline, then I must trust you as well. Take whatever measures you need to take but end this trouble - sooner rather than later. „." Wade sat back then looked at Foginet. Wade extended his hand. "I apologize for not rising, General, but I'm sure you understand. By the way, please join us for dinner this evening and make sure Lisa comes along. The first lady is dying to talk her ear off — about you, General," they both laughed.

As news of Foginet's promotion spread across the South, the Redeemers began to huddle once more. They knew now the president was pulling out all the stops. The battle would come down to Southern blacks fighting for their lives and place in American society versus those who would deny them their birthright. Wade figured those whites who hated the ex-Confederates did not care what happened to them, and if blacks were the architects of their destruction, then more power to them.

However, Wade also surmised most whites felt the Civil War was fought to end slavery, and now that slavery was a thing of the past, it was time to move on. This thinking served the Redeemers well. However, what the Redeemers didn't bank on was Wade placing the military might of the United States in the hands of a black man who would turn out to be the Redeemers' worst possible nightmare.

Foginet wasted very little time getting down to business in his new role. His first act was to promote several captains to the rank of major and three majors to the rank of colonel of the SG. Each one would now serve as the top commander of the SG in each of the five Military Districts. Major Washington Rapier now would command the SG as a colonel in the First Military District of Virginia. Captain Hope would take command of the SG as a major in the Second Military District of North Carolina and South Carolina. Major Embry would now command the SG as a colonel in the Third Military District of Georgia and Alabama. Captain Lacy was selected to assist Embry and was given command of the SG as a major in Florida. Captain Spencer Lawrence would now command the SG as a major in the Fourth Military District of Arkansas and Mississippi, and Major Soule would now command the SG as a colonel in the Fifth Military District of Louisiana and Texas. Soule would also have control over the state penitentiary at Huntsville and Camp Wade. When news of his appointment hit the prisons, it sent shudders through the ranks of the prisoners in both places. Foginet also promoted Major Whitfield to the rank of colonel and placed him in command of the Grey Shirts and all special military operations.

Next, Foginet created the Office in Defense of Reconstruction or Unit Three of the SG. Its headquarters, located on the grounds at Madison Farms, would serve as the hub of his intelligence apparatus. He named Lisa Stewart as the director, and placed a thousand of the Southern Guard's best and brightest troops under her command as special agents. He also created a Telegraph Corps brigade made up of Union soldiers and private citizens and placed it under her control. Her office would also have the power to issue arrest warrants, and, if necessary, would have the support of the military police and local law enforcement to carry out her orders

With the thousands of civilian spies already at her disposal, Stewart was now the second most powerful figure in the former states of the Confederacy just behind Foginet. She would soon have eyes and ears in every nook and cranny in the South, the nation's capital, and the state of Tennessee. She even placed highly-trained moles in every company of the SG, the Grey Shirts, and select units of the Union Army in the South. She left nothing to chance.

When it was all said and done, Foginet had created a formidable military machine and intelligence apparatus to combat the Redeemers, who relied on guerilla tactics to defeat Foginet's army and reclaim the South. His next move was to build a political operation to secure long-term political power for the black masses in the former Confederacy. Thus, he turned to Randall McArthur, who, along with the recently murdered Lyle Davenport, had orchestrated one of the greatest political triumphs in the history of American politics. He sent McArthur an invitation to come as his guest to Madison Farms.

# TWENTY-SEVEN

# McArthur

The November elections saw the Republicans maintain their hold on both houses of the Congress. Wade was now walking, but with a slight limp. He knew he had to return to Washington in a few weeks, but his mind was on the upcoming special elections to fill the seats of the murdered congressmen. The election for their seats was pushed to December in order to give candidates vying for their seats enough time to run sufficient campaigns. Wade felt this was a good time to finally get out and meet the fine people of Alabama.

The President made a surprise visit to the State Capitol and was given a thunderous ovation from the black-dominated legislature. His appearance created a security nightmare, and the SG, Grey Shirts, and state militia had to be called upon to control the crowd.

While leaving the capital, he noticed several well-wishers in the crowd held up three different flags. He only recognized one of them: the Stars and Stripes.

"The color purple seems to be mighty popular in these parts," said Wade, observing the sea of purple flags.

"It's the people's way of expressing gratitude to the Southern Guard, sir," explained Colonel Embry.

"The purple flag with the two stars is how the people express their support for General Foginet," said Colonel Whitfield, who along with Colonel Embry, rode with Wade. For security reasons Foginet and Stewart did not escort the president.

"They add a star each time the general is promoted," said Colonel Embry.

"I see," said Wade. "Hell, at the rate the general is going, those flags may not have enough room to accommodate his stars," said Wade, laughing. The others laughed aloud. "What about that one?" said Wade pointing to a flag which had three bars: one red, one black, and one green.

"The flag you are referring to, sir — the red, black and green one over there," said Whitfield pointing, "that one has just started to appear in public recently. I believe a few members of the SG use it as their company colors, and now it's been adopted by some in the general public. My understanding is the red symbolizes the blood we shed during slavery. The black symbolizes the indelible mark of our people and the green represents the land we need in order to prosper. Some say the green represents our former homeland in Africa, sir."

"I see. Good God," said Wade, shaking his head. "Who would have ever thought?"

"Excuse me, sir," said Embry.

"I was wondering if those traitorous bastards ever thought it would come to this?" said Wade.

"Well, sir, we owe it all to your presidency — every bit of it," said Whitfield.

"I appreciate that, Colonel, but it's not over yet. Knowing these murdering sons of bitches like I do, it's not over yet. Not by a long shot," said Wade, smiling and marveling at the huge, predominantly-black crowd chanting his name. "Wade! Wade! Wade!"

Following the Thanksgiving celebration[94], which was recently restored by each of the states in the former Confederacy, the focus shifted to the December special elections to replace the seven murdered congressmen from the South. By this time, Randall McArthur had arrived and met with the President and Foginet on several occasions. His opinion mattered to both men.

After assisting with the re-election campaigns for each Republican candidate, he turned his attention to creating a political machine that could withstand any challenge from the opposition. McArthur knew none of it would matter if the Redeemers ever regained control of the South. He

---

[94] Every fourth Thursday in November. The federal holiday has been celebrated every year in the United States since 1863 when, in the middle of the Civil War, President Lincoln declared it a national day of "Thanksgiving and Praise to our beneficent Father who dwelleth in the Heavens." *For a book about Thanksgiving that enlightens both the Native American and the Pilgrim perspectives, read* 1621, A New Look at Thanksgiving *by Catherine O'Neill Grace and Margaret M. Bruchac, National Geographic Children's Books, 2004.*

knew they would disenfranchise black voters by force. But that wasn't his concern. He left such matters in the capable hands of Foginet and his friend Lisa Stewart.

His immediate concern was the infighting in the party and the questionable allegiance of party leaders, particularly in the upper Southern states of Virginia and North Carolina, along with Texas. In these states, whites outnumbered blacks by double-digit percentage points, and some white Republican officeholders were increasingly relying on white Democrats to secure victory at the polls.

While the vast majority of black officeholders served their constituents well, some began to become less and less reliable. McArthur felt what needed to be done, first and foremost, was to rededicate the effort to educate the black masses about electoral politics. He felt an educated and informed voter would trump the shenanigans of dishonest politicians. Interestingly enough, he chose the SG as the starting point for his political renovation. He strongly suggested Foginet use his most politically-sophisticated officers to serve as the political vanguard for the SG. He argued, rather successfully, the SG represented 50,000 votes and it was prudent to make sure "our side" controls every one of them.

After placing select SG officers in an intense political education program, McArthur assigned them to every company in the SG. The officer's job was to keep his company informed as to current events as well as to maintain political discipline and loyalty. Of course, these officers worked with SG officers and enlisted soldiers assigned to Unit Three and assisted in ferreting out those who displayed less-than-enthusiastic support for the regime.

These officers would soon be recognized by a specially-designed gold patch they wore on the left arm of their uniform. They were also respectfully referred to as "MBs", for "McArthur's Boys." While serving as an SG officer carried tremendous prestige, even more so than regular army officers, those SG officers assigned to political duties or Unit Three were the cream of the crop. Their loyalty was unwavering.

This was a brilliant move by McArthur. Now the SG was not just a military force but it had become a political juggernaut. McArthur then created political clubs in every county in the former Confederacy. He made it mandatory for party members to join these clubs and become active in the affairs of these entities. He even teamed with the local colleges, which provided students who were properly trained to educate party members about the basics of electoral politics.

In addition to the basic curriculum, states mandated high school students to learn the basics of electoral politics. This prevented students from being manipulated when it came time for them to vote. Many party members enthusiastically embraced McArthur's plan and many felt a new sense of empowerment.

The fact the clubs and the political education classes were open to women also made McArthur's plan unique. This shook up the entire political establishment, but nothing could be done about it because it had the backing of both the President and Foginet. The idea served each man's political agendas. McArthur's efforts made him the undisputed titular head of the Republican Party in the South. After Foginet and Stewart, no individual held more sway in the South than Randall McArthur.

Before leaving to oversee the implementation of the plan throughout the former Confederacy, McArthur met with his old friend Lisa Stewart. The two had met years ago in Boston. McArthur had planned to study medicine, but after earning his college degree, he decided instead to work with the abolitionist movement helping escaped slaves make their way to Canada. Lisa had been working in the Boston area when she met McArthur, who was about eight years older than her. The two had hit it off right away, and now they were back in each other's company. Both were now powerful individuals with tremendous responsibilities..

"It's been a while, Lisa," said McArthur.

"Yes, it has, Randall," said Stewart.

"Why do you always say my entire first name?" said McArthur laughing.

"Why do you say mine?" said Stewart laughing.

Fair enough, Lisa."

"Randall, I'm so sorry about your loss."

"Lisa, they cut him up into small pieces, then shoved his penis down his throat," said McArthur. Stewart cringed, listening to the description of Lyle Davenport's death.

"I miss him so much, Lisa." Tears began to roll down McArthur's cheeks. Stewart grabbed his hand and pulled her chair closer to his.

"Lisa?" McArthur asked.

"Yes, Randall?"

"I want to thank you for always accepting me for who I am. Most people don't. Most people didn't accept Lyle, either. Poor Lyle," McArthur paused. "Does the general know about me, Lisa?"

Lisa just gave McArthur a look that answered his question in the affirmative.

"How does he feel about it, Lisa?"

"Randall, if Aurelius — the general — felt differently, you would not be his guest. The general prides himself on tolerating those who are different. He respects your brilliance and competence, and I advise you to live up to his expectations of you," Stewart said half-jokingly.

"Aurelius?" McArthur asked with raised eyebows. "Word has it the two of you are an item," said McArthur.

"Is that a question, Randall?"

"I guess so. And please, I must know all the details," McArthur hastily positioned himself to hear Stewart's story.

"Well, it isn't much to tell. We met at a dinner in Washington — at the Executive Mansion about three years ago, and we kept in touch."

"Wow, Lisa - the White House?"

"Stop interrupting, Randall."

"Okay. Okay. I'm sorry, dear. By all means continue."

Lisa was beaming. "After my tour of the South with Douglass, we spent a lot of time together in Tennessee and South Carolina. He calls me his gift from the Creator." Stewart stared at the ceiling.

"Go on," said McArthur.

"Well, he proposed last year, but we initially kept it a secret for my own protection," said Stewart.

"Well, the secret is out, my dear,"

"I know, Randall."

"So when is the big day?" McArthur started to shift his body.

"He promised me some time next year," said Stewart. Stewart wore a radiant smile and pushed down on her thighs with her hands while leaning her head back.

"Oh, this is so, so wonderful, Lisa. I'm so happy for you. Did you pick out a dress? What about the arrangements? And..."

"Hold on, Randall," before McArthur could say another word, Stewart informed him that the ceremony would most likely be private, under the circumstances.

"Aw, shucks," complained McArthur. "You will make an absolutely stunning bride, Lisa," said McArthur.

"Why thank you, Randall. That is a kind thing to say," said Stewart.

"Oh, please, Lisa — you're gorgeous and everyone knows it. Lisa?"

"What, Randall?" Stewart had an idea what the next question her old friend would ask.

"Does he know about Lloyd?" Stewart rubbed her fingers through her thick kinky hair.

"I will tell him in due time, Randall," said Stewart, looking exasperated.

"Dear, you're the smartest person I know, so please don't take this the wrong way, but it's not healthy to start off a marriage with those kinds of secrets. I'm just trying to be helpful, Lisa."

"I know," said Stewart. "And what about you? I see you've spent the last few days in the company of Colonel Embry, and I hear he's escorting you back to Georgia. He's extremely handsome," said Stewart.

"That he is," said McArthur.

"Well?" said Stewart.

"Well, what?" said McArthur, laughing. "You're embarrassing me, Lisa."

"Well, here's some advice for you, Randall," said Stewart. "Be careful. He is a colonel in the SG, and you're a major political player as well. Don't get sloppy, Randall. Not everyone is as tolerant of these matters as the general and myself."

"I understand, Lisa, and thank you for caring about my welfare. I'm lucky to have you as a friend."

"Likewise," said Stewart. "Now don't get sloppy, Randall." Stewart warned McArthur again.

"I heard you the first time, Lisa. Trust me, I heard you." The two friends gave each other a big hug.

# TWENTY-EIGHT

# Hortensia

The special elections bore no surprise results. Wade was elated. He celebrated the Christmas holiday with family and friends at Madison Farms. After Christmas dinner, a special guest was escorted into the dining room by General Foginet.

"Mister President, this is Holly Curtis, the woman you asked about. She defended you against your attackers," said Foginet. Curtis was a young, petite, attractive woman. The President extended both arms. While he remembered being assisted by a woman, he vaguely remembered her appearance.

"Well, I'll be. Come over here, young lady. Tell me again, what is your name?" asked Wade, as he hugged the woman.

"My given name is Hortensia, but my friends call me Holly. You can call me Holly as well, Mister President," said Curtis. The room exploded in laughter.

"Why, thank you Holly. I will do just that. Although Hortensia is a fine name," said Wade. "Holly, this is my wife Caroline."

"It's a pleasure to meet you, Hortensia," said Caroline.

"You may call me Holly as well, ma'am," said Curtis.

"Well, thank you, Holly, and thank you for saving my husband," said Caroline.

"Yes, Holly, I owe you much, and I thank you from the bottom of my heart for saving my life. Please forgive me for not recognizing you. Things happened so quickly that day," said Wade, his voices fading.

"That's ok, sir. I was doing my job. It's what they trained me fo', Mister President," said Curtis.

"Well, your training certainly paid off for me. Will you please join us for dessert?"

"Thank you kindly, Mister President. It's not every day a person can say they dined with the president of the United States," said Curtis, as Wade and the group laughed aloud.

"I like you, Holly," said Wade.

"I like you too, sir, and you too, ma'am," said Curtis, not forgetting the first lady.

"Can someone get our special guest a chair?" ordered Wade.

Douglass arrived shortly after the New Year's celebration. "Any news on the conspirators?" asked Douglass. Douglass and Stewart met alone in a private meeting room.

"Well, we made some progress," said Stewart. "We know much of the planning for the attacks took place in Washington and Tennessee, and we know the White League and the Red Shirts were deeply involved," Stewart continued.

"What about the attack on General Foginet?" asked Douglass.

"We have a couple of individuals in detention in Texas who are willing to testify Wright gave orders not to repair the communication lines when it was brought to his attention they were down. We also have a cook who said he was paid to pour some 'homemade' syrup on the general's bread the morning of the assault. He's positive he saw one of the men who paid him talking with Wright a few days before," said Stewart.

"Where's Wright now?" asked Douglass.

"He's being held in an undisclosed location in Virginia," said Stewart.

"Why Virginia?" asked Douglass.

"He caught a train there and was held by the SG after the lines were restored," said Stewart.

"I see," said Douglass. "And what about the murderers of Higginson, Davenport, and the Congressmen?"

"We think Wright has most of those answers," said Stewart.

"And you think he will give them up?" asked Douglass

"The SG can be very persuasive if need be. Wright also does not want to be brought back to Texas under Soule's authority," said Stewart.

"Hmm, I see," said Douglass. "Well, Lisa, when do you think we can wrap this up?"

"I'm guessing by March, Fred. But we still believe more attacks are being planned. At least that's what our people are telling us in the field."

"You trust the information?" asked Douglass.

"Let's put it this way, Fred, we have the most thorough intelligence-gathering system in the country. We hear just about everything," said Stewart, slightly boasting.

"Except in Tennessee and the District," said Douglass.

"We don't make the rules Fred – we simply follow them," Stewart absorbed the dig by Douglass.

"Good afternoon, Mister Douglass," said Foginet as he entered the room.

"General?" asked Douglass. "Lisa has been filling me in on matters regarding this damn conspiracy. She tells me we should complete the investigation by March," said Douglass, with a hint of disbelief.

"Well, if the Director," referring to Lisa by her new title, "says we should complete it by March then who am I to doubt her, Mister Douglass," said Foginet.

"I'll leave the two of you to yourselves. There's much work to be done," said Stewart as she gathered some items and made her way out the huge door of the meeting room.

"General, you know we're counting on you to handle this down here. The public up north wants the bastards responsible for organizing the attack against the president, Higginson, and Davenport brought to justice. They don't care much about a few dead Negro congressmen, but I do," said Douglass.

"And so do I, Fred," said Foginet. Douglass gave Foginet a cursory glance. It was the first time Foginet referred to him in the familiar. Douglass didn't know whether Foginet realized it or not. "Mister Douglass, at some point I may need the support of the president to get Tennessee under control. I need you to help convince him to put that damn rebel state under my jurisdiction. Much of the planning is taking place right there under our noses," argued Foginet.

"I'll talk to him. Have you mentioned anything to him yet?" asked Douglass.

"On more than a few occasions, through several correspondences. Fred, I could break these rebels if I got control of Tennessee," said Foginet.

"I'll see what I can do, Aurelius," said Douglass, looking down at the floor then at Foginet. Both men started laughing at the obvious gibe.

"General, I don't know how to say this, but what I say remains here," said Douglass.

"Speak freely, Fred," said Foginet.

"You know you possess the power to declare a state of emergency in these parts if you so choose?" asked Douglass.

"Of course, I know that, Fred," said Foginet.

"Well, don't hesitate to use your power if the situation becomes necessary," said Douglass.

"Three things must happen, Fred. First, I need a damn good reason to do it. Secondly, it means nothing if Tennessee isn't under my authority, and thirdly, I need you to make sure the President extends my authority beyond the 120 days when the time come," Foginet's response floored Douglass.

"I see you thought this thing through, General," said Douglass.

"Can you help me, Fred?" asked Foginet, ignoring Douglass' comment.

"Haven't I always?" asked Douglass.

"Yes, you have," said Foginet. The two men embraced, then shook hands. Both men knew at that moment they had formed a bond of both brotherhood and struggle that neither man would ever break.

"Good luck, General," Douglass shook Foginet's hand, and made his way to the door.

"Take care of yourself, Mister Douglass, and take care of our mutual friend, as well," said Foginet, referring to Wade.

"Will do," said Douglass. The next time the two men would see each other, the mood in the country would be very different, and Foginet would be at the height of his power.

On January 15, 1875, the president and first lady arrived back in the nation's capital with all the pomp and pageantry befitting an American president. His entourage included Frederick Douglass and Holly Curtis as well as over fifty impressive troops of the Grey Shirts. Many whites were flabbergasted at the sight of blacks carrying weapons in the nation's capital, but times were changing, and most whites knew it. In any event, Wade did not care.

The scene of armed blacks in the nation's capital was consistent with a major goal of his presidency, giving blacks the tools they needed to be self-reliant and safe from those who meant them no good. He was proud of his "Praetorian Guard," as he called the Grey Shirts. He laughed when the headlines of the local papers blared, "Wade Arrives in Capital with Negro Guard." Little did they know the Grey Shirts would remain with him for the remainder of his life.

"Aurelius, can we talk?" asked Stewart.

"Certainly, dear. What seems to be the problem?" asked Foginet. It was a month since the First Family left Madison Farms, and things were finally getting back to normal. Stewart had wrapped up her investigation and had prepared the list of all suspects. Her agents in the field made preparations to round up these individuals as soon as they received the word, but Foginet played it cool. It was a chilly February evening, and Stewart and Foginet just returned from having dinner with their good friend Colonel Soule, his wife, Constance, and their two sons. Constance, or Connie, as she was called, and Stewart had developed a close friendship.

"There's something I need to tell you," explained Stewart.

"Well, go on," said Foginet.

"I need you to sit down," said Stewart.

"Uh oh, I don't like the sound of this, Madame Director," said Foginet, calling Stewart by her official title.

"Why must you call me that when we're by ourselves?" asked Stewart, sounding a little annoyed.

"Honestly? I like the sound of it. Besides, haven't you called me by my official title in private?" Foginet was relaxed and in a good mood.

"I suppose, but please, Aurelius, come sit down," said Stewart. Foginet, sensing the urgency in her voice, poured himself a drink and sat down next to Stewart.

"Okay, Lisa, what exactly is on that brilliant mind of yours?" asked Foginet.

"This isn't easy for me, Aurelius. I mean, I've never shared this with anyone." Foginet looked puzzled, now realizing the matter was most likely of a personal nature.

"Talk to me, Lisa. Just talk to me." Foginet's tone changed. He took a sip of his drink then inched closer to Stewart.

Stewart proceeded to tell Foginet about her previous relationship with Lloyd Taylor, a runaway slave who made his way north via the Underground Railroad[95]. She told him they met in Boston in the early spring of 1864 when she was sixteen. He was nineteen.

---

[95] The Underground Railroad was an extensive network of secret routes, abolitionists, and safe houses used help slaves escape from slave states to Northern Free States and Canada. It is estimated that at its peak, nearly 1,000 slaves per year escaped from bondage using the Underground Railroad. *For first hand narratives of escaping slaves on the Underground Railroad, read* The Underground Railroad: Authentic Narratives and First-Hand Accounts *by William Still, Dover Publications, 2007. William Still was the son of slaves, and an abolitionist.*

A year before they met, Taylor had attempted to join the 54th Massachusetts Infantry Regiment[96], but was unsuccessful due to an eye injury he'd sustained when he was eleven years old. Due to the large number of black recruits who answered the call to enlist, the army decided to weed out the recruits by authorizing a rigid medical exam. Taylor failed to make the cut.

In February of 1864, just prior to meeting Stewart, Taylor tried his luck again in New York. He attempted to join the 20th Infantry Colored Regiment[97], which was being organized on Riker's Island. But once again, he was turned away due to his medical condition. Frustrated, he returned to Boston where he decided to become a seaman.

The young couple was together for over two years and had planned to marry when tragedy struck. While at sea, performing rigging duties aboard a sailing vessel, Taylor was knocked overboard. Unconscious, he was unable to respond to the determined efforts by his fellow crew members to rescue him. He subsequently drowned. Stewart was heartbroken. She told Foginet while she had dated since then, she never loved another man like she loved Taylor until she met him.

"I haven't shared that story in quite some time, but I wanted you know Aurelius," Stewart said quietly.

"I appreciate you wanting to share that with me, Lisa. Are you okay?" asked Foginet.

"I'm fine, Aurelius. Are you okay?" asked Stewart.

"Lisa. We both had a life before we met each other. I've loved before and so have you. We both know what that means. I just want you to know I'm here if you ever need someone to talk to, about anything."

"I'm here for you, too, Aurelius."

"I know, dear."

Early on in their relationship, Foginet had shared with Stewart the trag-

---

[96]  The 54th Regiment Massachusetts Volunteer Infantry was one of the first official African American infantry regiments used during the Civil War.

[97]  This regiment was part of the United States Colored Troops (USCT), established during the Civil War. When members of the USCT were caught by Confederate soldiers, they suffered an abnormal degree of violence. The Confederacy enacted a law stating that blacks captured in uniform would be charged with slave insurrection, a capital offense with an automatic sentence of death. Despite this added risk, however, by the end of the Civil War there existed 175 USCT regiments that constituted about one-tenth of Union Army manpower. *For more information on the USCT, see* African American in the Civil War: USCT 1862-66 *by Mark Lardas, Osprey Publishing, 2006.*

ic story of Binta, his fiancé, from Senegal, who died in France while giving birth to his only child. The child survived the delivery but died shortly thereafter. Following their deaths, he decided to leave France and travel the world.

Foginet paused and took a deep breath. "Well, then, the matter is settled. Now I have a surprise for you," said Foginet. A smiling Stewart placed her hands on her cheeks and sat up straight. Foginet walked over to his dresser and opened the bottom drawer. He pulled out a beautifully wrapped box and handed it to Stewart.

"What is it?" Stewart gasped. "It's a bit too heavy for jewelry," Stewart thought to herself. Then she quickly unwrapped the package. It was a rectangular wooden chest. On top, the words "The Wizard" were magnificently engraved. The interior was decorated with a dark purple velvet cloth. Tucked in the cloth were two pearl-handled double-barrel Derringer pistols, each engraved with the initials L.S.

Stewart's eyes flew open. "I heard you're a good shot," said Foginet.

Stewart let out a scream, followed by laughter. "Who told…?" Stewart laughed. "Never mind," said Stewart, not bothering to complete the question.

And without prompting the other, they both stated in unison, "The SG is everywhere."

"Thank you, Aurelius. It's a wonderful gift. And now I have something for you."

"And what would that be?" asked Foginet, appearing more than interested.

"Well, I thought we would play our favorite game first," said Stewart.

"Our favorite game? Now which one would that be?" asked Foginet, laughing aloud. He knew exactly what Stewart was talking about. Foginet quickly grabbed her and cuddled her in his powerful arms. "If I recall, I won the last time we played," said Foginet.

"That's because I let you," said Stewart. The two of them laughed and kissed each other passionately.

# — TWENTY-NINE —

# Dictator of the South

In February of 1875, both the House and Senate voted to make Tennessee part of the Third Military District. On Monday, March 1, 1875, the president signed the bill. Tennesseans were outraged. Most whites in the state felt their sovereignty was being trampled — and it was — but the mood in the North and in Congress was anything but sympathetic.

The president's and Secretary Chandler's assailants were all identified as being from Tennessee. General Higginson was murdered in Nashville and a clear assassination attempt took place against Foginet at the Southern High Command at Hickory Hills. General Wright, Higginson's executive officer stationed in Tennessee, was identified as being part of the conspiracy. Tennessee would now pay for its transgressions. It would serve notice on the other states of the former Confederacy as well as those would-be assassins as to the penalty for engaging in such acts of treason.

Foginet had quietly moved 2,000 SG troops near the Tennessee border and another 2,000 regular army troops in and around Nashville. Stewart had already set up her intelligence gathering apparatus, and it worked better than she expected. While ex-Confederates across the South knew better than to send messages via telegraph, the citizens of Tennessee were not quite familiar with the tactics of Foginet, Stewart, Embry, and the ruthless Soule, but they were about to get a lesson firsthand.

When the Senate voted to amend the Fifth Reconstruction Act, thereby placing Tennessee under the jurisdiction of the military governor of the Third Military District, Foginet prepared for the worst.

On Wednesday, April 15, 1875,- the tenth anniversary of Lincoln's death, General Foginet declared a State of Emergency in Tennessee and every state in the former Confederacy. He ordered all state and county militias on full alert. The SG quickly set up shop for all three units of its operation in Tennessee.

All ex-Confederates in Tennessee were made to take the Ironclad Oath, which effectively broke the power of the Democrats in the state. Most Tennesseans knew about Purple Sunrise and did not want any part of the SG, so those who refused to take the oath relinquished their office without a fight. The SG already had a list of Confederate sympathizers in Tennessee. Thus, it made little sense to lie. Foginet shut down the Nashville Banner newspaper and every newspaper in each state of the former Confederacy that remotely displayed any previous sympathies for the ex-Confederate cause.

Foginet, supplied with a list from Stewart ordered Unit Three or "U3," as they were now called, to begin making arrest of all suspected terrorists and those tied to Red Harvest. Many ex-Confederates fled north to escape capture. The prison compounds Foginet ordered built in 1872 filled to capacity except in the Fifth Military District. U3 agents were relentless in tracking down and capturing those suspected of terrorist activities. Many members of the SG lost loved ones and friends during the Red Harvest. Thus, the effort of tracking down the terrorists, for many, was personal.

In some cases, ex-Confederates caught by U3 were handed over to the locals. Many locals had no mercy. Ex-Confederates were tarred and feathered. Others were lynched. Some had a limb or two hacked off. Some were shot in front of family members. A few towns erected public whipping posts and those deemed terrorists were whipped mercilessly. U3 had free reign and most blacks either assisted them in the performance of their duty or stayed out of their way. In the eyes of most blacks, the vast majority of whom were former slaves, the racial terrorists got what they deserved.

When the news reached Washington, Wade rhetorically asked a confidant, "I wonder how those traitorous bastards feel now that their former slaves are holding the rifle and whip?"

Few Northern papers sympathized with the plight of the ex-Confederates. One which did, ran the headline, "Foginet Declares Himself Dictator of the South." The subtitle beneath it read, "Are We Next?" The question wasn't a subtle one.

While many Northern whites blamed Southern whites for starting the Civil War and the subsequent effects the war had on the country, many still held the view blacks were inferior to whites and thus had no right to be in charge of white people anywhere. But the Negro problem wasn't a problem for Northern whites. It was a problem for Southern whites to deal with, and it would be no small feat.

Foginet's next move was considered, by all accounts, one of the boldest ever undertaken by a military officer in the United States to date. On May 5, 1875, three weeks after declaring the State of Emergency, Foginet instituted General Order 265, which made it a crime for anyone who did not take the Ironclad Oath to possess a gun of any kind. This order sent tremors throughout the former Confederacy. For hundreds of years blacks were forbidden to possess firearms of any type under penalty of death, and now the tables were turned against the white men who had enforced such laws so vigorously.

In every town in the former Confederacy, U3 agents conducted door-to-door searches of the homes of ex-Confederates. Those found in possession of a firearm were immediately placed under arrest. Local militias and ordinary black citizens were the law's biggest supporters and many assisted the SG in ferreting out those who violated the law.

By mid-June 1875, all was quiet in the former Confederacy. Tennessee was under tight control, as was every state in the former Confederacy. Most blacks could not remember a period in their lifetime when they felt so at peace and unafraid. In fact, many Northern blacks, upon hearing the turn of events in the South began to migrate back to the states of the former Confederacy.

All three units of the SG were operating at maximum capacity. When Foginet finally issued a call to increase the ranks of the SG, many young blacks took up the call. Many recruits saw this as the opportunity of a lifetime. Gaining membership in the SG offered them status and an opportunity to serve in the "great struggle," as many began to call it, not to mention, gain a quality education, which was a strict canon of the SG. Many recruits felt they had nothing to lose.

The detention centers in many districts were soon undermanned. The commander of each military district had control over the prisons in his respective district and thus had free reign to run their prisons as they saw fit. With the lone exception of the Fifth Military District under Soule, most commanders used militia and regular army troops to serve as guards at their respective prisons. This would soon prove to be a mistake.

Overall, Foginet was pleased with the present state of affairs, however, he knew there was still much to be done. The Redeemers were not finished yet. But for the time being, the new dictatorship was in total control of the former Confederacy. His immediate challenge was to find a way to extend the emergency decree. That would be the only way he could effectively destroy the Redeemers once and for all.

In early July, he met with a team comprised of his most trusted advisors. As the meeting was winding down, there were four knocks on the door.

"Come in Alma" said Foginet, responding to the knock signal between him and his his trusted secretary.

"Lieutenant Rose is here to see you, sir."

"Send him right in, Alma," Foginet said to his secretary.

"Right this way, Lieutenant." Alma motioned the lieutenant to enter the room. Seated in the room with Foginet was Lisa Stewart, Colonel Soule, and Colonel Embry — the hierarchy of the South's military establishment.

"Welcome back, young man. How was your trip?" asked Foginet.

"Interesting, sir," said Rose.

"Whenever someone responds in such a way, I think the person is itching to tell me something. So what is it, Lieutenant? Oh excuse me, Lieutenant, have you met Director Stewart?" asked Foginet.

"I am an admirer of yours, Miss Stewart," shaking her hand and bowing his head slightly.

"And this here is Colonel Embry," said Foginet. Rose snapped to attention.

"You can dispense with the formalities, Lieutenant," said Embry. "I understand you had an opportunity to visit the detention camps in each District."

"Yes, I did, sir," Rose appeared nervous as Embry sized him up.

"And, of course, you know Colonel Soule?" asked Foginet.

"Uh, yes, I do, sir." Rose was clearly intimidated by the presence of Soule and the other figures in the room.

"Now Lieutenant, about your visit." After receiving complaints from various officers in the SG about conditions at some of the prisons, Foginet had sent Rose on a fact-finding tour of the facilities in each of the five military districts.

"Sir?" asked Rose.

"Your visit, Lieutenant — to the camps," Foginet appeared eager to hear from Rose.

"Well, sir, I thought we would speak in private."

"We are speaking in private, Lieutenant," Foginet informed Rose.

"Would you like something to drink, Lieutenant?" asked Stewart, trying to settle Rose down.

"Oh, yes, Madame Director. That would be perfect right about now," said Rose. Stewart motioned to Colonel Embry who went to the door and called Alma.

"Sit here, Lieutenant," said Stewart, motioning to a place next to her on the plush red couch. She then turned and looked at the others in the room. Soule began making his way towards the door.

"General, I must be going. I have an appointment I cannot be late for. Let's talk later on. Good meeting you, Lieutenant," said Soule.

"Colonel, will you and Connie join us for dinner tonight?" asked Foginet.

"That will be terrific. I believe it will do Connie some good to be in the company of the Director," said Soule.

"Likewise," said Stewart.

"Colonel Embry, it's always a pleasure. Good day."

"Take care, Colonel, and give the wife my regards," said Embry.

Soule shook Embry's hands as he made his exit.

A few minutes later the group was served with a pitcher of lemonade.

"I best be going as well," said Embry.

"If I didn't know any better, Colonel, I would think you hung around for our amazing lemonade," said Foginet. The others in the room started laughing.

"You are a mind reader indeed, General," said Embry. "But I do have some work to complete," said Embry.

"Please join us for dinner, Colonel," said Foginet.

"Sorry, General, I've made other plans," said Embry.

"Well, breakfast in the morning?" asked Foginet.

"I'll see you then. Good day Lieutenant. Madame Director," Embry politely bowed his head in Stewart's direction then made his way to the door.

"Well, Lieutenant, does this suit you better?" asked Foginet.

"Excuse me, sir?" asked Rose.

"Half my company is gone," said Foginet, smiling.

"Oh, this is much better, sir," said Rose, shaking his head nervously and glancing at Stewart.

"Tell us what's on your mind, Lieutenant," said Stewart.

"Well, sir, I don't quite know how to put this, but--" Rose began.

"The truth, Lieutenant. All I want is the truth," stated Foginet.

"Sir, I have some concerns about the camps in the Third Military District," said Rose.

"Go on," said Foginet.

"Well, sir, it seems as if we have some overzealous members in our ranks," said Rose.

"Explain, Lieutenant," said Foginet.

"Most of the abuse, sir, seemed to be directed at the white prisoners, sir," said Rose.

"I'm listening, Lieutenant," said Foginet, turning and walking to the nearest window.

Rose went on to explain how he witnessed prisoners in one Georgia prison being subjected to the gauntlet or the lash. He explained how some prisoners, upon first entering the prison, were forced to walk through two lines of men who would then beat the prisoners with clubs and other instruments. Others received twenty-five lashes upon arrival.

He said while the prisoners in general were well-fed, some of them were denied food as punishment. Some prisoners he said were forced to sleep in their leg irons while some were denied a bed altogether. Most of the prisoners were given adequate clothing, but some were given clothing that was tattered and dirty.

Rose also explained how some guards would allow select prisoners to have a guest if they could pay. Others would offer to accommodate a visit request from the wife or girlfriend of a prisoner in exchange for sexual favors. Rose concluded his report by telling Foginet while he found abuses in each of the military districts, with the exception of the Fifth, the Third Military District was by far the worst. Rose also expressed surprise at the relatively small number of prisoners in the Fifth Military District.

"What do you make of all of this, Lieutenant?" asked Foginet.

"Well, sir, when you asked me to undertake this mission back in April, I didn't expect to see what I found."

"Meaning what, Lieutenant?" asked Foginet, now perplexed.

"Well, sir, I joined the SG because of the professionalism it displayed and the emphasis it placed on education and physical grooming. So I guess I expected to see such qualities in every soldier under your command. But the behavior I witnessed from some Union Army and militia troops — black and white — well, sir, was not in keeping with what I feel you — or should I say we — expect in our troops, sir," said Rose.

"I see," said Foginet.

"I mean, sir, is it okay for us to become like them?" asked Rose.

"You mean like savages, Lieutenant?" asked Foginet.

"Sir?" Rose was taken aback by Foginet's response.

"Are you asking if it's alright for us to become like those who enslaved us for 300 years and fought a war to keep us enslaved and who are still determined to maim and kill innocent men, women and children as a means to restoring themselves to their former status as masters over us?" Foginet drove the point home. "No, it's not alright for us to become like them," said Foginet answering his own question. "And I won't pretend to know what motivates an individual to act in the way you have described. But I do know some folks are driven by a personal quest for revenge, Lieutenant."

"What drives you, sir? If you don't mind me asking." Foginet paused, then looked at Stewart. It was a bold question.

"The future, Lieutenant. Our future. The future of the black race in this country."

"Sir?" Rose was looking for more.

"Lieutenant, if we fail in our mission and the Redeemers reclaim the South, our people will suffer immeasurable harm for decades to come. It would be catastrophic. In fact, Lieutenant, white supremacy will once again become the law of this land, this country. At best we will be relegated to second-class citizenship. So while I'm not pleased with the news you bring to me because it reeks of lawlessness, chaos, and confusion, which by the way, is never productive, I would be lying to say I take pity on these savages."

"What makes a person human, sir?" Rose began to dig deeper. Stewart sat up, interested in the conversation and the question. She never saw Foginet challenged in such a way. Foginet took a deep breath and exhaled.

"I believe it begins with having a bond with humanity — even nature — wanting for others that which you want for yourself. That is how we begin to build the perfect society," said Foginet.

"And those who don't think along such lines, sir?" asked Rose.

"Well, let's just say, I would assign them to a lower level on the evolutionary scale," said Foginet.

"Does that make them savages, General?" asked Rose.

"Not necessarily, Lieutenant. But it does makes them developmentally delayed, and they are to be tolerated as long as they are unable to infect a greater number with their backwards thinking to the point where it becomes a danger to our collective well-being," said Foginet.

"And the savage, General?" asked Rose.

"The savage is myopic, Lieutenant. They can't be tolerated because they are irrational beasts, consumed by the urge to subjugate and, if necessary, destroy those who they feel are less than them. They don't see humanity as a single entity. They only see superior and inferior. They have no respect for differences," said Foginet.

"Sir?"

"Yes, Lieutenant?"

"Why are there so few prisoners in the Fifth Military District?" The question caught both Stewart and Foginet off guard.

"Lieutenant," interrupted Stewart as she gently grabbed Rose by the hand, "the general has another appointment. Let's see if we can finish this interesting conversation another time. Shall we?" both Stewart and Rose were now standing.

"Well, thank you, sir, for indulging me,"said Rose.

"No, thank you, Lieutenant. I look forward to our next meeting." Foginet walked Rose to the door held open by Stewart.

"Madame Director, it was a pleasure," said Rose.

"Likewise, Lieutenant. Good day."

"Oh, Lieutenant?" Foginet stepped out the doorway and into the hallway.

"Sir?" asked Rose.

"Are you familiar with a writing called the 'Remarks concerning the Savages of North America,' by Benjamin Franklin[98]?"

"Can't say I am sir."

"I own a copy. It's somewhere in here and when I find it, I'll let you borrow it, Lieutenant."

"Why thank you sir. I look forward to reading it."

"And Lieutenant?"

"Yes sir?"

"Please have the report regarding your travels on my desk as soon as possible." Foginet presented a friendly smile.

"Will do sir," said Rose.

As the door closed behind them, Stewart and Foginet stared at each

---

[98]  See *Benjamin Franklin Papers*

other. Both knew the answer to Rose's last question was a bit complicated. The Fifth Military District was under the command of Colonel Andre Soule. Unlike the SG commanders of the other military districts, Soule relied on SG troops to serve as prison guards in the Fifth Military District. Thus, his prisons were spared the acts of lawlessness found in many of the other prisons.

However, the SG in the Fifth Military District were given strict orders to shoot on sight select individuals targeted for arrest. Soule had no interest in wasting "precious" state resources or time in a courtroom on men who felt it was okay to maim and kill innocent black women and children. He literally took few prisoners. Many ex-Confederates in his district knew his policy all too well and chose to leave his district rather than face Soule's notion of justice.

"Dear, are you alright?" asked Foginet, as Stewart gathered her belongings.

"Oh, it's nothing, Sweetheart. Just feeling a little queasy. It's nothing, I'm sure,"

"If you say so." Foginet suspected something wasn't quite right with his fiancé.

"If you don't mind, Aurelius, I'm going to lay down for a while before dinner. Okay?"

"Sure, beautiful. I need my right hand to be at her best at all times. Would you care for some warm milk or something delivered to the room?" asked Foginet.

"That'll be fine. I'm sure it's nothing." As Stewart started to make her way past Foginet, he gently grabbed her by the arm and pulled her close to him.

"I love you, Lisa Stewart."

"I love you more, Aurelius." Stewart rested her head on his shoulders. He held her and kissed her gently.

# — THIRTY —

# The First Couple of the South

O n July 11, 1875, several black politicians recently elected in special elections held after Tennessee became part of Third Military District, were assassinated. This included the first black lieutenant governor of Tennessee, a state senator, two state representatives and the state's first black commissioner of education. A popular captain in the SG was also gunned down.

While Foginet would never wish death upon the likes of those who were murdered, their deaths presented him with the opportunity he hoped for. If the Redeemers planned it that way, they had made a colossal error. Why, he wondered, would they give him the excuse he needed to get an extension of his emergency powers? It didn't make sense. He concluded it must have been a rogue element among the ex-Confederates who didn't give much thought to the consequences of their actions.

Prior to his execution for treason, General Wright had warned his SG interrogators the Redeemers would stop at nothing to reclaim their homeland. He told them their plan was a long-term one.

"The Red Harvest was a surprising success," said Wright. "Sure, we would have loved to kill that son-of-a-bitch Wade, but we got the other two," Wright said, referring to Higginson and Davenport. "Hell, all we have to do is win the presidency and our nigger problem will disappear."

He had told his black interrogators had it not been for the presence of the Grey Shirts at Hopefield, Arkansas, both Douglass and Stewart would never have made it to Tennessee alive. The plan was to kill them once they got off the train or while on the ferry, but there were too many Grey Shirts.

When asked why he chose to betray Higginson and the Reconstruction effort, Wright was direct. "Higginson was an idealist. He believed in all that equal rights bullshit Wade and those Radical Republicans were talking. He allowed you niggers to climb too fast. Hell, you niggers started building a Utopia right here in the white man's homeland. It's not supposed to be this way. As a white man, I couldn't stomach you niggers struttin' round here actin' like you smarter than us white folks. It's not how it's supposed to be. Heck, y'all just niggers."

On July 12, 1875, Foginet requested an extension of his emergency powers. On July 26, 1875, his request was granted. This extension not only gave him unprecedented military and political power but this power could not be rescinded unless he chose to do so himself or the president and three-fourths of the United States Senate decided the State of Emergency should be terminated.

Thus, in order for the Emergency Decree to be rescinded, not only would Wade have to turn against him, which was highly unlikely, but so would seventy-five percent of the Senate. The Senate at the time had seventy-six members. Twenty-two of those members came from the former states of the Confederacy. Foginet had both a powerful ally in Wade and a numerical advantage. This meant Foginet as the military's supreme commander of the Southern states could effectively serve in this capacity for as long as he believed the conditions in the former Confederacy demanded it.

Immediately following the granting of this request, Foginet was summoned to Washington for a meeting with the president. Before leaving, he and Stewart were married in a private ceremony in the Alabama State Capitol. Senator Lafayette Inge performed the ceremony. The bride wore a stunning liquid gold dress that hugged her attractive figure without betraying her pregnancy. The groom wore a combination of the Union Army's uniform and black evening wear with a gold sash. His outfit was so well-liked, it became the standard for high-ranking army officials at formal functions. The couple made a regal appearance. Colonel Soule and his wife, Connie, served as best man and matron of honor respectively.

Among the small group of guests was Colonel Embry, Governor Bainbridge, Randall McArthur, Major Whitfield, and Foginet's secretary, Alma. Afterwards, a small reception was held in the couple's honor at Madison Farms. As word spread, an enormous crowd gathered around the compound. The couple briefly appeared and waved. Many onlookers left flowers and other gifts as a show of appreciation and affection for the powerful couple. The next day the local newspaper headlines announced the news. "General Foginet and Director Stewart Tie the Knot!"

At first, Stewart was reluctant to go to Washington due to her condition. She didn't want to take any chances. But she knew it was important for her to be with her husband for this particular meeting. Besides, she and the first lady had become well-acquainted through their correspondences, and she would probably not see her again for some time.

Travel arrangements were kept top secret. Accompanying the couple on the trip were McArthur and Embry. Soule was left in charge of all matters pertaining to the SG and militia units, and Alma would hold down the office while Foginet was away. Stewart left her able assistant Captain Weaver in charge of her office.

When the train arrived in Washington, there were no crowds. The press was not given any advance notice of their arrival. Although they had maximum security, they were able to sneak into the nation's capital undetected. The cover story was they were on their honeymoon somewhere in Louisiana. The following day, Wade announced their arrival, and a parade was held in their honor two days later. Thousands of SG troops from Virginia were allowed in the District for the festivities. Grey Shirt troops and regular army personnel assisted the SG troops in guarding the parade route. The crowd was enormous.

As the procession made its way toward the Capitol, onlookers were straining to get a peep at the First Couple of the South. One man yelled out, "Lisa, you broke my heart." The crowd erupted. Stewart smiled and blew him a kiss. While some held the flag of the United States, many blacks held a purple flag bearing two stars. They were everywhere. There were also a few sightings of the red, black, and green colors. One protester in the distance held up the Battle Flag of Northern Virginia, which had long been banned in every state of the former Confederacy. Needless to say, it didn't take long for that protester and his flag to disappear.

The SG had to do their best to keep the crowd at bay. At one point a black man broke through the SG's human barricade. He was immediately grabbed by Grey Shirt troops who walked alongside the couple's carriage. Foginet motioned the troops to let the man come closer, he leaned over and shook the man's hand. The man was ecstatic, and after jumping around for a few seconds, he waded back into the crowd.

When the procession reached the Capitol, a huge cheer came from the predominantly-black crowd. While many white faces appeared in the crowd, black faces clearly dominated the event. When the couple came to the podium, they were met by Wade, the first lady, Frederick Douglass, Senator Inge, and other dignitaries. Both Stewart and Foginet began smiling when the president alerted them to the presence of Hortensia, who was now the president's personal bodyguard and standing nearby.

The crowd erupted into chants of "Foginet!" Foginet! Foginet!" Wade took center stage. He began by praising the couple for their significant contribution to the South and the Reconstruction efforts. He then bestowed the Congressional Gold Medal[99] on Stewart. It was, at the time, one of the highest honor any U.S. civilian could receive. Stewart was the second black and first woman to ever receive the award. Douglass was the first black to receive the award.

The crowd erupted.

"We love you, Wizard!"

"May God bless you, Lisa!"

"Lisa, you are so beautiful."

Stewart graciously accepted the award from the president and thanked him. Next, Wade asked Foginet to step forward. He then opened a small box which was handed to him. The box contained two stars. He then summoned Colonel Embry and Douglass and asked both to place the stars on each epaulet. Foginet was now a lieutenant-general. The crowd went wild. One could even see a dozen purple flags bearing three stars. Foginet later learned the president had the flags made in advance for the occasion.

Back in the Executive Mansion, the president met with Stewart, Foginet, and Douglass. "Folks, I'm getting a little too old, and my enemies are sniping at my heels. I've decided not to run for re-election," said Wade.

Foginet and Stewart were stunned. They'd counted on Wade to make another run but completely understood his age and health wouldn't allow it.

---

[99]  At the time of the late 19th century the Congressional Gold Medal was the highest award possible for a civilian in the United States. The Presidential Medal of Freedom, its contemporary equivalent, is awarded to "individuals who have made especially meritorious contributions to the security or national interests of the United States, to world peace, or to cultural or other significant public or private endeavors," according to the White House official website.

"The party is gonna put up Rutherford Hayes[100] in my place. Don't trust him. So whatever you gonna do, do it and be done with it," said Wade. "He knows you hold the political power in the South, and he knows he needs you, but the man will do anything to occupy this house. Don't forget what I'm telling you. And I mean anything. The folks back home tell me he's one slippery fellow," said Wade.

The president was aging right before their eyes. Both Stewart and Foginet felt sorry for him. They had grown to care deeply about the man who they both considered a political savior for black people.

"The key here is to never allow those Confederate bastards back in power. I hear they're building political alliances all over the North," warned Wade. "Don't ever concede an ounce of power to these rebel bastards, ya hear? Excuse my language, Lisa," said Wade coughing. "What are— excuse me folks," Wade said as he coughed again. "What are your immediate plans, General?" asked Wade.

'Well, sir, I plan on granting women the franchise for municipal and state elections starting next year," said Foginet.

"That's a brilliant idea, General. Fred mentioned you said something like that some time ago," said Wade.

"We've also discussed the possibility of expanding our intelligence apparatus," said Stewart.

"My God, Lisa, folks up here in Washington are afraid to say or write anything negative about you guys. I hear down there they are so petrified, folks barely talk about politics publicly or privately," said Wade chuckling.

"Only the traitors are petrified, sir," said Stewart. Everyone laughed.

"Well, both of you are doing a damn good job. Keep up the good work. And, by the way, General, make sure our little lady here is well provided for — with her condition and all. It's driving Caroline crazy," said Wade.

Foginet and Stewart both agreed to inform the president and first lady of Stewart's condition prior to their arrival. "Don't worry, sir, she's in good hands. Maybe you can convince her to slow down a bit, Mister President," said Foginet.

---

[100] As 19th President of the United States, elected in 1876, Hayes oversaw the end of Reconstruction. Hayes' election, however, was controversial: he lost the popular vote to Democrat Samuel Tilden but won the electoral college vote after a Congressional commission awarded him 20 contested votes. The result was the Compromise of 1877 in which the Democrats agreed to Hayes's election on the condition that he end all U.S. military involvement in Southern politics. *For a look at Hayes' vision as president, see* Rutherford B. Hayes: And His America by Harry Barnard, *American Political Biography Press, 1994.*

"Oh no, Aurelius. I'm not getting in the middle of that," said Wade, using Foginet's first name for the first time in his presence.

"You're a smart man Mister President," said Stewart. The group laughed.

"Besides, I have my own battles with Caroline," Wade continued to the group's amusement. "Congratulations to the both of you," said Wade, his tone becoming serious. "And listen, what you folks do now with the power you possess, will determine the future of your people for years to come. Do what you must. I believe I've given you everything you need, eh? Wade asked rhetorically. "Now, let's go eat. I'm starving."=

"So are we," said Stewart, gently rubbing her belly. Everyone laughed.

As they were leaving the president's study, Foginet pulled Douglass to the side.

"Listen, Fred, thanks for everything. I know none of this would be possible if not for you," said Foginet.

"Aurelius, the president has placed a great deal of trust in you. You represent his vision and his legacy. People are saying he's become obsessed with the South. Members of his cabinet say that's all he thinks about these days. Personally, I think the man believes he has a divine calling to correct the gross injustice of slavery. He once said to me he believes by lifting up the black race he can purify the souls of whites and save this country from eternal damnation. This is what he told me. Something is driving the man, Aurelius, and he has chosen you to be his instrument in pursuit of some divine salvation. You must understand what is being asked of you. Do you?" asked Douglass.

Foginet just stared at Douglass, who appeared to be looking straight through him. "You cannot fail, Aurelius. This is it. We'll never have an opportunity like this again — ever." Douglass shook his fist and lightly tapped Foginet's breast with it. "And, like the president, I'm convinced now more than ever their next move will strictly be a political one. Make sure you're ready, Aurelius," said Douglass.

Foginet was surprised by Douglass' comments. For as long as he had known Douglass, the man preached moderation. On this day he sounded like a radical. He sounded like Stewart and himself.

"I've made my plans, sir," said Foginet.

On the train ride home, Foginet asked Stewart to accompany him to Texas before returning to Alabama. He told her it was a matter of great importance. Although Stewart wanted desperately to get back to work and return to the comfort and familiarity of Madison Farms, she agreed to travel further south with Foginet. When the train pulled into the newly constructed Beaumont station, SG troops were everywhere. A young lieutenant escorted the couple to a waiting carriage. Embry and McArthur had taken another train to Georgia, so Stewart and Foginet rode alone.

"Where are we going, darling?" asked Stewart.

"We'll be there shortly, dear," said Foginet.

"What is the big secret, Aurelius?" asked Stewart, now sounding a bit anxious. As a cool breeze blew across her face, Stewart felt a sense of relief from the hot Texas air.

"Wow, that feels good," said Stewart.

"We're just about there," said Foginet, pretending not to hear her. The carriage finally turned off the road onto a long, well-manicured private road shaded by huge pecan trees lining each side of the road. Ahead stood a beautiful stately three-story mansion held up by large Greek columns, each adorned with subtle decorative designs. The house had a spacious wrap-around deck on the first two floors. At the top of the house sat a white-ribbed cupola trimmed in black.

"Well, what do you think?" asked Foginet.

"Aurelius, it's beautiful," said Stewart.

"It's going to serve as our headquarters and our home," said Foginet.

"But how," before Stewart could answer she was be helped out of the carriage by a member of the SG. Another soldier escorted her up the steps which led to the entrance. When she got close enough, Foginet opened the door.

"Surprise!" yelled the small crowd in the house. Stewart was dumbstruck. In the crowd was her assistant Captain Weaver, Alma Sinclaire, Colonel Soule, Connie, and many of the other familiar faces from Madison Farms.

"Welcome to Riverside Manor, my dear," said Foginet.

"Oh, Aurelius, you've made me so happy," said Stewart, as she draped her arms around her husband.

"And you've made me equally happy, my dear," said Foginet, as the room applauded and celebrated the moment.

Riverside Manor once belonged to a wealthy landowner. It was used as a temporary headquarters for the Union Army during the Civil War. Foginet had it restored to its original beauty and added a few modifications to the interior. He also built a state-of-the-art barracks, stable, and carriage house. The huge grounds were also decorated with a half dozen cottages that had a gothic flair. These would serve as guest houses for out of town visitors. Surrounding the perimeter of the property was a well-designed eight-foot brick wall with several guard houses and numerous cannons in between various sections of the wall. For all practical purposes, Riverside Manor was a beautiful fortress. Foginet had chosen Beaumont because of its close proximity to the Naches River and the Gulf of Mexico. These two bodies of water would serve both an economic purpose and a military one.

Rumor had it, Foginet had made a sizeable fortune in his ventures overseas in France. It was said he made most of his fortune from the shipping trade and as the owner of several hundred acres of vineyards in the Bordeaux region of France, where he owned a successful wine-producing Chateau. Only a few individuals, including Stewart and Soule, knew his background, which he guarded jealously.

For much of the fall season, things were relatively quiet in the former Confederacy. Stewart's dreaded U3 had curtailed most dissent. It was estimated that one out of every four citizens in the former Confederacy worked in some capacity for U3. Most citizens did not say or write anything that would bring attention to them or members of their families. Whites, to the delight of most blacks, were terrified of U3. Many whites adopted the custom of flying the Purple Flag or what was commonly referred to as The General's Flag, a purple flag emblazoned with three gold stars, on their homes.

Black women took particular comfort in the fact that they could confront a white man who through his body language or spoken words made them feel uncomfortable. These confrontations usually resulted in an apology from the man who feared being beaten in the street by a male relative of the woman or worse, being arrested by the local constable and handed over to the SG.

After centuries of being at the mercy of white men, black women wasted no time taking advantage of their new social status. Lisa Stewart-Foginet was at the very top of the political-military food chain, and that meant they were too. To most black women in the former Confederacy Lisa Stewart-Foginet was royalty — a powerful queen, and like their queen, they expected to be afforded a similar deference by all men.

# — THIRTY-ONE —

# Welcome to the New South

O n Christmas Day of 1875, the political status of women took a
giant leap forward. As planned, Foginet announced all women
eighteen years of age and over, in those states of the former Confederacy
would now have the power to vote and run for office in both state and
municipal elections.[101] Additionally, his edict stated the wives and relatives
of all ex-Confederates would have to take the Ironclad Oath.

This decree virtually doubled the black vote in the former Confederacy
while keeping the white vote unchanged. The act stunned political observers in the North and South. While some feminists praised the move,
others frowned upon the decision to hold Southern white women to the
same standard as their husbands and male kin. Foginet ignored their crit-
icisms, arguing it didn't bar every white woman, just those sympathetic to
the Confederacy. Further, he argued, he did not want ex-Confederates to
use their wives as proxies. Black women were ecstatic.

The decree also meant whites would no longer dominate the legislatures and municipalities of Virginia, North Carolina, Tennessee, and Texas. While the Republican Party dominated these legislative bodies, most
of the power was in the hands of white members of the Party, who became
increasingly unreliable. Thanks to the decree, political power in those

---

[101] Women's suffrage — the right for women to vote for and hold political office — was guaranteed in the United States with the ratification of the Nineteenth Amendment on August
18, 1920. Catherine Helen Spence of Australia, Annie Besant of Britain, Mary Ann Müller of
New Zealand and Marie Goegg-Pouchoulin of Switzerland were prominent voices for women's
rights in their respective countries. *For a comprehensive overview of women's suffrage, see* Century
of Struggle *by Eleanor Flexner, Belknap Press, (3rd edition) 1996.*

states would soon effectively be in the hands of blacks.

McArthur's efforts at voter education and political mobilization would soon be put to the test. He wasted no time. He identified candidates for office and created a brilliant strategy for the upcoming municipal elections in several states. These elections would serve as a test. Needless to say, the Redeemers were furious. This act by Foginet was but another nail in their collective coffin. Desperation set in for the Redeemers.

Foginet's decree established the fact he held undisputed power in the former Confederacy. Although he allowed state legislatures to make laws as they saw fit, every governor and legislator knew as Supreme Commander of the military, he retained veto power that could not be overridden. Foginet also had the power to dismiss legislators he felt were corrupt or not acting in the best interest of their respective constituencies.

While it was rare for him to dismiss a sitting legislator, he did it on four different occasions. He balanced this power by allowing for special elections to be held to fill the vacancy. Foginet was careful not to abuse the power bestowed upon him by his emergency decree, but he was not afraid to exercise it.

Foginet's judicial use of his broad powers earned him the respect of blacks and whites, male and female, in the North and South. Even foreign diplomats were impressed by his political and military skills. After issuing the decree that allowed women to vote, Foginet received congratulatory correspondences from feminists throughout the world. Catherine Helen Spence of Australia was one of the first to send congratulations. Young British activist Annie Besant sent a letter to Stewart praising her and Foginet. Mary Ann Müller of New Zealand also sent a correspondence lauding Foginet's bold move as did Marie Goegg-Pouchoulin of Switzerland.

But not everyone was impressed. When the British ambassador was asked what Queen Victoria thought of the decision to allow women to vote, he informed the press "the Queen has no interest in such matters" and therefore would not comment. Many opposed to granting women the franchise in this country applauded the Queen's silence on the issue. For them it was a small victory.

Shortly thereafter, Foginet was invited to a state dinner by Hassan I, Sultan of Morocco to discuss "political, military and other matters." Foginet wrote to inform the Sultan he would take him up on his invitation as soon as he could find time for a vacation.

Years ago, as a seaman, he had spent time in Morocco with his friends

Kamal and Amadou. Kamal was a native of Morocco and taught him how to speak Arabic, and Amadou was from Senegal and taught him the Wolof language. Both men practiced Islam and while Foginet was not a religious man, he adopted many of the customs of their faith. He missed both men dearly.

In the former Confederacy, a cult-like movement appeared to be developing around Foginet and Stewart. They were viewed as royalty. Neither, however, ever allowed themselves to become sidetracked by their enormous popularity. Both knew their mission to ensure a safe future for blacks was far from over.

In early February 1876, Foginet restructured his military. He dismissed the military governors in each of the other four military districts. In addition to serving as Supreme Commander of all United States Southern Forces, he was still the military governor in the Fifth district. He replaced these men with the commanders from the SG. He promoted those who held the rank of colonel, including Whitfield, Soule, and Embry to the rank of brigadier-general. Foginet gave Soule his old post as military governor in the Fifth military district and Soule was also given command over all prisons in the former Confederacy, in part because of the report provided by Lieutenant Rose.

Embry, while lacking the skills of a prison warden, was an excellent military strategist, was given command over all U2 troops who were transferred to assist the regular army on the border of the former states of the Confederacy. Foginet had concluded the state capitals were pretty much secured and were no longer in need of thousands of SG troops maintaining security. Although he left about 2,000 SG troops in each state capital, he moved approximately 3,000 troops from each state to the frontline. Military observers were perplexed by these moves, but Foginet was fully confident in his decision. It was Embry's job to serve as the gatekeeper for the former Confederacy, and with 30,000 SG troops under his command and over 20,000 regular army troops at his disposal, he was more than prepared to carry out his duties.

Embry established Welcome Centers in every state of the former Confederacy. Each state had at least four. With the assistance of U3, these Centers not only helped to identify visitors and new residents to the state, the Centers also served as a deterrent to would-be terrorists. Most visitors including those seeking to establish new residency cooperated with the new system. Those who attempted to enter the state without passing through a Welcome Center and receiving the proper credentials ran the risk of being deported or worse, arrested and thrown into prison.

An account of one boy's impression of a Welcome Center appeared in a New York paper.

"As we approached the large brick structure that served to welcome guest to the state of Georgia, I noticed hundreds of Union troops on post or milling around. Everyone seemed so busy. Those troops wearing the colors and insignia of the SG appeared to be the most intense. They did all the questioning of those seeking to enter the state. They checked all the carriages. They were all about business. At least four adult males were arrested on the spot and taken to the back of the station. I never saw them again during my brief stay.

The arrests were carried out so quietly most of the people passing through hardly noticed. My dad presented his travelling documents to the captain of the SG, and after a brief inspection by SG troops, our family was directed to leave our belongings with our carriage. My father was handed a slip of paper with a number on it, and we were ordered to proceed to the doors leading to the entrance of the building.

The space inside the building was enormous. Desks were neatly arranged and were occupied by men and women, black and white. Each member of my family was interviewed separately. There were five of us. We were questioned about our family background and our reasons for moving to Georgia. Since my little cousin was under the age of twelve, he was not questioned, but my parents, my sister who was fourteen, and myself, being fifteen, were all interviewed. After the thirty-minute interview each of us was given identification papers, which stated our name, age, the date of the interview, a brief description of our physical appearance, and a number that followed the initials GA. My cousin also received his papers even though he was not interviewed.

We were then taken to a large hall, and upon entering the room, an aroma of fried chicken and cornbread filled my nostrils. Upon observing my reaction, a lieutenant in the SG whispered to me, 'you should have been here for breakfast, son.' He then winked and smiled at me. While we were not charged for the meal, there were neatly-dressed girls and boys who would walk around the hall soliciting donations. I recall my father leaving a generous donation. After eating our meal, we were allowed to leave the building.

It was a sunny afternoon, and when the doors swung open, I could not believe my eyes. The landscape was dotted with huge trees and colorful cabins that served as temporary shelters for new arrivals. Purple flags swayed alongside the flag of the United States. More than a few cabins had a red, black, and green flag flying from their building.

SG troops were positioned strategically throughout the area. Black people were everywhere. It seemed as if every one of them wore new clothes. Most appeared to be happy and each one appeared to be free of the fear that enveloped every black man, woman, and child at some point during our lives. Each member of my family was given a flag and a care basket full of essential items like soap, new blankets, and a bell, as a gift. We were later told the bell was used as a personal warning device or to alert others to any approaching danger. My father was then directed to the stable where he could retrieve our carriage and belongings.

It is very difficult to describe how I felt, but it was as if I walked into a different world — a black world. It was the happiest day of my life."

Foginet promoted Captain Weaver to the rank of major, and gave him control of all SG troops in U3. Weaver would now be the top commander in U3 and would answer only to Stewart or Foginet. Those regular army troops not assigned under Embry's command were dispersed throughout the former Confederacy, and with the help of local militias and law enforcement, would mainly protect the armories, highways, train depots, and rural roads of the South. Those who possessed special skills served as military advisers and observers.

Soule wasted no time in his new role. He quickly began to empty the prisons throughout the former Confederacy. At the time, there were about 5,800 prisoners in the former Confederacy. Alabama claimed the most, followed by Mississippi and Arkansas.

Those who were held on minor charges and cooperated with the SG were allowed to leave prison on the condition they leave the former Confederacy and never return. Nearly half of the prisoners fell into this category. These were the lucky ones. All others were subjected to a military court-martial.

Several hundred arsonists and vandals who caused no loss of life were given prison sentences between five and ten years and sent to the Texas State penitentiary. Those who were convicted of committing atrocities prior to and/or during the Red Harvest faced a firing squad or death by hanging. Soule was merciless toward such individuals. He truly believed he was justified in eliminating those who brought so much pain to black people.

It was estimated that nearly 2,000 ex-Confederates were put to death as a result of Soule's tribunals. Over 100 blacks were also executed for their role in aiding the ex-Confederates, including the black cook who attempted to poison Foginet at Hickory Hills. Nearly twenty percent of the prisoners who faced a military tribunal were found innocent. Some legal observers were amazed by this figure. Most did not hold Soule's tribunals in such high regard. But Soule knew some prisoners were victims of personal vendettas and other shenanigans he refused to accommodate. He wanted only those who were guilty to pay.

For Soule, his small bloodbath was nothing compared to the thousands of innocent black men, women, and children who were terrorized and/or murdered prior to and during the Red Harvest at the hands of white vigilante groups. Soule aimed to send a simple message to those who were still at large: "If you harm or attempt to harm black people by your terrorist activities, the penalty for your crime will be death."

By the time Soule had finished the last court-martial, he was the most hated man in the South among the white citizens. A few blacks loathed him as well, but the vast majority of blacks loved Soule. After Foginet and Stewart, Soule was arguably the most celebrated black in the former Confederacy. Many whites referred to him privately as the "Louisiana Butcher." He took pride in the title.

# — THIRTY-TWO —

# Joy and Pain

On March 12, 1876 Stewart gave birth to twins — a boy and a girl. The boy was named David Benjamin after the 19th century black abolitionist David Walker[102] who wrote The Appeal, and the president. The girl was named Araminta Caroline after the great Harriet Tubman, who was born Araminta Ross and Caroline Wade. The First Couple of the South was overjoyed.

Well-wishers from all over the country and throughout the world sent congratulatory letters. Stewart's mother arrived just prior to the birth to assist her daughter. Connie Soule was always a regular presence. She and her husband were asked to be the God-parents and of course accepted.

"Congratulations, big daddy," said a smiling Soule, while creeping up on Foginet who was in his private office. "Alma said I could find you in here."

"Hey there, General," said Foginet, teasing his dear friend about his new rank.

"Cut it out," said Soule. "How do you feel, old friend?"

"Well, brother, I feel like a blessed man. I'm happy for Lisa. With so much going on, I want her to take it all in as a new mom. But the woman is such a fighter and I know she feels torn between her duties. It would

---

[102] David Walker was an African American abolitionist. In 1829, he published a pamphlet entitled *Walker's Appeal, In Four Articles; Together with a Preamble, to the Coloured Citizens of the World, but in Particular, and Very Expressly, to Those of the United States of America.* The pamphlet, undoubtedly one of the more radical pieces of abolitionist literature, called for slaves to revolt against their masters. *For further reading, Walker's Appeal is easy to find online - many universities such as the University of North Carolina have published the resource online for free.*

help a lot if you and Connie would just encourage her not to worry about our struggle against these – " Foginet paused and looked at Soule.

"Savages," said Soule, finishing Foginet's thought.

"Thank you, good brother," said Foginet. "She only hears it from me."

"What do you think, Aurelius? Are you concerned?"

"Right now, 'Dre," Foginet referred to Soule by a nickname he had given him. "They are gaining allies in the North. If they somehow pull off a victory in the upcoming presidential elections, it could complicate matters for us." Foginet wore a look of concern on his face.

"How far are you willing to go, Aurelius?" asked Soule.

"You mean for those little ones upstairs and your little ones and future generations of our people? 'Dre, we must all be prepared for the worst. I will never hand over this land to these sick, twisted bastards willingly. I will not go down in history as the one who faltered and failed our people in the hour when they needed me most. I've already made my move," said Foginet.

If anyone knew what Foginet meant it was Soule. While he was well aware of — and even proud of — his own reputation, he knew it was a mistake on the part of the opposition to discount the ruthlessness of Foginet. Like others who studied the man, Soule knew there was something about him which made him different from most men. Foginet possessed a beautiful spirit — a quiet spirit — but there was also an internal fury which laid dormant in the man. Maybe that's what Higginson, Douglass, and Wade saw in Foginet. Soule sensed it as well. He knew Foginet better than anyone except Stewart.

Soule recalled Stewart once telling him, "behind my husband's quiet veneer is a burning rage." His handsome, dark face and strong features rarely betrayed his secret. Foginet had learned to control it. This was part of his genius. His climb to the top was by no means an accident. It was his destiny, and the life he lived prepared him for it.

The official name of Foginet's government was the General Government of the Southern United States of America or G.G.S.U.S.A.. It even had its own official seal. The words, "The Seal of General Government of the Southern United States of America" occupied the entire rim of the seal. In the center of seal was the image of a black woman, wearing a dress and holding a torch in her right hand and cradling a book in her left. The woman represented liberty. The torch represented progress, and the book represented knowledge. Under the torch appeared a rising sun with eleven rays and a purple horizon. This symbolized the day known as "Purple Sunrise." The eleven rays emanating from the sun represented the eleven states of the former Confederacy. At the woman's feet laid broken chains, which represented the former period of chattel slavery. But what struck most observers as audacious was the dagger that hung from the sash tied around the waist of the woman. Its meaning varied, but popular belief said it represented the people's willingness to defend their liberty by any means necessary. Many also said the woman on the seal represented a tribute to Lisa Stewart. The year "1875" represented the year the G.G.S.U.S.A. came into existence.

Unbeknownst to the Redeemers, another plot was being hatched, which had nothing to do with their plan of winning the presidency. The plotters were seeking revenge, and their target was the tall, debonair general named Andre Soule. The group was made up of a few blacks but mostly whites. Each had lost a relative, or two, or three, as a result of Soule's effective, yet brutal tactics in ridding the South of Confederate sympathizers.

Lieutenant Governor Ulysses J. Pratt was patiently waiting his term to be Louisiana's next governor. A black man born into slavery, Pratt knew full well the horrors of the slave system. Immediately following the cessation of hostilities between the North and South, Pratt made his way back from Tennessee to his home state of Louisiana after being honorably discharged from the army.

At first, like many newly-freed black men, Pratt sought to earn his keep by seeking employment in various trades. He spent his evenings learning to read and write. Early one evening, after working twelve hours during the day, he decided to skip his usual lessons and chose instead to attend a political rally hosted by the local Republican Party in Tensas Parish. Afterward he confided to a friend, "I found my niche." After working on several campaigns, he decided to run for public office himself.

In his first bid, he succeeded in defeating a white Democrat for a seat as a county commissioner. After a couple of years, and with the backing of the SG, he became a member of the Louisiana House of Representatives. Pratt served his constituents well, and he was rewarded by the voters each election cycle. After Pinchback's term as governor came to an end in 1873, blacks elected Patrick Kellogg as the first black elected governor in Louisiana's history. Kellogg, who served in the House with Pratt, chose him with the backing of the SG and the state political apparatus as lieutenant governor.

At some point in early April of 1876, General Soule received word by secret courier his presence was requested at a meeting with Pratt. The correspondence suggested it was of the utmost urgency the meeting take place. Given that the presidential election was on the horizon and the request was from Pratt, a loyal Party member, Soule's interest was elevated more than usual.

A cautious man, Soule reviewed the intelligence coming out of Baton Rouge, the capital, for any hint of sabotage. He found nothing. He then conducted a thorough background check on Pratt to determine his acquaintances and his comings and goings. He found it odd Pratt attended two meetings with Republican Party officials from New York, who were travelling through the South. He also learned Pratt was having an affair with a recently-divorced white woman. Pratt was married.

After much contemplation Soule decided to meet with Pratt, but on his own terms. He would meet him in Calcasieu Parish on the outskirts of Lake Charles. The site of the meeting would be revealed to Pratt just prior to Soule's arrival. Pratt would be escorted by a squad from the local SG, and no one, other than Pratt, would be allowed at the meeting. The plans changed several times before the meeting was to take place. Soule knew there was a price on his head, and he wasn't taking any chances. If it was anyone else other than Pratt he would have dismissed the matter entirely, but Pratt appeared desperate to reach out to him and nothing in Pratt's background suggested he was a traitor. Besides, he was in line to be the next governor of the state. Why would he risk that for anything?

The men met at a remote cabin on the outskirts of Lake Charles. Pratt informed Soule he had received news from Washington that a plot was underway to torpedo the dictatorship. According to Pratt, with Wade out, the next president was likely to end the State of Emergency. What was needed was control of the Senate. Several Northern Republican senators had pledged their support and the conspirators counted on Kellogg, the outgoing governor, to deliver two dependable votes from Louisiana in the U.S. Senate.

Soule knew something was afoot, and so did Foginet, but now there was confirmation. Soule knew if the plotters were successful in regaining control of the U.S. Senate, they could easily dismantle the regime. Absent an emergency decree, power would shift back to Washington D.C. This was serious. The fact that U3's vast intelligence apparatus didn't catch it made it even more unnerving.

The meeting lasted a little over an hour. Soule made the decision to take Pratt back to Beaumont with him. He knew Pratt's life was now in danger and so was his own.

"What if Kellogg..." before Soule could finish his sentence, gunfire could be heard coming from all directions. Some of the SG troops who escaped the gunfire rushed in to take cover, but it was too late. The frail wooden structure was hit by a barrage of bullets. Bodies were dropping everywhere. Soule caught Pratt just before he hit the dirt floor. Soule managed to lay him gently on the ground and started to return fire. Seconds later, men dressed as civilians entered the cabin. There were at least a dozen, and it appeared a dozen more were outside.

"This is for Clark, you son of a bitch," yelled one gunman before firing into Soule's upper torso.

"For Billy and Bobby Lee, nigger," yelled another. By this time, Soule was on both knees pitched backwards. He raised his sword in a last desperate attempt to strike down his aggressors.

"This is for my daddy, nigger," screamed a white boy who was barely sixteen. His shot caught Soule between the eyes. Soule's lifeless body just fell limp.

It was a brazen attack. One SG soldier guarding the perimeter of the meeting site followed orders and upon hearing gunshots, managed to slip away and race back to headquarters in Beaumont, Texas. As word filtered out, scores of SG troops descended on Lake Charles in the hours following the tragic event. Word spread quickly throughout the South, finally reaching the nation's capital. Flags were ordered to be flown at half-mast throughout the South. In the North, a sense of uneasiness filled the air. Killing the third most celebrated individual in the regime came with a price. No one knew what that price was going to be.

Back at headquarters, Stewart consoled Connie, Soule's widow. Foginet did the same with his young sons. The air was thick. Many were openly weeping for the loss of such a powerful figure and stabilizing force. In Soule, the black masses saw the mighty sword of justice and retribution for the years of pain and torture suffered at the hands of their white masters. Sure, Soule was brutal in his ways, but he had to be, most blacks reasoned. "How else do you tame savages?" This was the question asked by Bainbridge and many blacks in the South. For them, the answer justified Soule's ruthlessness and now he was gone.

# — THIRTY-THREE —

# Patience

Thousands turned out for the funeral of General Andre Soule, including many local and national politicians. Douglass came on behalf of the President Wade. Foginet had put the entire SG, as well as state and local militias, on full alert. Thousands of whites fled the South in anticipation of retribution by blacks for the death of Soule.

Sensing the political winds, Foginet decided to play it cool.

"Patience, brothers and sisters. Patience is what we need now." These were the words used by Foginet when he addressed the high-ranking officers of the SG. For most blacks in the South, and some whites, Foginet was like God on earth. His word was law and to disobey was to invite unwanted retribution.

At Soule's funeral, held in his hometown of New Orleans, Foginet gave a rousing eulogy. The text of his speech was printed in newspapers across the country and throughout the world. His speech was designed to immortalize Soule and give credibility to the dictatorship. It succeeded on both accounts. Condolences poured in from all over the world. Soule was hailed as a champion for justice, a crusader for the downtrodden, and a warrior for the people.

Pratt's funeral took place in his home district of Tensas Parish. While not as well-attended as Soule's, he did receive a home-going service worthy of a high-ranking state official. Stewart made sure to send as many intelligence agents to the parish to begin her investigation. U3 turned the parish upside-down seeking insight into the murders of Soule and Pratt. She even sent agents north to interview the two Republican Party officials who last communicated with Pratt. Those familiar with U3 knew better than to provide false information. People either had information to give or they did not. Giving false information or withholding information could land a person in prison or worse — six feet under.

Stewart sent her best team of agents to interview Pratt's mistress. In the end, the entire story came together just as Pratt had conveyed to Soule. However, one big piece was missing. How did the enemy know how and where to ambush the two men? Stewart began to think it was an inside job. She surmised the communications could easily be intercepted by the right people in the right places.

After talking over the matter with her most trusted agents, she met with her husband to discuss her plan, at least most of it. She was given the green light to execute it. In the early morning hours on July 31, 1876, Stewart issued an arrest warrant for five Union telecommunication officers. A warrant was also issued for Phillip Baptiste, a white man and the powerful head of Louisiana's Republican Party. The final warrant was issued for Patrick Kellogg, the sitting governor of Louisiana. All were taken by train under heavy guard to Camp Wade in Texas. Stewart took the trip as well.

Each man was placed in his own cell and provided a pen with ink and paper. They were all instructed to write what they knew about the conspiracy to kill Soule. While none of the Union officers wrote about the matters pertaining to the upcoming presidential election, at least four admitted they were paid to intercept information and pass the information along to Baptiste and Democratic Party officials. Baptiste admitted to receiving the information about the meeting between Pratt and Soule, and passing it on to Kellogg.

Baptiste was a former slave owner. When the war broke out, he remained loyal to the Union and left Louisiana and found safe haven in Tennessee. After the war, he was able to recoup some of his financial losses, thanks in large measure to his allegiance to the Union. However, not unlike General Wright, his sympathies rested with Southern whites. Although he did not support the rebellion, it offended him deeply those he and fellow slave owners once held in bondage now controlled matters in the former Confederacy. It was too much for him to swallow.

He decided to play it cool until an opportune moment presented itself. The upcoming election of 1876 was his moment, or so he thought. As the head of the Republican Party in Louisiana, he represented the interest of the national party's conservative wing in the state. After promising Kellogg a few favors, he was able to persuade him to go along with the plan to undermine the regime's support in the U.S. Senate. Since the state legislatures appointed U.S. senators, he needed Kellogg's support.

Kellogg admitted to receiving the information. A week or so prior to getting the information, he had heard representatives of the Republican Party from the North, while visiting the state, mistakenly provided details of the conspiracy involving the Senate to Pratt. When he learned Pratt was meeting with Soule, he knew Pratt would betray the plan. For the Democrats, Soule's death was a matter of revenge. Pratt's death was inconsequential. For Kellogg, once the plan was exposed to Soule by Pratt, both had to perish. He joined forces with Baptiste and those elements in the Union Army loyal to the Democrats.

On Tuesday, August 8, 1876, a little more than a week following the arrest and imprisonment of the "Gang of Seven," as the prisoners became known, a heavily-guarded carriage pulled up to the front entrance of Camp Wade at around 2 A.M. A striking, graceful figure draped in a long black cloak with a hood descended from the carriage, carrying a purse.

The cloak hugged the body of its owner, betraying her shapely figure. Two armed SG soldiers, accompanied her. They were met at the gate by several other SG troops. Two more armed SG soldiers were selected to join the group. The five individuals led by the woman disappeared down a long hallway leading to an isolated section of the prison. Once inside they made their way to the cell holding Governor Kellogg. The jailer was ordered to open the cell. The woman walked in the cell and removed her hood. The cloak and hood were lined with purple velour. "Lisa, is that you?" asked the governor, straining to see the person standing before him as he struggled to his feet.

"Yes, Governor, it's me, and you know what you must do." Stewart then reached into her purse and pulled out her pearl-handled Derringer pistol and laid it gently on the desk in the cell.

"But... but I don't understand," said Kellogg, who was now starting to grasp the full meaning of the Director's visit.

"You have five minutes, Governor," said Stewart, as she exited the cell. The group then went to the adjacent cell, which held Baptiste.

"I have nothing to say," said Baptiste, who turned his back to the group.

"We did not come here to address you, and we certainly have no interest in hearing anything further from you, Mister Baptiste," Stewart said. She then reached into her purse and pulled out a second pistol, which appeared to be an exact duplicate of the first. "You have five minutes, sir."

Stewart then placed the weapon on the desk in his cell.

"What the hell? You black bit..." The cell door slammed shut as Baptiste struggled to find his words.

As she stood outside the cell, waiting for Baptiste and the governor to take their own lives, Stewart replayed in her head the words spoken by Lafayette Inge following the Red Harvest: " How we handle this situation will determine the future of black folks in the South in particular and this nation in general for generations to come." She then turned her thoughts to her children.

After five minutes, Stewart re-entered Baptiste's cell with her two guards, both of whom had drawn their weapons. She noticed her pistol remained untouched on the desk. Baptiste now faced his jailers. As a trembling Baptiste raised both hands, attempting to negotiate a deal, Stewart calmly lifted the pistol off the desk, and positioned herself directly in front of the much larger Baptiste, who was sweating profusely. Stewart then placed the pistol to the center of Baptiste's forehead and pulled the trigger.

The white man's heavy body dropped to the floor. Her guards cast a quick glance in her direction, then stared at each other before turning their attention to the dead prisoner lying on the floor in a growing pool of his own blood. Stewart motioned to one of the guards to retrieve her weapon. She then left the cell as calmly as she walked in.

Just as the guard was about to unlock the cell holding Gover Kellogg the group heard a loud bang. Upon immediate inspection, they found Stewart's pistol lying beside the corpse of Kellogg. The guard then retrieved Stewart's pistol and handed it to her. She took one last glance at the dead man before exiting his cell.

Right before boarding her carriage, she turned to the captain of the guard. "Make sure the others meet a similar fate by firing squad tomorrow morning," she stated in a rather calm voice.

"On whose orders, Madam Director?" asked the Captain. "On the orders of my husband, the Supreme Commander. Do you have a problem with the order, Captain?" Her voice was no longer calm.

"No, ma'am. No problem at all."

"I didn't think so," said Stewart. Stewart then instructed her driver to take her to the station to board her private train that would take her home to her husband and children.

## — THIRTY-FOUR —

# Unit Four

66 What's troubling you, Aurelius?" Stewart moved purposely about the spacious room in Riverside Manor. Her tone suggested this conversation was all business. It was a little more than two months since the arrest and execution of the "Gang of Seven." While the white Northern press played up the executions to spark outrage toward Foginet's dictatorship, black Southern newspapers reported the "facts" as presented by the G.G.S.U.S.A.. The editorials vilified the Gang of Seven as "traitors" determined to help return blacks to involuntary servitude.

The vast majority of Southern blacks considered any support for the Redeemers as tacit support for turning back the clock on all they've accomplished since Wade had assumed the presidency. Besides, many blacks reasoned, the murder of Soule justified the regime's act of retribution.

Life at the time was never so good for blacks in the South, and any threat to their newfound freedom had to be extinguished by any means necessary. Foginet and the leaders in the regime understood this fact more than anyone. The regime's leaders knew if the Democrats were even remotely successful in ending the dictatorship and removing federal troops from the region, life for blacks in the South would be altered in ways that were unimaginable. Thus, they were not only unapologetic for the brutal tactics employed by their regime, they frowned upon any delay in using such tactics when it became necessary.

"I was approached the other day by General Embry," Foginet began.

"And?" asked Stewart.

"He informed me that Captain Rose..."

"Yes, I remember that interesting conversation we had with the Cap-

225

tain. He was a lieutenant back then. Are we talking about the same person, Aurelius?" Stewart was curious.

"Yes, Lisa, the same. As I was saying, Captain Rose suggested to General Embry all federal troops, Southern Guardsmen, state and local militia should be made to take a loyalty oath to the regime — to me — the Supreme Commander of the G.G.S.U.S.A.. What do you think?"

"Well, Aurelius," Stewart began, you recently purged the Union Army. You sent thousands packing to the North."

"Where they belong," said Foginet. His face displayed a deep frown.

"But 28,000 remained — including 5,000 white soldiers," said Stewart.

"What do you make of the idea, Madam Director?" asked Foginet.

"Most want to serve under your command. You have been good to them, Aurelius. The regime has been good to them. They believe in what we are doing here."

"So what are you saying?" asked Foginet.

"I like the idea of a loyalty oath. Let them swear loyalty to you and our cause. Most will honor it. We'll root out those who don't," said Stewart.

"What about its impact on the presidential elections?" asked Foginet.

"You know as well as I do we will probably lose most of the North. So the act of your soldiers swearing allegiance to you might send an unpleasant message in the North, but it will also send a powerful message in the South and the rest of the world," added Stewart. "Politics aside, Aurelius, no matter what happens in November, are you going to turn over the South to these savages? I would rather rot in hell before I let that happen," said Stewart.

"Just so you know, I couldn't imagine such a beautiful creature such as yourself rotting anywhere." Foginet wore a faint smile.

"Aurelius!" Stewart raised her voice and ignored the compliment, "we have to think worst case scenario. If we lose the presidency, or if we win and Rutherford is what Wade claims he is — and there is no reason to doubt the president, our options are limited." Stewart stared at Foginet. He stared back while rubbing his beard.

"I'll be meeting with General Whitfield tomorrow," said Foginet.

Stewart looked at Foginet. "Do you want me there?" asked Stewart.

"I think it's best if I see him alone."

"I understand perfectly," replied Stewart.

The following morning, Foginet and Whitfield met at Riverside Manor, or as it was called by the locals, "The Manor."

"How are things, General?" asked Foginet.

"Things are coming along well, sir," said Whitfield.

"General Whitfield, I never thanked you for your efforts in making the Grey Shirts one of the finest military units in this country. The president and first lady certainly appreciate them," said Foginet.

"Just doing my duty, sir, and by the way, I never thanked you for all you've done for me personally, sir and our people down here. Trust me when I tell you, it hasn't gone unnoticed," Whitfield repaid the compliment.

"Thank you, General Whitfield. I'm just doing my duty as well." Foginet was apprehensive. "Ako," Foginet was now using Whitfield's first name, at least a condensed version of it. General Whitfield's first name was Akocha, the Chickasaw word for "sunrise."

"I have to plan for the absolute worse. If either Tilden or Hayes wins this election, even without the support of the U.S. Senate, they could still remove the federal troops and weaken the regime.

"How many federal troops accepted your offer to transfer north?" asked Whitfield.

"Sixteen thousand, mostly white. We have a total of about 28,000 active federal troops, 5,000 of whom are white."

"Do you trust, if it came to it, they will obey a presidential order to leave the South?"

"I don't know, Ako, I don't know. It's a chess match now."

"When I gave the troops the option to leave the South, I knew most of the white troops would do so. I knew the blacks wouldn't. They've cast their lot with our brethren down here. This move weakened the Democrats' military presence in the South. They recruited officers and enlisted men who were in key positions to undermine us."

"The Gang of Seven?" asked Whitfield.

"Yes, five were officers in the regular army." Foginet was now slowly pacing the room. "I suspect there were more — a lot more. A few are still within the ranks of those who stayed behind," said Foginet.

"Do you have an idea who they are?" asked Whitfield.

"We'll find them. The Director has increased the U3 presence among their ranks. She put some of our best agents among them. Most of the traitors will be exposed in due time, but I suspect the Democrats and their Republican friends have a two-fold strategy. The key is removing the federal troops, but if that proves to be too tenuous, they hope to have the votes in the Senate to end the State of Emergency," explained Foginet.

"Killing the regime," Ako interrupted.

"Exactly." Foginet stopped and looked at Whitfield. "Once they end the State of Emergency, they can chip away at the pillars of the regime until the whole thing comes tumbling down. Now without the votes in the Senate, they will have no choice, and in desperation they will order the removal of the troops."

"You seem certain of these tactics, General. Why?"

"Because that's what I would do," said Foginet.

"General, assuming the federal troops obey the president's directive, we still have the SG and the local and state militia, a quarter of a million men and women, sir." Whitfield sounded confident.

"The SG — well they are unquestionably loyal and dependable. But with the exception of the militias in Alabama, Louisiana, and Arkansas, the other state militias might become a bit fickle in the face of 100,000 Union troops," said Foginet.

"Excuse me, sir." Whitfield finally began to comprehend what Foginet attempted to convey.

"General, I said," Foginet began to speak.

"I know what you said," Whitfield interrupted again. Foginet was not giving up the South without a fight. "Sir, do you think the new president would mount a military offensive — another war? Do you think they're capable?"

"General, these are desperate times. We're all desperate. Southern whites desperately want things to go back to what they once were or close to it, and we're equally desperate to prevent that from even remotely happening. The problem for us is they have more allies up North than we do. Many Northern whites did not like slavery, but as you well know, Ako, they never saw us as their equals. Our success down here over the last few years is an affront to their white sensibilities. To answer your question, not only are they capable, Ako, but many are determined to put us back in our place."

"What do you plan to do?" asked Whitfield.

"I've dispatched ambassadors to our European friends. I don't expect much — not now anyway. The Europeans will of course play this one very carefully. It's a long shot, but I would be derelict in my duty if I didn't reach out to them."

"What do you need from me, sir?" asked Whitfield.

"What is the readiness of Unit Four, General?"

"As ready as they will ever be, sir. Just give me the word and the lists."

"Very good, General. Very good." Foginet made a fist with one hand and punched the palm of the other.

Unit Four was a clandestine military unit within the G.G.S.U.S.A.. Only the upper echelon of the regime knew of its existence. The individuals who made up its ranks were hand-selected by the regime's top brass, including Foginet, Stewart, Soule, Embry, and Whitfield. They were men and women from all walks of life. Some were white, but most were black. The group also included a dozen Native Americans, two Asians, and at least a half dozen Mexicans. Each had a deep devotion to the regime. They were vetted thoroughly.

Created in 1874, Unit Four trained at a camp located in Booneville, Mississippi. The land once belonged to a member of the Chickasaw tribe. The training was quite rigorous. The agents of Unit Four or "U4" as they were called, were trained in outdoor survival skills; tracking; fighting; shooting; disarming; explosives; forgery; eavesdropping; the use of code as well as code-breaking; camouflage; and many other techniques that could aide them in a given mission. But much of their training focused on the art of assassination.

The Unit's motto was, "By Any Means Necessary." The words appeared at the bottom of their shield. Above these words appeared an image of a creased cloak, which dominated the shield. In the center of the cloak appeared an image of a dagger with the blade pointed downward. On one side of the blade appeared a torch, and on the side appeared a pistol.

After passing the twenty-month course, each agent was given a gold coin depicting the crest on one side and the number 18, which sat in the center of the coin, printed in small writing on the other. It was a tribute to Wade, the eighteenth president. Each agent was also given the opportunity to select a code name. Some chose names derived, in most cases, from a skill they displayed during the training. One individual called herself "The Scribe." Another called himself "The Chef." There was "The Czar," "The Doctor," "The Professor," "The Artist," "The Hunter," and "The Stranger," to name just a few. One woman called herself "The General," borrowing the nickname given to Harriet Tubman, who previously gave a lecture to the recruits during a surprise visit.

These men and women were talented. Their personal stories, in some instances, were as intriguing as their talents.

One evening after dinner, a small group of U4 agents was huddled around a campfire behind the main dining hall. One individual who called himself "The Fisherman" told the story of one of his earliest recollections of a family fishing trip. He was eight or nine years old at the time. His father, uncles, and cousins used to hunt alligators in the swamps of Louisiana. One day, he recalled, his uncle, a big burly fella, came to the dock carrying a sack. The youngster noticed a lot of movement in the sack, and thought it was an animal he captured in the woods.

"Did you git it?" his father asked.

"What do ya think?" the uncle replied. "Some feisty nigga gal gave me a rough time, but Lil' Joe the overseer just walked over and snatched it and dat was dat."

"What's our cost?" asked another uncle.

"Oh, Lil' Joe jest want some of da catch. Dat's all."

"Well, let's git on wit it," shouted his father. The boat made its way out to the middle of the swamp. The young boy kept his eyes glued to the sack. He couldn't wait to see the bait that would be used to catch the alligator. This was his first alligator hunt, and he was the most excited among the crew. The others on the boat watched the gaze of hungry eyes perched just above the water level. Some of the creatures began to encircle the boat. They could sense a meal was about to be served.

When the men reached just beyond the middle of the swamp, his uncle reached in the sack and pulled out a small, black baby boy who appeared to have a deformed foot.

"Bring it chere," screamed his cousin.

"Make sho ya tie the leg nice an' tight. This is our only bait. We probably can catch two, if not three, gators with this here little picaninny. Toss it in," yelled his uncle. The young Fisherman recoiled in horror. His cousin, slightly older, burst out with laughter.

"How do ya think we catch dees gators, boy?" His burly uncle asked. "It's only a crippled nigga baby boy who aint gonna be good to nobody. We just doing it a favor." His uncle put his arm around his shoulders and pulled him closer to him. As the baby splashed about, the small boat was suddenly surrounded by several hungry lizards.

"Pull it in," demanded his cousin.

The first gator was pulled on board holding the half eaten baby in its mouth.

"Is it still breathing?" asked his father.

"I think we got one mo' catch in it." One leg of the child appeared to be twitching. The alligator was bludgeoned to death, and the baby was ripped from its jaw. Its half-eaten body was flung back in the water to catch another gator.

"I knew at that moment, I would never grow up to be like the men I shared that boat with that day," said The Fisherman as he completed his story and lowered his head. The rest of the group sat in stunned disbelief. Not a word was spoken.

# — THIRTY-FIVE —

# "Sheer Anarchy"

The atmosphere was festive in Jefferson County, Alabama. The troops, numbering in the thousands, took their respective place on the parade ground. The area was under heavy guard, patrolled by members of the SG, Grey Shirts, and the militia. Stewart employed non-uniformed agents throughout the crowd. The regime left nothing to chance. Even the choice of Jefferson County was based on a thorough internal vetting process. No other state in the G.G.S.U.S.A. was more secure than the state of Alabama.

The dais was sparkling, as were the troops. Purple flags were everywhere. Flanking Foginet on the dais were Stewart, Connie Soule, and her two sons. The crowd, estimated at over 100,000, came from every state in the former Confederacy. Many wore purple attire. Soule's widow received a thunderous ovation. Tears streamed down her face but she managed a smile. A chant went up "Soule! Soule! Soule!"

Also on the dais was General Whitfield, General Embry, Randall McDaniel, who had just returned from the North, Governor Bainbridge, and the top commanders of the SG including Major Hope and Major Lacy. Frederick Douglass was even on hand to bestow a fourth star on Foginet, courtesy of the president. This would be one of Wade's last official acts as commander in chief.

Support for the regime poured in from capitals across the world. After reciting the loyalty oath given by Senator Inge, the troops and the crowd erupted in wild applause. Foginet now stood at the height of his power.

Following the ceremony, the crowd made its way to the scores of huge tents spread out across the parade ground. The G.G.S.U.S.A. hired local cooks to provide free meals to those who chose to remain and enjoy the occasion. It was a fun time for all.

"Where do we stand?" asked Foginet standing in a private tent a mile away from the festivities.

"Well, General, without the women's vote we can still win the South, but the North is problematic," said McArthur.

"How problematic, Mac?" Foginet was fond of giving individuals nicknames only he used. It made McArthur feel extra special to have the Supreme Commander refer to him in such a personal way. He regained his composure.

"I think we have a good chance to carry four or five states, General, maybe more."

"All due respect, Mac, that's not what I'm hearing," said Foginet.

McArthur glanced at Stewart, then continued. "General, not only did I put a lot of effort into organizing the base up North, but I've spoken to the people. Now, with the exception of Connecticut, I think we have a shot. Heck, the white folks up there, especially in some of those New England states, are your biggest supporters. They believe the ex-Confederates are getting just what they deserve. And for many of them, it's even sweeter because black folks are giving them a taste of their own medicine."

"Thank you, Mac. Let's hope you're right." Foginet was not convinced.

"Madam Director, any news yet?"

"Our operatives are working overtime, General. The minute I get something you'll know."

"Thank you."

"Excuse me Sir," Alma came rushing towards Foginet. "Mister Douglass would like a word with you."

"Tell him I'll be right there, Alma." Foginet followed Alma to an adjoining tent.

"Fred, sorry to keep you waiting," said Foginet.

"Impressive, General. The president sends his regards, but he's concerned," said Douglass.

"So am I, Fred," said Foginet.

"Aurelius, if we lose this election, we have few options." Douglass tugged at his beard and paced the small area.

"Don't you think I know that, Fred?" Foginet knew the stakes were high. But he refused to allow his external demeanor to betray his thoughts.

"The president wants to know the end game."

"He'll know soon enough."

"What does that mean, General?" asked Douglass.

"It means it's not over 'til we say it's over," Stewart walked in on the group and interjected. "Fred — I don't know how to say this, but I'll try. We're not giving up the South. The decision has been made. I think it would be best if you inform the president we might be needing him at some point, but now is not the time."

"Excuse me, Madam Director?" Stewart's words stung Douglass.

"Fred," Foginet paused. "Can everyone clear the area please?" Foginet directed everyone other than the top brass to leave the tent. "Fred, please sit down. Would you like a drink?"

"Some lemonade would be nice."

"Alma, please bring Mister Douglass a glass of your delicious lemonade."

"Thank you, General," Douglass said, while casting a less-than-admirable glance at Stewart. For her part, Stewart, rolled her eyes at Douglass.

"Fred, we appreciate all you've done, and certainly we wouldn't be where we are without the president, and you, for that matter. We get it. All Lisa is attempting to convey is there is nothing more you can do at this time. The president is a lame duck. The Party leaders have all but handed him his hat. Our plans have been made. We still need the president, but not right now. Trust us to handle the situation." Foginet tried desperately to be measured.

"Aurelius, this can only mean one thing — more bloodshed," said Douglass.

"Well, Fred, it's either our blood or theirs." Foginet's tone was now harsh.

"I just hope you know what you're doing, Aurelius. Contrary to what some around you believe," Douglass turned his head in Stewart's direction, "the answer doesn't always lie in the barrel of a gun."

"It does when you are dealing with a savage, Mister Douglass," said Stewart.

"I'll be leaving tomorrow morning, Aurelius. I'll report your position to the president. Tell Alma I'll try her lemonade some other time. Folks, til we meet again. Madam Director, Generals, good day." Douglass graciously bowed to his host and exited the area. Foginet followed closely behind.

"Safe travels, Fred, and give the president our regards," said Foginet.

"Will do, General."

On Tuesday, November 7, 1876, the numbers trickled in slowly. In the end, Democrat Samuel J. Tilden of New York beat Republican Rutherford B. Hayes of Ohio in the popular vote. Tilden had 184 electoral votes and Hayes had 165 with 20 votes unresolved. Hayes had swept the entire South and did better than expected in several Northern states, thanks to the efforts of McArthur, but Tilden controlled much of the North and the West thanks to the migration of Southern whites to both regions and the strong support of white Republicans. Wisconsin with 10 electoral votes, Connecticut with 6, and Rhode Island with 4, were all contested.

For weeks after the election, neither side would give in. Then the news struck like a thunderbolt. The Republicans, as Foginet expected, cut the deal. Before most of the world knew of the betrayal, Stewart's agents at the Wormley Hotel, where negotiations were being held, intercepted the correspondences which left no doubt a deal was struck. Hayes agreed to remove the remaining federal troops from the South in exchange for the contested electoral votes that would give him the presidency. Additionally, Hayes promised to deliver enough senators to end the State of Emergency, thereby ending Foginet's dictatorship.

Foginet's grip on the Senate was tenuous at best, but he was confident he could count on enough senators to maintain the dictatorship. But the removal of the troops would spell disaster. Wade was furious. In a face-to-face talk with Hayes, he scolded him and reminded him he was a Republican, and the deal he made would wreak havoc on the black population of the South.

"What's done is done, Mister President." Hayes reportedly told Wade. "And by the way Mister President, tell your little general his days are numbered."

"So are yours," Wade reportedly shouted back.

Hayes flashed a polite grin and left the Executive Mansion.

On February 21, 1877, Foginet moved the capital of the G.G.S.U.S.A. to Pittsboro, North Carolina. Two weeks later, Foginet did what most observers called the unthinkable. Foginet issued Executive Order 111 — an order to defend the G.G.S.U.S.A.. Its code name was "Operation Deo Vindice." The name represented the motto of the Confederacy during the war. It meant "Under God, our Vindicator." The words were also found on the Confederate seal.

As the Supreme Commander of the G.G.S.U.S.A., Aurelius Foginet ordered the murder of over 700 individuals loyal to the Redeemer cause and prohibited anyone not named from offering those targeted assistance of any kind. With a list supplied by Stewart and made available to every publication in the G.G.S.U.S.A., Foginet made it legal to hunt down and kill everyone his government deemed to be an enemy of the regime. While the order only applied in the areas governed by the G.G.S.U.S.A., it had widespread repercussions.

The names of leading members of the planter class, Confederate sympathizers, Democratic Party leaders, mid-level and high ranking officers in the Union Army loyal to the Democrats and traitors within the Republican Party, black and white, all were placed on the list. No one was spared. Foginet was determined to put an end once and for all to any notion of restoring the Redeemers to power in the South. It would be over his dead body or a lot of other dead bodies. He chose the latter.

As far as Foginet was concerned, the South now belonged to those who worked its lands, built its plantations, and made its landowners some of the richest people in the world. It belonged to those who wore the indelible mark of the ex-slave. The South belonged to its black majority. He would not voluntarily relinquish his grip on the former Confederacy.

Foginet's actions were unprecedented. The bloody dagger of the regime was now exposed for the world to see. A few nations issued protests through their ambassadors in the United States. The protest fell upon deaf ears.

"Where were your letters of protests when the black race was catching hell in bondage?" said Wade to one European ambassador.

"Foginet Legalizes Murder" one white Northern newspaper headline read. "PROSCRIPTION" shouted another, referring to the term used in ancient Rome when the dictator Sulla put his enemies to death, and again under the Second Triumvirate consisting of Octavian, the great nephew of Julius Caesar and future emperor, Mark Antony, and Marcus Lepidus.

Black Southern newspapers boomed "Foginet Orders Death to the Traitors." Fear gripped the entire nation. Most citizens in the South cooperated with the SG, U3 agents and local law enforcement who were active in every town searching for those listed as enemies. Those on the list sought safety wherever they could. Some wore disguises. Many abandoned personal dignity and hid in outhouses, barns and wells. Those who could fled west or to the North. Some left the country altogether. Some were fortunate to escape death but most were not.

U4 agents were dispatched all over the country with a primary concentration in the North and South. These men and women were given the most dangerous assignments and targeted the most wanted individuals on the list. Former Democratic Senator Andrew Garner was found in a remote cabin near his home with his throat slit and a rose planted neatly in the wound. He also had a rectangular shaped piece of wood tied to a rope draped over his neck. Scribbled on the wood were the words "Deo Vindice." It was the work of the female assassin they called the Gardener.

The senator's body wasn't discovered for several days. This caused the rose, which was initially bright red, to turn a very dark red — almost black in color. The press mistakenly stated his killer left a black rose. From that point on, all killings associated with Operation Deo Vindice were deemed to be the work of a secret organization created by Foginet, known as Black Rose.

As hundreds of whites and dozens of blacks were hunted down across the country, race riots broke out in Northern cities. Foginet anticipated such action. Prior to giving orders to Whitfield to unleash his terror campaign, he dispatched envoys to the North. Now he ordered these envoys to convince each city's respective leaders to give blacks safe passage out of the cities to the "Freedom" trains heading south. This was accompanied by a promise from Foginet no harm would come to the leaders or their family members. Foginet's tactic saved thousands of lives. However, many black lives were still lost to Northern mob violence.

Fed up with what he described as "sheer anarchy," the new president and former Union Army general began to call up federal troops. Ironically, many of those volunteering to fight for the Union were ex-Confederates soldiers who left the South.

Upon hearing the news, Foginet closed the border of the G.G.S.U.S.A.. General Embry was ordered to mobilize all 30,000 SG troops and all 20,000 Union Army troops under his command as well as the state militias of North Carolina, South Carolina, and Virginia. 25,000 troops were positioned on the border of West Virginia. The country now stood on the brink of a second civil war.

# — THIRTY-SIX —

# The Texas Compromise

I n 1859, the eyes of the nation had been fixed on Harpers Ferry, Virginia. Abolitionist John Brown and a small band of freedom fighters had been determined to engage in armed insurrection to end the slave system in the United States. He was betrayed, and his noble plan failed. Brown met his end by hanging shortly thereafter. On the morning of April 10, 1877, the eyes of the nation were once again fixed on Harpers Ferry, which was now located in the newly-created state of West Virginia, for an even greater event.

Former President Wade accepted an invitation by the nation's new President Rutherford B. Hayes to mediate a crisis, which if not resolved, could lead the country down the path to another civil war. The location was selected by Wade who guaranteed the safety of all federal officials attending, including the new president.

As Hayes' carriage made its way down a dirt road past troops loyal to the G.G.S.U.S.A., he was in awe. He could not believe the arms these troops had at their disposal.

"Who armed these nig-" Hayes caught himself. "Where did the dictator get the resources to arm these troops, Colonel?" Hayes was addressing Colonel George Smith, his military attaché and like Hayes a veteran of the Civil War. The new president hated Foginet and was quite in the habit of using disparaging terms to describe him.

"Well, sir, our intelligence informs us the G.G.S.U.S.A. has a special fund for such purposes. Additionally, sir — General Foginet has influential friends in certain European capitals." Unlike, Hayes many high-ranking officers in the Union army like Smith, had a profound respect for Foginet, not because he cared for him as a person but because of his military acumen and his commitment to his troops and people. To many of them, leaders like Foginet appeared once in a generation.

"I'd say the intelligence is right," said Hayes. "Damn, and they look so professional. How many are there, Colonel?"

"We estimate they can put close to 50,000 well-trained troops in the field, and double that within weeks, sir," Smith drove the point home.

"Good God, Colonel. What we have is a formidable opponent."

"The army agrees, sir." Hayes turned quickly to his attaché and looked away with disgust.

"By the way, Mister President, we received word troops from the Louisiana, Alabama, and Arkansas militias have massed on the borders of Missouri and Kentucky. We've also learned some of the Welcome Centers are being stocked with hospital supplies. "

"What?" yelled Rutherford. "Is there anything else the army has kept from me?"

"Well, sir, one last thing."

"Go on," demanded an exasperated Rutherford.

"Sir, the state Republican Party leaders of New York and New Jersey were found murdered in their homes yesterday," Smith seemed to take solace in bringing Hayes one bit of bad news after another.

Many Union officers and regular army troops opposed the idea of a second civil war. For many of them, too much blood was already spilled to save the Union and now Hayes and his political allies dared to risk more bloodshed to help restore the enemy-secessionists to power in the South. The idea created a mutinous atmosphere within the Union Army.

"My God. Tolliver? Jackson?" Rutherford was shocked. Two of his most trusted political allies were now gone. He rode the remainder of the short distance in complete silence and deep in thought.

The meeting space was a newly-constructed building equipped with rooms of all sizes and with all the latest amenities. Foginet and Stewart arrived around 10 a.m., two hours after all the other participants. They were housed in a secret location a few miles away. When the couple arrived, pandemonium broke out around the town. Their carriage was besieged by curious onlookers. Purple flags bearing four stars waved side by side with flags bearing the seal of the G.G.S.U.S.A.. There were even quite a few flags bearing the colors red, black, and green. Only a few American flags were held by the mostly black crowd. The Grey Shirt and SG troops numbering over 250 did a credible job in managing the perimeter around the actual area where the meeting was to take place.

Wade was the first to greet the couple as they exited their carriage. Foginet gave the former president a big hug and held his frail hand, then raised Wade's arm up to the crowd. Stewart planted a kiss on Wade's cheek. She then stood in the middle of both men and held the hand of each before raising both men's arms. The small crowd erupted at the sight of the mighty trio. The group then made their way inside the meeting hall, where they were met by an audience of select newspaper reporters from across the country. Fifteen Grey Shirt troops stood silently around the room. Stewart also had several U3 agents pose as reporters for additional security.

Unbeknownst to most, the federal delegation, which included Hayes and Tilden among others, was taking the celebration in as each sneaked a peek at the couple's arrival from behind the curtain in their respective rooms. To say they were intimidated would be an understatement.

The meeting began shortly after lunch. After introductions, Wade opened the meeting by thanking everyone for agreeing to be part of this historic event. He then began slowly and deliberately.

"General Foginet, here is what the federal government is proposing. The G.G.S.U.S.A. is to immediately end the State of Emergency; discontinue the use of the Ironclad Oath; rescind Executive Order 111; disband Unit Three; and phase out the Southern Guard. Upon doing so, the federal government agrees to partition the State of Texas into two states: East Texas and West Texas. The latter will be open to all citizens who no longer desire to reside in the area under the control of the G.G.S.U.S.A..

Although much of the plan had been worked out, there were a few sticking points concerning deadlines.

Foginet countered. "We agree to the following, Mister President: The Ironclad Oath will be rescinded for women immediately and phased out in five years for select white men. The SG will be phased out in three years. Unit Three will be disbanded in one year. The proscription will end immediately, but Union troops will remain under my command for another three years. As for Executive Order 265 — those whites who were stripped of their right to bear arms will be barred from bearing arms for the remainder of their lifetimes if they choose to remain in the states that make up the G.G.S.U.S.A. "

After several hours of discussion, Wade suggested the parties meet again in the morning to finalize the deal. As Foginet and Stewart were about to board the carriage to take them back to their secret location, Wade slowly made his way over to them.

"I think we are almost there, but I'm concerned this matter with Unit Four is going to be a major obstacle for the other side." He was talking in a hushed tone. Stewart and Foginet looked at each other, then thanked the former president for his leadership and friendship. "We'll give it the utmost consideration, Mister President," said Foginet.

Prior to dinner, Foginet and Stewart received a surprise guest.

"Welcome, Fred. How delightful," exclaimed Stewart.

"I don't think we left on the best of terms the last time we were in each other's company, Madam Director," said Douglass.

"Fred, tensions were high. I apologize if I was a bit short with you. I have nothing but the utmost respect for you and what you've meant to the General Government," said Stewart.

"Thank you, Lisa. It means a lot hearing you say that," said Douglass.

Foginet appeared relieved. He knew both Stewart and Douglass had strong personalities. Each was extremely valuable in the struggle at hand. The mission was much better served when the key components were on the same page.

"Aurelius, the other side is concerned about this Black Rose business," said Douglass.

"Fred, I can't acknowledge having any control over such an entity."

"My god Aurelius, you issued an order that sanctioned state-sponsored murder." Douglass appeared dismayed.

"True, and I would do it again. But I will not give credence to some shadowy outfit that leaves roses in the sliced throats of its victims."

"Fred," Stewart began, "as far as we're concerned, Black Rose is a vigilante group operating free of the auspices of the General Government,"

"Lisa, who's going to believe that? You guys run an operation more sophisticated than the federal government. The only reason they agreed to sit down with you is because they respect your capacity to inflict enormous harm against any force sent against you. They know your capabilities, and they also fear Black Rose. Fighting a war at this point isn't worth it for them, but that can change." Douglass attempted to reason with thepowerful duo.

"Fred, thank you, but if admitting a link to Black Rose is a deal-breaker, then we might as well not show up for the meeting tomorrow. The best we can offer is to use our influence to prevent any more killings by U...," Foginet caught himself.

"You were saying, General," said Douglass sarcastically.

"That's the best we can do." Foginet finished his thought.

Stewart and Foginet both knew Unit Four was their secret weapon. As long as ex-Confederate sympathizers knew an entity such as Black Rose could come knocking at their doors, they were less apt to step outside of prescribed boundaries. The leaders of the regime believed Black Rose was the only thing that would keep "the savages" in check once the dictatorship ended.

"DEAL REACHED — WAR AVERTED." The major dailies in the North and South all printed a similar headline. In the end, Hayes and his allies did not have the stomach for another war. Foginet's forces were too well-equipped and prepared for war. Most importantly, the morale of the troops fighting for the G.G.S.U.S.A. could not be matched by the troops of the Union Army. The former were fighting for their very lives. It wasn't so clear-cut for the latter.

Hayes had also received word the G.G.S.U.S.A. received a commitment of support from several foreign governments regarding supplies and manpower. Thanks in large measure to General Whitfield, the vast majority of the Native American nations aligned themselves with the G.G.S.U.S.A.. Most of their leaders felt they had far more to gain in alliance with the black South than the white North.

Hayes accepted Foginet's promise to do his best to rein in Black Rose. The terms of the deal was a death blow to the Redeemers who felt they were betrayed by Hayes and their Northern allies and for the most part, they were. Not only did they lose the presidency but they also lost the South. It was now in the hands of their former slaves. All they could do was relocate to the new state of West Texas and begin a new life in a different America.

When Foginet and Stewart arrived back in Pittsboro, it took them two hours before they could leave their private train. The crowd was enormous. The conductor suggested the train temporarily leave the station, but Foginet and Stewart wouldn't have it. It was a time to celebrate. Besides, the couple was beyond anxious to hold their lovely twins.

Foginet and his regime broke the backs of the Redeemers for good. General Whitfield, who travelled with the couple, was elated.

"Thank you, Ako. I thank you from the core of my being," said Foginet, turning and hugging Whitfield. Stewart also gave the General a strong hug.

"We did it," said Stewart.

"Yes we did it, Madam Director," said Whitfield.

"Please join us for dinner, Akocha."

"If you insist, Madam Director."

"Call me, Lisa, General."

"Yes, Lisa, and I get a chance to see those adorable twins."

"And they would love to see Uncle Ako," said Foginet. Laughter filled the air. The three most powerful members of the regime had every reason to celebrate. All that was left was to create safe passage for those who chose to leave the South and head west to the new state of West Texas.

Foginet knew in due time the Redeemers would attempt a comeback, but it wouldn't happen in the former home of the Confederacy. The Texas Compromise gave the Redeemers and their supporters an opportunity to start over again in the West. As for the South, the land belonged to black people and that's how it would remain for the foreseeable future.

# THIRTY-SEVEN

# East Texas

On January 1, 1878, the state of East Texas became the 39th state of the United States. West Texas became the 40th. The line was drawn from Hardeman County in the north to all of Dimmit County in the south. All counties east of the line connecting the two counties made up East Texas. Most whites packed up and left the South as soon as the State of Emergency ended. Some headed north, and many headed west.

The East Texas legislature was housed in Austin, the former capital of the state of Texas. Blacks dominated both chambers and the executive branch. Many had wanted Stewart to run for governor, but she refused because she considered her duties in dismantling the regime and particularly U3 more important.

For his part, Foginet began to incorporate the SG into their respective state military apparatus. He encouraged SG members to join their local and state militias. In the end, all twelve states created an official state militia made up of former SG troops and state and local militia members. Each maintained an extraordinary degree of professionalism. Agents from U3 were also absorbed by the individual states and came to form the early police apparatus of each state. The Grey Shirts were also absorbed by the individual states and served as security for government facilities and high-ranking elected officials.

Foginet, Stewart, and Whitfield decided to make Unit Four a secret society. It would be called by a familiar name: "Black Rose." The society would be funded through private donations. Its primary goal would be to eliminate any threat whatsoever to the black majority hold on power in the South. It would also guard against any acts of internal corruption that could interfere or undermine the spirit of communal living and good governance in the former Confederacy including the new state of East Texas.

Members would be recruited by other members and subjected to a rigorous vetting and training process. Like the SG, it would be everywhere. Stewart would see to that. In years to come it would become one of the most powerful entities on the planet.

Foginet's greatest accomplishment after the end of the dictatorship was the creation of the Southern Regional Council. The S.R.C. was made up of representatives from each state who represented a particular department in their respective state's government. Thus, the governor of each state was expected to select an individual who would represent his or her state's agricultural interest. This would allow each state to work in harmony with the others to develop best practices regarding agricultural production and trade. Foginet created independent councils for each major sector, including banking, education, communication, transportation, health, public safety, judicial, housing, and government. There were ten in all.

Each council would meet separately to discuss and approve matters pertaining to its particular interest. However, it was the S.R.C.'s Executive Committee, made up of the governors of each state or his/her designees, who had the final say on regional agreements. The S.R.C. Executive Committee was headed by a chairperson who would be given a five-year term. This individual could not be an elected official. Foginet was initially offered the job but turned it down. He was still a military officer, and there was much work to be done in the sphere of military matters. He did inform the group if the offer was still on the table, he would strongly consider it when his military service was up.

The experiment was a resounding success. This structure allowed the South's economy and infrastructure to grow at an explosive rate. The South's standard of living surpassed most countries in Europe and put the northern part of the country to shame. But on March 2, 1878, life in the South came to a grinding halt. News reached the region that Benjamin 'Bluff' Wade had died.

The black majority in the South was stunned. He was their president. The only American president who ever truly recognized blacks as human beings, as equals. A man who'd understood the need for blacks to possess the power to defend themselves against the terroristic acts of armed whites; a man who'd empowered black leaders to serve black people and raise them up to the status of first-class citizens; a man who many blacks believed was sent by God as an act of divine intervention.

Every town throughout the South held a vigil in honor of the country's eighteenth president. Many blacks began to name their newborn sons "Benjamin" in his honor. They felt it was the least they could do as The First Couple of the South had already done.

The South's First Couple travelled to Ohio under heavy guard to pay their respects. Both Stewart and Foginet accepted invitations to speak at the funeral. Douglass gave the eulogy. Following the private funeral, the couple dined with the former first lady and Douglass before heading back home to Riverside Manor. The train ride home was unusually quiet. Foginet finally spoke.

"Lisa, what if we changed the name of the East Texas state capitol to Bluff City and the county in which it sits to Wade County?"

"I think that's a wonderful idea, Aurelius. Can you get it through the legislature?" Foginet gave Stewart a cursory glance. Stewart smiled.

As the train pulled into the station Stewart turned to her husband.

"Aurelius, do you ever think of your own death?"

"Sometimes I do, dear. More often than you might realize. What about you?"

"I do, but then I think about the twins, and the idea of death quickly leaves my mind."

"It's not that easy for me, Lisa. I mean, I love the twins dearly, and I love you mightily, but when I do think about death, the thought haunts me for a while."

"Are you afraid of death?" asked Stewart.

"It's not that, because I've been taught to believe in the concept of life to life. I don't know. I guess I want to be sure we've completed the task our Creator put before us. I just want to be sure we've fulfilled her will."

"Wow, Aurelius, so you believe God is a she?" Stewart was pleasantly surprised.

"Not only do I believe God is a she, Lisa, but I believe if God appeared, she would be the embodiment of you."

"That's the nicest thing anyone has ever said to me, Aurelius."

"I mean it, Lisa."

"Do you think the people are safe, Aurelius? I mean, do you anticipate any problems in the immediate future?"

"I think the immediate danger has passed, Madam Director," Foginet flashed a grin. "But you never know, dear."

"What about you, Lisa? What do you think?" asked Foginet.

"I think we won this war, Aurelius, but in due time we will have to contend with the West and their supporters in the North."

"And how do you think we should prepare for that inevitable show-down, Lisa?"

"Do you want to see my plans?" Stewart smiled.

"I should have known, Madam Director. We could save it for later, my dear," said Foginet, laughing.

"Are you happy, Aurelius?"

"I've never been happier, Lisa, and you?"

"Do you have to ask, General?" Lisa flashed her beautiful smile, and the couple embraced. The doors opened and once again the crowd cheered.

## — THIRTY-EIGHT —

# Home Sweet Home

"I hope you enjoyed our stay with Uncle Ben."

"I had a wonderful time, Mom. Thanks, Mom. That was a good decision."

"Why thank you, Pumpkin." The train was on its way to Beaumont. "How's the book coming along, sweetie?"

"I should be done by the time we get to Beaumont. I was able to do a lot of reading at Uncle Ben's place."

"I hope you didn't ignore the little girl from next door," said Tina.

"Nah, Mom. You taught me better. Rainy was cool. She talked a little bit too much at times, but other than that she was cool."

Tina just smiled and shook her head. "Rainy — That's a unique name," said Tina

"Her real name is Lorraine but her family and friends call her Rainy for short. "Mom, what are grades?" Cody switched subjects quickly.

"What do you mean, grades? Like the grades you get in school?"

"No, Mom. Rainy said she was going to the eigth grade, and she asked me what grade I was going to, and I didn't know. I told her we do things differently down here."

"In the North, the school system is different, Pumpkin. Students are promoted each year to the next level or grade. In the South we keep our students in sections until they are reading above a certain level and can master certain writing and math skills. The age of the student doesn't matter. We also separate the girls from the boys to avoid unnecessary distractions."

"Which way do you think is better, Mom?

"I like the way we do it, Pumpkin."

"Why, Mom?" Cody was curious.

"Well, the way we do it ensures every student who receives a diploma from one of our high schools can hold his or her own in the real world. They can read and write sufficiently and they have a basic understanding of real-world mathematics. We also teach our students how to think critically. Most importantly, Cody, the teachers in the South have high expectations for our students. They believe in each student's ability to learn. That's important, Cody."

"Mom, Rainy said her parents are saving up money so she can go to college. Do you have to pay for me to go to college?"

"No, Pumpkin. Down here, college is free for every student who completes the majority of his or her elementary and secondary education in a public school located in the South. Education is a big deal in the South. Now, you may not be able to go to any college you want. Your choice of college will depend on how well you do on your high school exit exams." Tina chose not to go into detail about the particulars regarding which Southern states were included. In reality, only those students who attended public school in one of the eleven states represented on the C.S.G.S. were afforded free tuition for college.

"Do you think I will be able to go to Powell like Uncle Ben?"

"You are very bright, Cody, and if you study hard and work hard, I don't see why not."

"Mom, Rainy said there are not a lot of black people in the North where she lives."

"That's true, Cody. Most black people in this country live in the South. It's been that way for many years now. Blacks used to escape to the North during slavery but after the 'great struggle'... well, read the book, sweetie."

"Have you been to the North, Mom?" Cody continued his questioning.

"Yes, I have, Cody. Our family owns land on Martha's Vineyard."

"Where's that, Mom?"

"It's a small Island off the coast of Massachusetts."

"Do you like the North, Mom?"

"Some things are okay, but nothing is like the South, Pumpkin. This is our own little paradise. Besides, it's too cold up there," Tina flashed a grin and hugged herself, pretending to be cold.

"Do you think I can go there one day?"

"Absolutely, sweetie. I'll make it a point to take you there soon."

"Will they bother us up there because we're black?"

"Who told you that, Cody?" Tina frowned.

"One of my friends at school said there are certain places we can't go in the North, and he said we definitely can't go to West Texas."

"Cody, you should be careful any time you travel by yourself, but I think we'll be fine in the North." Tina never bothered to discuss the reality for blacks in the state of West Texas. The state was unwelcoming for blacks.

"Can Uncle Ben or Uncle Stew come with us?"

"I'll certainly invite them."

"Thanks, Mom. I love you, Mom."

"I love you too, Pumpkin, so much." Cody opened his book and turned to the chapter marked, "Welcome to the New South."

Five hours later the conductor's voice awakened Tina from a sound sleep. "We'll be arriving in Beaumont in twenty minutes. Next stop Beaumont in twenty minutes."

"Cody, are you ok, dear?"

"Yes, Mom. I'm just thinking."

"About what, dear."

"About our family. I just finished the last chapter. Mom, why didn't you tell me how famous our family is?"

"Well, Cody, I didn't think it was that important. Besides, I knew you would figure it out one day."

"Is that why people treat you a certain way, Mom?"

"Like what, Pumpkin?" Tina acted as if she did not know what her son was talking about.

"People are always speaking to you no matter where we go. They treat you special. They ask for your autograph. You know, Mom." Cody sounded exasperated.

"People are just being kind, Cody."

The sun began to set as the train pulled into the Beaumont train station.

"They must be waiting for us, Mom." Cody eyes followed the two white men on the platform as the train slowed down.

"Who, Cody?"

"The guy over there holding up the sign that says 'Tina and Cody.'"

"I guess so," said Tina, laughing.

The family's estate was located almost twenty-five minutes away. Tina got comfortable in the limousine that was sent to retrieve her and Cody. Tina began reminiscing about her summers spent at Riverside Manor. If she could do it all over again, she would. Her mother, Constance Jean Hamilton, grew up on the estate then went off to college at Wheatley in Florida. After college, she met her husband Ulysses Forrester. Within seven years she had two children: Tina and her brother Ben.

Education was her field of expertise, and she held several high-level administrative positions in the Department of Education in the state of South Carolina. At one point, she served as the state's education representative to the C.S.G.S.. Her mother, Araminta, arranged for her to take a high-ranking position in the federal government, but after a little more than twenty-five years in the field of education, she decided to retire and move back to Beaumont. Her husband subsequently joined her after his retirement as a successful businessman. The couple was extremely wealthy. Connie Forrester, as she was known to friends, soon became the most prominent socialite in the state of East Texas.

The car made several turns and before anyone knew, they were travelling on the back roads of Beaumont. The city's landscape disappeared. Up ahead, Cody could see the family's sprawling estate.

"Mom?"

"Yes, Cody." Tina came out of her trance.

Cody motioned her to move closer to him in the back seat of the car. "Does everybody in our family have a pin like you, Uncle Stew, and Uncle Ben?" Cody whispered.

"What are you talking about, Cody?"

Cody just looked at her.

"Mom, you know; the pin with the cape and the knife on it? They talk about it in the book?" Cody was still whispering.

"Cody, where did you see that pin?" Tina's voice was low, but took on a serious tone.

"I saw one inside the glass paperweight on the dresser in your bedroom. I also saw one in the paperweight on the desk in Uncle Stew's office, and in the glass paperweight on the desk in Uncle Ben's study." His tone remained hushed.

"Cody, one day you will learn a lot more about our family, but today is not the day. You must promise me you will never mention what you just said to me to anyone else. Do you hear me, Cody? Do not mention it again. It will be our secret. Okay Pumpkin?"

"Sure, Mom. Not even to Grandma Connie or Grandma Ari?"

"Especially not to them. We'll talk about it later."

"Okay, Mom."

Just then, the limousine pulled into the circular driveway of Riverside Manor. Under the huge columns, in the doorway of the front entrance to the main house, stood her mother and father, waving. The handsome couple was splendidly dressed. Several members of the racially-diverse house staff joined them.

Tina was able to see her grandmother in the distance. Araminta rocked slowly in her chair on the porch of one of the large cottages adjacent to the main house.

"Is that Grandma Ari?" Cody noticed her too.

"Yes it is, Pumpkin."

"So this is where she and her twin brother were born," Cody whispered to his mom.

"Yes, Cody — David is his name — your great-great uncle."

"Wow, Mom. This is the home of the First Couple of the South and their children."

"Your family, Cody." Tina reminded him. "This is where it all began." Tina's smile was dim.

"When can I talk to Grandma Ari, mom? I have so many questions to ask her."

"Soon, Pumpkin. I'm sure she has a few questions for both of us as well." Tina kept staring in her grandmother's direction.

"You think so, Mom?" Cody became excited.

"I'm sure of it, sweetie." At that moment, the driver opened the back door of the limousine, and Tina and Cody exited the vehicle. They were greeted with hugs, kisses, and an imposing gaze from a short distance away.

...TO BE CONTINUED

Made in the USA
Middletown, DE
17 January 2019